ALSO BY PHILIP R. CRAIG AND WILLIAM G. TAPPLY

First Light: The First Ever Brady Coyne/J.W. Jackson Mystery
Second Sight: A Brady Coyne/J.W. Jackson Mystery
Third Strike: A Brady Coyne/J.W. Jackson Mystery

ALSO BY PHILIP R. CRAIG

THE J.W. JACKSON MYSTERIES

Vineyard Stalker
Delish!: The J.W. Jackson Recipes
Dead in Vineyard Sand
. Vineyard Prey
Murder at a Vineyard Mansion
A Vineyard Killing
Vineyard Enigma
Vineyard Shadows
Vineyard Blues
A Fatal Vineyard Season
A Shoot on Vineyard Holiday
Death on a Vineyard Beach
A Case of Vineyard Poison
Off Season
Cliff Hanger
The Double Minded Men
The Woman Who Walked into the Sea
A Beautiful Place to Die
Gate of Ivory, Gate of Horn

ALSO BY WILLIAM G. TAPPLY

THE BRADY COYNE MYSTERIES

One-Way Ticket
Out Cold
Nervous Water
Shadow of Death
A Fine Line
Past Tense
Scar Tissue

Muscle Memory
Cutter's Run
Close to the Bone
The Seventh Enemy
The Snake Eater
Tight Lines
The Spotted Cats
Client Privilege
Dead Winter
A Void in Hearts
The Vulgar Boatman
Dead Meat
The Marine Corpse
Follow the Sharks
The Dutch Blue Error
Death at Charity's Point

OTHER NOVELS

Thicker than Water (with Linda Barlow)
Bitch Creek
Gray Ghost

BOOKS ON THE OUTDOORS

Those Hours Spent Outdoors
Opening Day and Other Neuroses
Home Water Near and Far
Sportsman's Legacy
A Fly Fishing Life
Bass Bug Fishing
Upland Days
Pocket Water
The Orvis Guide to Fly Fishing for Bass
Gone Fishin'
Trout Eyes

OTHER NONFICTION

The Elements of Mystery Fiction: Writing the Modern Whodunit
A Half Century with the Fly Casters 1946–1996

THIRD STRIKE

A Brady Coyne/J. W. Jackson Mystery

PHILIP R. CRAIG
AND
WILLIAM G. TAPPLY

SCRIBNER

New York   London   Toronto   Sydney

SCRIBNER
A Division of Simon & Schuster, Inc.
1230 Avenue of the Americas
New York, NY 10020

First Scribner hardcover edition December 2007

For information about special discounts for bulk purchases, please contact Simon & Schuster Special Sales: 1-800-456-6798 or business@simonandschuster.com.

DESIGNED BY ERICH HOBBING

Text set in Sabon

Manufactured in the United States of America

1   3   5   7   9   10   8   6   4   2

Library of Congress Control Number: 2007009103

ISBN 13: 978-1-4516-2493-9

for Jane Otte and Fred Morris

Revenge, at first thought sweet,
Bitter ere long back on itself recoils.
MILTON, *Paradise Lost*

You can observe a lot by watching.
YOGI BERRA

THIRD STRIKE

THIRD STRIKE

Chapter One

J.W.

The first death was that of a striker named Eduardo Alvarez who, according to the morning *Globe*, had been killed by an explosion he'd apparently detonated in the engine room of the *Trident*, a small trimaran car and passenger ferry that had been tied up for the night in Vineyard Haven, between trips crewed by scabs trying to make some good money while the Steamship Authority ships weren't running. Alvarez had gotten his head and ribs crushed by flying pieces of metal.

"Hoist with his own petard," said Manny Fonseca, not unsympathetically. Manny, unlike many on Martha's Vineyard, wasn't angry with the striking crewmen who had caused the ferries of the Steamship Authority to grind to a halt in mid-August, just as 100,000 summer visitors wanted to leave the island so their kids could return to school. And unlike many a quoter of Shakespeare, Manny, who lived, breathed, bought, sold, repaired, shot, and probably dreamed of guns, actually knew what a petard was.

Zee and I and the kids were sitting with Manny in the Dock Street Coffee Shop, finishing breakfast and

1

reading the Boston paper, which had just broken the news of Alvarez's death. Zee had dined on a bagel and one fried egg with her tea. The kids and I had had full-bloat breakfasts: juice, coffee for me and milk for Joshua and Diana, sausage links, eggs over light, fried potatoes, and toast.

"Sounds like this fellow Alvarez messed up the timing device," I said. "It wouldn't be the first time something like that happened."

Up until now, the strike hadn't meant much to me because my family was little affected by it. We lived in the Vineyard woods, ate a lot of fish and shellfish we caught from island waters, and grew most of our vegetables. We had no need to go to the mainland and less need than most for the goods normally brought in from there. Alvarez's death had changed our attitude. What had previously been akin to comic theater had suddenly become tragedy.

Manny finished his coffee. "This is not going to make things any easier for the union, J.W. They already got more enemies than they need. I'm on their side, though."

"How come?" asked Zee. "You're not a union man. You work alone."

"True enough," said Manny, who was a fine cabinet maker and finish carpenter and owned his own shop, "but I'm always for the workers instead of the bosses. The people who do the real work on every job get paid chicken feed, while the people who do the least live highest on the hog. Always been that way and probably always will be, but I don't have to like it. Well, I'm out of here. See you later." He put money on top of his tab and started to walk toward the door, then paused, turned, and said, "We still on for tomorrow morning, Zee?"

"Nine o'clock," she said.

Manny nodded and went away.

"You have another competition coming up?" I asked Zee.

"Up in New Hampshire in a couple of weeks," she said. "If I can get off the island by then, that is." She drank the last of her tea and touched her lips with her napkin. "I'm a little rusty."

Even a rusty Zee was a better shot than I would ever be, though I'd briefly been a soldier and later on a cop with the Boston PD. Manny was her pistol instructor, and she was his prize pupil. At home, Zee kept her trophies in the guest room closet.

"Does he still want you to try out for the Olympics?" I said.

"The subject comes up pretty often. He's bringing his Feinwerkbau tomorrow, so I can see what I think of it."

"And?"

"It might be fun to try out," she said. "I haven't decided. I'd have to be away from home."

"The kids and I can get along without you for a while."

"Thanks a lot."

"You know what I mean."

"I know." She smiled the smile that still melted me after ten years of marriage, and put her nose back in the paper. "One thing this is going to do," she added, "is bring Joe Callahan here to try to mediate this strike before there's any more violence. Too bad he didn't get here before a man got killed."

I agreed. Joe Callahan, in spite of a couple of foreign policy blunders early in his first term as president, had emerged from Washington with an almost JFK-like halo around his head. If he hadn't mistaken a young African revolutionary for a potential savior of his country instead of a worse dictator than the one he'd replaced, and if he'd been quicker to cut off the aid the preceding administration had given to right-wing militias in Central America, he might have been granted sainthood. In spite of those and other flaws in his record, however, he still had a major influence in politics because both workers and bosses trusted him. And because of his fondness for the Vineyard, his favorite vacation site during his presidency, he had reportedly been watching the strike with interest and concern. The explosion and Alvarez's death had made it certain, according to the press, that he'd soon be here to help end the standoff.

The waitress came by. "More coffee?"

I put my hand over my empty cup. "Not for me, Jenny. Is this strike having any effect on your business?"

"You mean are we running out of bacon and eggs?" She shook her head. "Not yet. I hope it ends pretty soon, though. This man's death isn't going to help things, and the August people are already getting restless."

Actually, many of the August people were getting angry, which was bad news for the police, since under the best of circumstances the island's August visitors are more trouble than the June people or the July people. Just why this is so is a matter of ongoing debate, but it's a fact that no cop on the Vineyard looks forward to the coming of the August people.

And now, thanks to the striking ferry crewmen, those August people were trapped on the island. The middle class and the poor among them, that is. Rich visitors and residents were barely inconvenienced by the strike, since they could afford to fly or take their own boats back and forth between the island and the mainland.

The arguments about the strike were the usual ones. The prostrike faction—a minority on Martha's Vineyard, where unions were few and antiunion sentiment was strong—held that the strikers were more than due an increase in wages, job security, and benefits, especially since they'd been working for over a year without a new contract. The antistrike faction, the vast majority of Vineyarders—or at least the far noisier portion—compared the strikers to Communists, socialists, and other suckers of the public blood, and opined that they should all be fired on the spot and replaced, some said, by members of the island's large Brazilian community, who would be glad to work for a lot less money and who could certainly do the crewmen's jobs at least as well as the strikers, which wasn't saying much. There was also a lot of talk that the strikers were not only ruining a perfect island summer, but were also wrecking the island's reputation and thereby destroying the future livelihood of everyone dependent upon the tourist economy, which meant most of the Vineyard's permanent population.

Patients with medical problems had difficulty getting to their doctors on the Cape. Store shelves emptied and prices climbed. There were concerns about depletions in the supply of gasoline and propane, even though those fuels were brought to the island by vessels and barges having nothing to do with the ferry strike. To no one's surprise, the canny fuel suppliers had also jacked up their prices, justifying the raises by arguing that as other prices went up, their costs also went up, and they couldn't afford to hold the line on their own products.

There had been pushing and shoving between strikers and antiunion men, along with name calling, threats—reportedly, mostly anonymous phone calls—and more than one fistfight, mostly in Oak Bluffs and Edgartown, the only two island towns with bars where angry people could become fighting drunks. There had been those stories in the papers that Joe Callahan was being asked to mediate the strike but was holding back, hoping that the parties could resolve it themselves. But now there was a dead man, and the latest scuttlebutt was that Callahan would soon be using his charm and political savvy to bring labor and management to a rapid agreement.

Though most people were unhappy with the strike and hoped for a rapid resolution, there were a number of other people who wished that it would last forever. These were the owners and leasers of the boats, mostly trawlers and draggers and other fishing craft, that now shuttled back and forth between the island and the mainland bearing people and goods. They were making more money than they'd ever been able to make on the fishing grounds.

The larger of the fishing boats, including the largest of them all, the big and burly *Neptune,* carried cars on their decks. Their owners charged astronomical prices for the service, but these being abnormal times, drivers clenched their teeth and paid their pennies to the ferryman.

Island merchants also paid through the nose for the goods they required to remain in business and passed the costs on to their customers, who had no choice but to pay up in their turn.

Privately owned barges were busy carrying fuel, semitrailer trucks loaded with lumber, housing modules, and everything else imaginable. The water between the island and the mainland was a highway of commerce, but in spite of all the traffic, there were not enough private boats to carry many of the August people and their automobiles back to America.

A few island visitors actually enjoyed being stranded. It heightened their feelings of excitement and made their vacations seem like genuine adventures, akin to being shipwrecked on a desert island or being in a castle threatened by an army outside its curtained walls. All this, of course, without their being in any real danger. They even had excuses for not going back to work. What could be better?

For most tourists and year-round islanders, however, tempers rose.

But mine did not, nor did those of my family, because we lived lives mostly centered on ourselves, our cats, Oliver Underfoot and Velcro, and our immediate friends, not upon the larger world. To us, the strike had been something like a theater production, a noisy drama with us in balcony seats looking down upon it from afar.

Until now. Now death had entered, stage left, the sinister side, and everything had changed.

"Well, well," said Zee, sticking her face farther into the newspaper. "Here's an interesting tidbit. Guess who owns the *Trident*."

"I haven't any idea," I said. "Donald Trump?"

"Nope. Julius Goodcamp."

The name seemed familiar. "Isn't Goodcamp the CEO or whatever of the Steamship Authority board? Don't tell me he owns the *Trident*."

"Arthur Goodcamp is the chairman, not the CEO, and it's his cousin, not Arthur, who owns the *Trident*, but the idea of the chairman's cousin making money from the strike is going to raise some eyebrows."

"We live in a complex world," I said, wondering how many people already knew who owned the boat.

As we left the coffee shop and climbed into my rusty old Land Cruiser, Zee became thoughtful. "Manny was right," she said. "This is bad for the union. People will paint the guys with a broad brush. They'll be seen as terrorists, willing to blow up boats to get their way. Most people will think this dead man deserved what he got."

I thought she was right. On the other hand, some of the more fanatic union people and leftist revolutionary types, of which there was a fair share on the island, would think of Alvarez as a martyr. I said as much to Zee.

"I know," she said, "but the crewmen and their

wives that I've met aren't the martyr types. They're just working people. They went on strike because they want to get ahead. I wish this Alvarez guy hadn't decided to do what he did. Sabotage isn't the answer. He not only killed himself, he just made things worse for the strikers."

We pulled out of the parking lot in front of the yacht club, inched across Dock Street, being careful not to run over any of the tourists who use Edgartown streets as sidewalks, eased up to North Water, took a left onto Winter Street, thence to Pease's Point Way, then right on Main, and on out of town. As we passed the Post Office, the morning traffic eased.

"Pa?"

"What, Joshua?"

"Is somebody really dead?"

"Yes."

"Who is it?"

"We don't know him," I said. "A man named Alvarez."

"What happened to him?"

"He was killed in an explosion."

"When?"

"Last night, according to the *Globe*."

"I know a girl named Mary Alvarez," said Diana. "She's in my class." She paused, then said, "She's my friend."

In the fall, Diana would be in the second grade. I supposed there were a lot of Alvarezes on the island.

"Didn't Mary come over to play in the tree house?" asked Zee. "Doesn't she have yellow hair and brown eyes?"

"Yes," said Diana. "She's really pretty, and she has nice dresses."

Diana was a miniature of her mother, and like Zee, had little consciousness of her own beauty, though she had a sharp eye for the looks of others.

"I'm sure I met her mother at Parents' Day at school," said Zee. "Maybe you should invite Mary over again before summer vacation ends."

"That would be excellent!" said Diana. "Can I call her when we get home?"

"Yes."

We turned off the paved road onto our long, sandy driveway and drove down to our house. The property had once been a hunting camp where whiskey had flowed more often than shots had been fired. When my father bought it and its surrounding few acres, land in that part of the island was cheap. Since then, first he and then I had slowly transformed the cabin into the rambling house it was now, with its lawn and its flower and vegetable gardens, its shed out back, and its balcony that looked out over Sengekontacket Pond and Nantucket Sound. The latest addition to the Jackson place was the tree house in the big beech, which was a popular recreation stop for our children and their friends.

In our yard there was nothing to suggest the tensions elsewhere on the island. Beyond the gardens, the green waters of the pond and sound were lovely under a pale blue sky. A gentle southwest wind sighed through the trees, and the morning sun was climbing through a thin scattering of summer clouds.

Paradise. But with serpents just out of sight.

We climbed out of the truck, and Diana tugged at Zee's hand. "Come on, Ma. Let's call Mary and see if she can come over. Can she stay the night, Ma? Please?"

"One thing at a time," said her mother. "First, we'll see if she can come over to play."

Oliver Underfoot and Velcro, who had been snoozing in the sun, yawned hello and came to meet us, asking where we'd been in their catty voices.

Zee and Diana gave them pats and went into the house, and our eldest, Joshua, said, "Can I have somebody over, too, Pa?"

"Why not? Who do you have in mind?"

"Jim Duarte. Pa, if he can come over, can we go to the beach?"

It was a beach day, for sure. "Maybe your mother and sister and Mary would like to come, too."

"First, we have to find out if Jim can come. I know his number." He started for the house.

"Your mother's on the line right now," I said. "You can call him when she's through with the phone."

While we waited for Zee or Diana to come out and give us a report on the Mary call, Joshua said, "Can we take fishing rods?"

"We always take fishing rods when we go to the beach," I said, "because you never know when there might be some fish swimming by. We'll take quahog rakes, too, and a couple of wire baskets. We can go down to the far corner of Katama Bay. If the waves aren't too high, you kids can swim on the ocean side of the beach and I can do some clamming in the bay. If it's rough water outside, we'll go on over to East Beach."

11

I looked at the door just as Zee emerged. Her face had an odd set to it.

"I just talked with Gloria Alvarez," she said in a quiet voice. "Eduardo Alvarez was her husband. She says he would never have tried to blow up that boat. I'm going over to see her. She needs to have someone with her. I'll take Diana with me. Mary needs a friend, too."

Joshua and I watched them drive away. Although the sun was bright, the world seemed darker.

"Pa?"

"What?"

"Can I still call Jim? Can we still go to the beach?"

I looked down at his innocent face. For him, Eduardo Alvarez's death had no meaning. Joshua's world had not changed.

"You can ask him over," I said, "but I think we'd better stay here so we'll be home when your mother and sister come back."

"We can play in the tree house," said Joshua agreeably, and I watched him trot into the house to make his call. He was a happy boy.

I thought that we humans must be the only animals who grew up to believe that death intruded on life.

Chapter Two

Brady

Around seven o'clock on a sultry Thursday evening toward the end of August, Evie and I were sipping our second round of gin and tonics in our little patio garden behind our house on Beacon Hill. A gang of goldfinches and a few song sparrows and nuthatches were swiping sunflower seeds from the feeders. Henry David Thoreau, our Brittany spaniel, was sprawled on the bricks, absorbing the accumulated warmth from the day's summer sunshine and eyeing the songbirds without much interest.

I had swapped my lawyer pinstripe-and-tie for jeans and a T-shirt. Evie had shucked off her business suit in favor of blue running shorts cut high on the hip and a skimpy pink sleeveless tank top. Bare feet, no bra. All but naked. She was slouched in one of our Adirondack chairs with her long golden legs splayed out in front of her, and when the phone rang from the kitchen, she was yawning and stretching her arms up in the air, exposing a delicious patch of flat belly and zinging dirty thoughts into my brain.

She opened her eyes. "You want me to get that?"

"Get what?" I said.

"The phone."

"I didn't hear anything."

The phone rang again.

"You heard it that time," she said.

"I choose to ignore it."

"It might be important," she said.

"What could be more important than our quiet togetherness after a noisy day at our offices? What could be more important than our gin and tonics?" I waggled my eyebrows. "Know what I was just thinking, speaking of important?"

She cocked her head and narrowed her eyes at me. "Of course I know what you were thinking," she said. "I was thinking the same thing."

The phone rang a third time. Evie sat up.

I held up my hand. "Let it go, honey. If it's important, they'll leave a message and we can call them back." I patted my lap. "C'mere."

"Brady, really," she said. "I can't just . . ."

It rang again, as if it was determined to wedge its two cents' worth into our conversation.

Evie blew out a breath, took a quick sip, and put her glass on the table. "I can't ignore it," she said. "You know me."

"Just leave it."

"Sorry, babe. Can't." And she unlimbered her long sleek legs, stood up, patted my cheek, and trotted into the house.

Henry lifted his head and watched her go. Even a dog couldn't take his eyes off her.

I sighed, tilted my head back, and gazed up at the sky.

A minute later Evie came out. She was pressing the phone against her stomach. "It's for you," she said.

"Come on, honey," I said. "I understand and tolerate your compulsion to answer any ringing telephone, but couldn't you at least take a message, tell them I'd call back?"

"He's on a pay phone. Says it's important. *Urgent* was his actual word. It's . . . Larry Bucyck?" She made his name a question.

"Larry Bucyck," I said. "No kidding?"

She nodded. "Do I know him?"

"No. Hm. I haven't talked to Larry in . . . I don't know. Years. What's he want?"

She shook her head.

"Calling from the Vineyard?"

She shrugged. "Didn't say that, either." She thrust the phone at me and mouthed the words, "Talk to him."

I took the phone from her and put it to my ear. "Hey, Larry," I said. "Long time. What's up? Everything okay?"

"You're still my lawyer," he said, "right?"

"Depends," I said. "Did you murder somebody?"

"Not yet."

"Hey, listen—"

"I'm kidding. Jesus, Brady. You used to have a good sense of humor."

"Just wondering why you didn't call the office, that's all."

"You never were big on trying to make people feel better," he said.

"Hey," I said. "I'm a lawyer. I cherish the truth.

15

Truth and justice. If it hurts, too bad. Just giving you a context here. I told Evie not to answer the damn phone, but as usual, she does what she wants."

"Look, okay," he said. "I'm sorry about that. I had to pedal my bike about four miles—well, okay, maybe a mile, but it's a crappy old bike—to get to this damn pay phone, and then there's some fat lady with orange hair beat me to it, should never be seen in public wearing a bathing suit, kept making phone calls, some August person complaining about the price of groceries and she can't find a babysitter, and no matter how much I sighed and paced around glaring at her, the old bag wouldn't hang up."

"You still living off the grid down there?" I said. "No phone? Can't even spring for a cell?"

"Brady, listen. I wouldn't bother you if it wasn't important."

"I know. You wouldn't be comfortable if I didn't bust your balls a little, either. So what's up?"

I heard him sigh. "I got a real problem, man." His voice was low, as if he was trying not to be heard. "I—it's something bad. I think I might be in trouble."

"Talk to me, Larry."

"I can't. Not on the phone. There's something I need to show you."

"This got anything to do with . . . what happened?"

"No, no. Nothing like that."

"So what kind of trouble?" I said. "You're scaring me."

"Yeah, well, I'm kinda scared myself, so that makes two of us."

"What do you want me to do?"

"I hate to ask . . ."

"You need a lawyer, why don't you—"

"I need you, Brady. You're the only—"

"There are plenty of lawyers on the Vineyard." I glanced at Evie. She had her head back and her eyes closed and her gin-and-tonic glass resting on her bare belly, pretending not to be listening. "I can recommend somebody," I said to Larry.

"My point is," he said, "I don't know who I can trust down here these days. So I don't trust anybody. Lawyers are as bad as anybody."

"I can't argue with you there," I said. "But you can't expect me to just . . ."

"Yeah," he said, "okay. Right. Sorry. I get it. I'm a thoughtless jerk, and I don't have any money to pay a fancy Boston lawyer anyway. You're pretty busy, there, with your girlfriend and your gin and tonic and everything. Forget about it. Sorry I called."

"Come on, Larry. Lighten up. Anyway, I'm not that fancy. And you know better. It's got nothing to do with money. I was only—"

"I sat around all day just trying to summon up the courage to call you," he said. "Stupid me."

"You really in trouble?"

"You think I'd grovel like this if I wasn't?"

"I didn't notice you were groveling."

"Well, what else would you call it?"

I hesitated, then said, "Okay."

"Whaddya mean, okay?"

"I mean," I said, "okay I'll be there. Tomorrow. Can it wait till tomorrow?"

"Yeah, sure. Absolutely. Tomorrow would be great."

Evie had sat up. She was waving her hand at me.

I arched my eyebrows at her.

She mouthed something that I didn't understand. I frowned at her and shook my head, and she rolled her eyes and sprawled back in her chair.

"Tomorrow's Friday," I said to Larry. "I'll try to get away in the afternoon. We can make a weekend of it. Maybe do some fishing."

"Fishing," he said. "Sure. That'd be fun. You remember where I live?"

"I guess I can find it. It's been a couple years."

"More like five years, actually," Larry said.

"You're in the woods down there in Menemsha," I said. "I remember that. I guess you better remind me how to get there."

"Coming from Vineyard Haven, Oak Bluffs?"

"That end of the island, yes."

"Okay," he said. "So you pick up South Road in West Tisbury, follow it into Menemsha. Other side of Middle Road, South Road becomes Menemsha Cross Road. Stay on it, you go, oh, less than half a mile on Menemsha Cross, you come to a left turn. First road on the left. You with me so far?"

"I'm with you. I got the map in my head. I guess I'll recognize it when I see it."

"Take that left, go half a mile, maybe, past some new houses that weren't there last time you came down. You come to another left, little dirt road going back up into the woods," he said. "Follow it all the way to the end. Hundred yards or so. My driveway—not much more than a pair of ruts—it angles off to the right. Look for the stone sculpture."

"Huh?" I said. "Stone sculpture?"

Larry chuckled. "You'll see."

"I'll find you one way or the other."

"Look for you around suppertime?" he said. "I'll dig some quahogs, make us a chowder."

"You don't want to give me a hint what this is about, Larry?" I said.

"I got people here getting restless waiting for the phone," he said. "Gotta go."

"Okay. Tomorrow, then."

"Thanks, man. You're a lifesaver."

I pushed the Off button on the phone, put it on the table between Evie and me, and picked up my drink. The ice cubes had shrunk to mothball size, but it still tasted good.

"You're going to the Vineyard, huh?" said Evie.

I nodded.

"That man's in trouble?"

"He called me a lifesaver."

"Wouldn't tell you why?"

I shook my head.

"He calls it urgent," she said, "and you take it at face value."

I shrugged. "I know. It might be nothing. Larry Bucyck's not the world's most stable person. Actually, he shows all the symptoms of a paranoid schizophrenic. Thing is, though, if I didn't go and something really did happen to him, I couldn't live with myself."

"He's your client."

I nodded. "He is my client."

"And he needs you."

"That's about it," I said.

"You should've been a social worker, you know that?"

"I'd've made a terrible social worker," I said.

"And this has nothing to do with slipping off to the Vineyard for a weekend, escaping the steamy city, getting away from your crabby girlfriend for a couple days, doing a little surf casting, huh?"

"Nothing like any of that," I said. "Something has seriously freaked the man out. Anyway, you're not that crabby. You're, um, challenging sometimes. And sexy always. But I wouldn't call you crabby."

Evie smiled. "So how exactly were you planning to get down to the Vineyard?"

I looked at her for a minute, then slapped my forehead. "I forgot about the damn strike."

"That's what I was trying to tell you. The ferries aren't running."

"God damn Larry, he never even mentioned it."

"You said he was living off the grid," said Evie. "Maybe he doesn't know."

"How could he not know?" I said. "The whole world knows about the ferry strike. Stupid me for not thinking of it. Just the other day ex-President Callahan was on TV saying he'd be available to mediate it if the two sides were willing to sit down. I guess if Callahan could bring those Middle East countries to the table, he ought to be able to get a ferry strike settled. Seems to me he's done more good peacemaking since he left office than he did while he was in the White House."

"So what're you going to do?"

"I can't not go," I said.

Evie smiled. "Of course you can't," she said. "Listen. The big-shot surgeons at the hospital wouldn't be caught dead riding the ferry with the riffraff even when it is running. They fly. You want to fly?"

"Sure. What's my choice?"

"No choice." She frowned. "What's the name of the . . . ? Okay. I remember. Cape Air. Several flights every day, Logan direct to the Vineyard. Want me to call them for you?"

"That," I said, "would be sweet."

"You go make us another pitcher of gin and tonics, then."

I took the empty pitcher into the kitchen as Evie was pecking numbers on the telephone. When I returned, the phone was sitting on the table beside her.

I filled both of our glasses, then sat down. "So'd you get me a reservation?"

She smiled. "Cape Air flies every hour on the hour starting at 7 A.M., something like ten flights a day, and the first available seat was next Monday. She said things've been crazy with the ferries not running, especially around the weekends. I did not reserve that seat for you. You said it had to be tomorrow."

I nodded. "It does."

"Can't he wait?"

"In the first place," I said, "Larry said he was in trouble, that this whatever-it-is was urgent. He kind of scared me. Second place, I don't know how to get ahold of him to tell him the plan's changed." I shook my head. "Now what do I do?"

"Call J.W.," Evie said. "If anybody can tell you what to do . . ."

"It's J.W.," I said. I took a sip of gin and tonic, then picked up the phone and called the Jacksons' number in Edgartown. Zee answered on the third ring. I told her I needed to get to the Vineyard tomorrow.

"Jeez, Brady," she said. "With the ferries not running, it's a zoo down here. A veritable monkey house. You sure you want to do this?"

"I don't have a choice. I've got to see a client. I was hoping J.W. might . . ."

"He's outside playing in the tree house with the kids. Let me get him for you. Hang on."

I waited, and a few minutes later J.W. came on the line and said, "You serious?"

"I've got a client in Menemsha," I said. "He's got some kind of emergency, wouldn't tell me what it was. I told him I'd be there tomorrow."

"You don't want to be here," he said. "Prices of everything are skyrocketing, tempers are flaring, and it's gonna get worse before it gets better. It's getting so bad I almost wish I was somewhere else."

"Well," I said, "it can't be helped. I was hoping . . ."

"It's a long swim, brother."

"What would you do if you were in my situation?"

"I guess I'd call me," J.W. said. "I know some people with boats, assuming you're willing to pay scalpers' prices."

"My client will pay," I said. "Just tell me who to call."

"Sit tight," he said. "I'll get back to you."

*　　*　　*

A couple hours later, just as Evie and I were finishing our take-out pizza—Vidalia onion and goat cheese for her, eggplant and sausage for me—J.W. called back.

"I talked to Zee about it," he said. "She agrees with me. Everybody who's driving boats back and forth from here to America's gonna charge you an arm and a leg. Except for me. So I'll come and get you in the *Shirley J.* How's that sound?"

"That's a lot to ask," I said. "I'm willing to pay."

"Come on," said J.W. "It'll give me an excuse to sail my catboat o'er the bounding main, you know?"

"In that case," I said, "thank you."

"We got a perfect morning tide," he said. "I'll meet you in Woods Hole around noon, okay?"

"Noon is great," I said. "I'll shut down the office. Nothing much going on in Boston law offices and courtrooms on Fridays in August anyway. Julie will be thrilled to get away from the office for a long weekend."

"You gonna need a car? What about a bed?"

"I hadn't gotten that far," I said. "But, yes, I'll definitely need a car. I suppose I'll stay with Larry. I'll figure that out when I get there, I guess."

"Larry being your client?"

"Larry Bucyck. Know him?"

J.W. didn't say anything for a minute. "I'm sure I don't know him, but the name definitely rings a bell. Lives in Menemsha, you said?"

"He used to pitch for the Red Sox."

"Not the guy who—?"

"That's him. The ninety-one playoffs."

"Larry Bucyck," said J.W. "Wow. A name to be

reckoned with. Right up there with Bill Buckner and Bucky Dent. Haven't heard that name in years. So Bucyck's down here on the island, huh?"

"Has been for the past fourteen or fifteen years. Lives pretty much like a hermit."

"Don't blame him," said J.W. "If I was him, I guess I'd want to crawl into a cave and never come out. So he's your client?"

"I negotiated his contract, and later on I did his divorce. I guess that makes me his lawyer. He seems to think so."

"So what's so important he's dragging you down here in the middle of a damn ferry strike?"

"I don't know," I said, "and if I did know, I couldn't tell you. All I know is, he says he's in trouble, he sounds scared, he's got something he wants to show me, and I told him I'd be there."

"Heigh-ho, Silver," said J.W.

"Aw, you're worse than Evie. I'm just a lawyer doing my job."

"I'll see you at the dock in Woods Hole, noon tomorrow," he said. "We'll have a nice sail, go to the house, have a beer, visit with Zee and the kids. You can use Zee's Wrangler for as long as you need it."

"I appreciate it," I said. "Thank you."

"Finish up with Mr. Bucyck," he said, "we can sneak over to Cape Pogue, catch us a mess of bluefish."

"That," I said, "is an incentive to finish up with Mr. Bucyck. See you tomorrow."

When I put the phone down, I caught Evie frowning at me.

"What's the matter?" I said.

"You better tell me who Larry whats-his-name is."

"If you're a true-blue Red Sox fan, you'd know."

"I've only been a Red Sox fan since I met you," she said.

"You've missed most of the angst, then," I said. "This was back in ninety-one. The Sox made up four or five games in the standings in September, didn't nail down the wild-card spot till the last day of the season. The media were resurrecting old Red Sox phrases like Cardiac Kids and Impossible Dream. It was pretty thrilling. Anyway, they called Larry Bucyck up from Double A in the middle of August. He was a right-hander, a power pitcher. Major-league fastball, nice quick-breaking little slider, decent control. Local kid, grew up in Waltham, pitched for B.C. Made second-team All NCAA, pretty obvious he was going to get drafted early, so my old buddy Charlie McDevitt, he was a friend of the Bucyck family, he recommended me. To handle Larry's contract."

"Like a sports agent?" said Evie.

I shrugged. "Larry was drafted in the third round. The contract was pretty much boilerplate except for the specific numbers. It was all routine, but I think Larry and his folks felt good, having me help out. So anyway, he spent two and a half years working his way up through the minors, getting people out at every level, and when the Sox called him up, everybody in New England was pretty excited about it. Local boy makes good, you know?"

Evie smiled. "What about you? Were you pretty excited?"

"Sure," I said. "I get excited by the Red Sox anyway.

But this kid was my client. That was very cool. So like I said, this was the middle of August, and the Sox were in second place, chasing the Yankees as usual, still in the hunt for a playoff spot. Larry pitched pretty decent in long relief, the Sox had that great September, and they put him on the playoff roster. He was the last man on the depth chart, didn't figure to get into a game unless it was already one-sided, just there to maybe absorb some innings, save the other arms on the staff. Lo and behold, the Sox kept playing well, winning playoff games, and they made it to the American League Championship. So it comes down to the seventh game. They're playing the Angels in Anaheim, and by game seven both pitching staffs are used up. So wouldn't you know, the game goes into extra innings. It's after our bedtime back in Boston, but of course all of New England's watching. So finally, the top of the fourteenth inning, the Sox manage to eke out two runs, and all they've got to do is get three outs and it's on to the World Series. Whoever they had in there pitching, can't remember his name, he goes back out there in the bottom of the fourteenth and promptly gives up a hit and then a walk to the first two Angels. Tying runs on base, nobody out. You look out to the bullpen, there's only one arm left out there."

"Larry Bucyck," said Evie.

"Pink-cheeked rookie Larry Bucyck himself," I said. "Our manager goes out, talks with the pitcher. I'm watching on TV—it's about three o'clock in the morning, the game out there on the West Coast—and I can see the manager and the pitcher both shaking their heads. So they bring in Bucyck. All the hopes and dreams of Red Sox Nation—don't forget, 2004 hasn't happened yet, the Curse of the Bambino's still a big black cloud of doom hanging over us—everything resting on young Larry Bucyck. Kid looks about twelve years old, and when the TV camera zooms in on him, he looks so scared he might puke."

"Your client," said Evie.

"I was so nervous," I said, "I thought I might puke myself. It was nerve-racking, but pretty cool, too, having this kid I worked with, my client—seeing him out there in this situation."

"That doesn't seem fair," said Evie, "bringing an inexperienced boy into a situation like that."

"Fair, schmair," I said. "He's all they've got. Anyway, look, he's a professional. He's got a job to do. Get three outs before they score two runs. Shouldn't be that hard. So, first guy, Larry strikes him out, good fastball in on his hands. Next guy hits a two-hopper to the shortstop, easy double-play ball, ballgame over, on to the World Series. Except the second baseman has trouble with the relay, can't get it out of his glove. We got the out at second, but the batter beats it out at first, so the Angels are still alive. By all rights, Larry Bucyck should be the hero, but instead there's runners on first and third and he's still gotta get one more out. The manager goes strolling out to the mound, talks to the kid, pats him on the ass, tells him he's doing great, don't worry about it, whatever. So the next batter, strike one, strike two, like that. All we need is that third strike and it's all over. But then the youngster makes the oh-two pitch too fat, typical rookie mistake, and the batter smacks a line shot to left, clean single. The Angel scores from third. Now we've just got a one-run lead. But still two outs. I'm watching on TV, I want to cover my eyes. I'm seeing Larry's body language, and I don't like it. So, sure enough, he walks the next guy, four pitches, not even close. Now they got the bases loaded. And, not to drag it out, four more pitches, he walks the next guy, too. Now the game's tied up. The TV camera pans on the Sox bullpen. Nobody's up and throwing, which the manager was gonna keep hearing about until he got fired two years later, but the fact was, they didn't have anybody, and the manager already made his allotted trip to the mound, so he can't even go out there and give the kid a pep talk. So anyway, to spare you the agony of it, Larry walks the next guy, too, four straight pitches not even close to being strikes, and the game's over."

Evie was smiling at me. "That was all those years ago, and you remember every detail."

"How could I forget? For a while, nobody forgot. Twelve straight pitches out of the strike zone." I shook my head. "Actually, I left out a lot of details, figured they'd bore you. That was the abridged version."

"I'm not sure I followed it all," she said, "but it sounds like Larry Bucyck choked."

"Oh, absolutely," I said. "You hate to say it, hate to accuse anybody of choking. But twelve straight balls? Walk in the tying and winning runs? That was awful. Worst thing you can do in that situation is not throw strikes. He coughed it up, just gave them the game. No doubt about it. Larry Bucyck shit the bed big time."

"I bet the media and everybody were pretty hard on him."

"Less than you might think, actually," I said. "They were a lot harder on the manager for putting himself in a situation where he had to bring Larry in with the game on the line, and they were pretty critical of the veteran second baseman for botching the double play. There was a shitload of analysis of that inning, needless to say. The manager—I can't even remember who it was, we had a whole string of unmemorable managers back then—he made a couple moves back in the eighth and ninth innings that were rightfully second-guessed. But, see, the subtext of it all was, Larry Bucyck wasn't good enough, over his head, never should've been in there in the first place, which wasn't exactly great for the kid's confidence. Anyway, none of that mattered, because Larry was harder on himself than all the fans and media put together ever could have been. It was like his whole image of himself had been destroyed in fifteen minutes on a September night in Anaheim."

"What happened to him?"

"They started him off back in Double A the following spring, trying to keep the pressure off him, let him find his groove again. He had a good arm, a good history, and they figured, give him more seasoning, he'd be a decent big-league pitcher. But after a few months down in Scranton or Wilkes-Barre or wherever he was, he couldn't get anybody out, so he went down to Single A, and after that they sent him down to an instructional league in Florida so they could work on his mechanics. But, of course, his problems had nothing to do with the mechanics of his arm and every-thing to do with the mechanics of his head."

"He was washed up, huh?" said Evie.

I nodded. "It's a pretty sad story. Kind of the oppo-site of the American Dream. A year after Larry Bucyck walked in the winning run in Anaheim, the Sox let him go, and nobody picked him up. I talked to him about pitching in Mexico or Japan, maybe, but he was cooked, and he knew it. He didn't even want to try it." I shook my head. "Fact is, he was relieved. He hated baseball. Then a year or so after he left baseball, I did his divorce for him. His wife got custody of the two kids, the house in Sudbury, their investments, and Larry got the shack in Menemsha. I could've done better for him, but that's how he wanted it."

"Guilt, huh?" said Evie.

"Guilt, self-loathing, you name it. I was pretty worried about him. Whenever I was on the Vine-yard after that, I'd make a point of dropping in on Larry, but it was pretty clear all he really wanted was to be left alone. He was trying to simplify his life, which I certainly respect, had no need for a lawyer, didn't seem to want a friend, even, or at least a friend who remembered that game against the Angels in ninety-one. After a while, well, a man who seems uncomfortable around you, you don't hear from him for a while . . ."

"You stop worrying about him," Evie said. "When did you last see him?"

"I would've said a couple years ago, but I guess it's closer to five or six. One summer when I was down fishing with J.W. It was pretty clear to me that I made

30

Larry uncomfortable. He couldn't wait for me to leave."

"What happened to his wife and kids?"

"Far as I know, he hasn't seen them since the divorce. He has visitation rights, I made sure of that, but he just went to the Vineyard and stayed there. Last I heard, Marcia—that was his wife's name—she'd remarried and moved to Vermont. I guess the kids—there was a boy and a girl—would both be out of high school by now."

"That's harsh," said Evie, "giving up your kids like that."

"I argued with him, of course," I said, "but it's how he wanted it. Larry figured when they got old enough to understand, they'd hate him as much as he hated himself. He thought they'd be better off if nobody, including themselves, connected them to the choke artist who gave away the ninety-one playoffs."

Evie shook her head. "That's terrible. It was only a stupid baseball game."

"Try telling that to a Red Sox fan."

Chapter Three

J.W.

Early that afternoon, while Joshua and his pal Jim were scrambling around the tree house, I walked up to the box at the end of the driveway and got the day's mail, which didn't amount to much but did include the week's edition of the *Vineyard Times,* which comes out on Thursdays. I wanted to get the *Times*'s take on the explosion, but the accident had happened too late the previous night for the story to make the paper. This meant that the *Vineyard Gazette,* which came out on Friday, and whose editorials almost always supported positions opposite those of the *Times,* would get the scoop and a temporary edge in the ongoing Vineyard newspaper duel.

I walked back down to the house, checked to see if both boys were still intact in spite of their swinging around in the big beech tree, and reread the strike stories in earlier editions of both island papers. Some of these reviewed the reasons for the strike, none of which were unusual: wages, job security, working conditions, benefits, and the like. Other stories were nostalgic recollections of the last ferry strike, in the spring of 1960, which I remembered hazily as a time of high adventure because it had been my first time across Vineyard Sound on a fishing boat. Other stories focused on the effects the strike was having on the local citizens and visitors. Some of these stories were comic, some were maddening, and some were quixotic. The editorials of both papers attempted to take the high ground, expressing sympathy for all involved and offering unctuous hopes that a just and rational solution to the conflicts would be quickly found.

As usual, the letters to the editors ranged politically from the hysterical, union-hating, right wing, to the hysterical, union-loving, left, with much pontificating on both sides, but little light to shed on the causes of the strike and few sensible proposals for its resolution. These letters seemed to bear out a study that I'd read about that indicated pretty clearly that partisans, no matter how intelligent they might otherwise be, responded to political issues emotionally and not rationally.

No surprise there. The only new information I had gotten from the study was that emotion was reflected by activity in one area of the brain, and reason was reflected in another area. I'd wondered if that meant, as I sometimes suspected, that free will is an illusion and that we are wired to act the way we do. It was a concept I didn't like at all, and refused to accept, even in the face of evidence that I might be wrong.

Was my refusal a choice? Or was I wired to refuse?

Did the editorial and letter writers have a choice about their views, or were they just writing what they were biologically predestined to write?

It was the old free-will issue that I'd never resolved to my satisfaction. Facing this dilemma, I'd decided to act as though I had a choice in my actions even if I in fact had no choice but to decide I had a choice.

There madness lay, but I ignored it.

By and large, both papers seemed glad that so many private boats had come to the island's rescue, even as both recognized that in the long run the Steamship Authority offered the only viable lifeline between the Vineyard and America. Reflecting classic island xenophobia, both editors also wanted to keep the Commonwealth of Massachusetts out of the matter. Better to sink beneath the sea than trust Beacon Hill to act responsibly.

I saw no solution to the strike other than whatever would be hammered out during the endless meetings between management and labor. Sooner or later, I was sure, a new agreement would be reached, and when it was, it would have both supporters and detractors venting their opinions in the island papers.

Meanwhile, an explosion had nearly sunk one boat, and a man was dead.

I put aside the newspapers, got a Sam Adams out of the fridge, and went outside to a lawn chair. The August sun was hot, and the beer tasted just right.

Joshua and Jim were crouching on the rope bridge between the beech and the oak, shooting make-believe arrows at make-believe enemies, apparently playing *Tarzan and the Leopard Woman*. It was a good game—much better than pushing buttons on some electronic gadget.

As I was finishing my beer, Zee's little Jeep came

down the driveway and parked beside the Land Cruiser. Zee and Diana got out, both looking unhappy. Zee pointed at the boys in the tree, and Diana seemed to cheer up a bit.

"Stay where you are, Jeff," said Zee. "We'll be right back."

They went into the house and a few minutes later came out again. Diana headed for the tree house, and Zee, carrying two bottles of Sam, came over and sat on the lawn chair next to mine. She gave me one of the bottles and took a drink from the other.

"I invited Mary over to play with Diana," she said, turning her bottle in her hands, "but Mary didn't want to leave her mother. Gloria is almost hysterical. She can't believe that Eduardo is dead. She says he would never use violence of any kind. She says something terribly wrong happened to him."

I thought that wives don't always know as much about their husbands as they think, and vice versa.

"How's the little girl?" I asked.

Zee looked down into her bottle, then took a sip. "She's afraid to leave her mother because something might happen to her, too. Her father left the house and now he's dead. She's afraid that will happen to her mother if she leaves her."

I thought about how I'd felt when my mother died. I was four and my sister Margarite was two. Later I learned that my mother had been the victim of a fast-moving cancer, but at the time all I'd known was that she was gone and wasn't ever going to come back. I'd been lonely and nervous for a long time, even though my father, suffering even more than we children were, and destined never to remarry, had made a deal with the fire department so he could stay home with us for a while.

"Tell Mary he's asleep," I said. "Tell her that he feels fine and will see her later."

"I want you to help Gloria," said Zee.

I was startled, because Zee usually doesn't approve of my getting involved in matters that might include a component of violence.

"How?"

Zee's dark eyes lifted and looked into mine. "Gloria's heard the speculation about Eduardo, that he killed himself when he set off that explosion on the *Trident*. She says he never would have tried to blow up a boat, that he was a pacifist. She says it's hateful for people to be saying such bad things. She says she can live knowing that he's dead, but that she can't stand the things people are suggesting. I want you to find out what really happened so she can find some peace."

Other people, knowing that I'd once been a policeman, had sometimes asked me to make informal investigations for them. But Zee never had. I said, "I doubt I can learn anything that the police can't learn."

Usually, that was an argument that Zee used when I was tempted to stick my nose in other people's business. But this time, she shook her head.

"Gloria says he wasn't the kind of man who would ever damage anyone or anything. I believe her. I want you to find out the truth."

"The police will be looking for that," I said. "Detectives will come down from the mainland to help. They'll want to know everything—who did it, where the explosives came from, why. Everything."

"I believe Gloria," said Zee. "I want you to help her."

I looked at her and saw suffering in her face. She was a nurse, and though she was tough enough to calmly tend terrible wounds that would paralyze most of us with horror, she had the classic characteristic of her profession—she was a born caregiver. She couldn't look at human or animal pain without trying to do something about it. As with most of our strengths, her tenderness also made her vulnerable.

I tried one last argument before giving in to her sorrow and concern. "Look," I said, "if I go out there, there's no telling what I'll find. I may find out that Eduardo Alvarez wasn't the saint his wife seems to think he was. What then? Do you think Gloria Alvarez is going to feel better knowing that her husband was just what people think he was—a guy who got blown up by his own bomb?"

"That's not what you'll find."

"You can't be sure."

"Gloria is sure of Eduardo," she said, "and I'm sure of Gloria." She looked at me, and my will was drawn into her eyes like Breachan into Corryvreckan.

"All right," I said. "But I have to have some place to start. I need to talk with Gloria."

She put out a hand and took mine. "I told her that you'd want to do that. She's expecting you."

"You know me better than I do," I said, and I felt a rueful little smile flit across my face. "Tell me where she lives."

Gloria Alvarez lived in a small house off Wing Road in Oak Bluffs. In spite of the mansionizing that's happening all over the Vineyard, there are still lots of small houses in every town. Most of them are getting along in years, but a few are still being built. The Alvarez house was one of the aging ones, but it was neatly kept and its yard was well-tended. There was a wooden swing set beside the one-car garage and a middle-aged Ford sedan in the driveway. Another car of similar age was parked at the curb.

I parked mine behind the Ford and went to the door. The woman who opened it was too old to be Gloria Alvarez. Sadness seemed to ooze out around her, seeping from the house like an invisible fog.

"I'm J.W. Jackson," I said. "I'd like to speak to Mrs. Alvarez."

"I'm Sarah Martinez," said the woman. "Gloria is very tired. Are you a friend?"

"My wife is her friend. Mrs. Alvarez is expecting me."

"She's had a terrible shock."

"I know."

She paused, then nodded and stepped back. "I hope you can be brief. This is a terrible day for all of us. George and I have known Eduardo and Gloria for years."

I went in and followed her to a small living room. The windows let in a lot of sunlight, but the room seemed dark. A young woman sat on a couch with a girl about Diana's age. The girl had yellow hair and brown eyes.

"Mr. Jackson is here," said the older woman.

The woman on the couch lifted her eyes to me. "Zeolinda said you'd come. Thank you." Her voice was exhausted by sorrow.

"I don't know if I can be of any help," I said. "But I'll try. I need to know where to start asking questions, so I'll need some information." I nodded toward the girl. "Should we talk in private?"

The child put her arm around her mother's arm and pulled herself closer.

Her mother looked down at her and said, "No, we can talk here."

I looked into the girl's angry, confused eyes. "Perhaps Mrs. Martinez can take Mary for a walk."

Gloria shook her head. "No. Mary wants to stay here."

"All right. Tell me about your husband. I know he was a union man, working on the ferries, and I know you don't think he caused the explosion on the *Trident*."

Gloria's voice was small but firm. "He would never have done such a thing. He didn't like all this fighting and trouble. He wanted the strike to end quickly so he could go back to work with George and the others. Something bad happened. Someone blew up that boat, but it wasn't my Eduardo."

"Why do you think he was there, then?"

She lowered her eyes. "I don't know. He was supposed to be working in the restaurant."

"What restaurant?"

"The Wheelhouse, in Edgartown," she said. "He got a job there in the kitchen to bring in some money while the union was on strike. He cleaned pans and cleared tables. The college boys had quit and they needed help, so Eduardo worked there nights."

It was a familiar phenomenon for college kids to get summer jobs and swear they'd stay until Labor Day but then bail out in mid-August so they could have a couple of weeks of party time before heading back to school.

"What work did your husband do on the boats?" I said. "Was he an engineer? Did he work on the engines?"

"No. He knew nothing about engines. He was an able-bodied seaman. He worked hard."

"Did he have any conflicts with his boss, or anyone else he worked with?"

She shook her head. "No. He was on strike, but even the managers liked him. He was a very gentle man." She touched a damp kerchief to her eyes, but it did little to block the tears.

I pushed on. "Did he have any special friends? I'd like to talk to them, if he did."

"My husband was his friend," said Mrs. Martinez. "George worked with Eduardo for years."

"Your husband is a union man?"

She nodded. "Yes, and proud of it. He's a bosun, but it's the same union."

"So he's on strike, too. I'd like to talk with him later."

"He had nothing to do with this explosion business," said Mrs. Martinez, "so you'll be wasting your time if you want him to talk about that."

I turned back to Gloria Alvarez. "Did your husband have any enemies? Was he on bad terms with anyone?"

"No," she said. "I told you. Eduardo had no enemies. He was too sweet for his own good, in fact. He was a pacifist. Did you know that? He was a conscientious objector. He didn't believe in fighting."

"Zee mentioned that he was a pacifist," I said. "Did he have any friends who might not be pacifists? Anyone who might know how he happened to be on the *Trident* last night?"

"He was everyone's friend. Everyone loved him. He's in heaven, but I'm in hell because of what people are thinking of him." More tears ran down her cheeks.

St. Eduardo.

"Did he have a favorite tavern?" I said. "A place where he could meet friends and talk?"

"Eduardo didn't drink alcohol or smoke. He didn't go to taverns."

"Did he go to church?"

"Every week, yes."

"Who is his minister, his priest?"

"Father Zapata," she said. "Why do you ask? I'm sure Father Zapata can tell you nothing about last night."

"You're probably right." I looked at Mrs. Martinez. "Is there a place where the union members meet, do you know? Some pub or coffee shop?"

"They're men," said Mrs. Martinez. "They like coffee and beer. George goes to the Fireside sometimes. I think he sees his friends there, and a lot of his friends belong to the union."

I wasn't getting much help from Gloria, but I tried another couple of questions. "Did your husband gamble? Did he argue with anyone enough to make that person angry?"

"No," said his widow, wiping her tears. "He wasn't a gambler. He would argue, but never so as to anger anyone. He was a good man. A very good man. No one would want to hurt him, and he would never hurt anyone."

And yet somehow Eduardo, like Jesus, had managed to get himself more than just hurt.

I thanked both women for their time, got Sarah Martinez's phone number, and departed. I didn't have much more to go on than when I'd left home, but I had some.

First, though, I drove to the Vineyard Haven police station. The station, which fronts the Stop and Shop parking lot, is pretty impressive from the outside and is a contender, with the Edgartown station, for the best-looking police station on the island. It almost overlooks the site of the explosion.

Inside, I asked a couple of questions and soon found myself sitting in an office across from Sergeant John Sylvester, a man about my age who looked to be fifty or sixty pounds over fighting weight. I'd seen him around town, but I didn't know him.

"What can I do for you?" he asked.

I told him the nature of my quest, and when I was through he said, "We won't know for sure until we get the ME's report, but everything we have now makes it look like Alvarez got himself killed when his own explosive blew up on him." He shrugged. "This strike

43

is getting rougher every day. There are hotheads on both sides, so something like this isn't a big surprise. That said, I think you should call it a day, go home, and leave the driving to us." He smiled.

"Are you treating his death like a homicide?"

"Until they rule otherwise," Sylvester said, "it's a state-police case." The way he said it made me think that he, like a lot of town cops, resented the idea that in Massachusetts the state police were responsible for investigating all homicides, or suspected homicides.

"Are you considering the possibility that Alvarez was a victim? That he didn't set the explosive?" I asked.

His eyes narrowed. "We're considering all of the possibilities."

"Mrs. Alvarez says her husband would never have blown up a boat."

"Al Capone's mother probably thought her baby boy was just misunderstood."

True enough.

"If you find out anything," I said, "will you let me know?"

His smile returned to his lips, but it didn't reach his eyes. "You can read about it in the papers."

I walked down to the harbor and looked at the *Trident*. She was a small, double-ended trimaran ferry boat such as I'd seen in photographs. The only sign of an engine explosion was a blackened area astern around a hatch. She was tied to a pier, and men were standing on the pier with their hands in their pockets looking at her.

I joined them.

"God damned strikers," a man was saying. "They ought to be shot."

His companion nodded. "This here boat carried eight cars at a time. Two, three trips a day. I guess they didn't want that happening. Served the guy right, killing himself like that, maybe. Bad business, though. I don't like it."

"Where'd this boat come from?" I asked.

They both looked at me, as though wondering who I was and whether they should like me or not.

"Down in Connecticut," said the man who'd damned the strikers. "Normally runs out to some little island down there. Came up here to make some real money. Now this happens. Damned shame."

"You're right about that," I said, and thereby seemed to make myself his friend.

He shared another nasty remark or two about the union and nodded knowingly as I left.

I was weary already, and I hadn't even really started to work. Tomorrow seemed soon enough, so I went home.

"Well?" said Zee.

"I told Mrs. Alvarez I'd try to help," I said. "I'll start in the morning. I have some leads, or at least a few places to begin asking questions."

She stood on her toes and kissed me. "Good. Go see what the kids are up to and I'll fix us some martinis. You can meet me on the deck."

I went out to the beech tree and looked up through the leaves. Joshua and Diana and Jim Duarte were all up there, still alive after the earlier attack of the leopard men.

"Come up, Pa!" yelled Diana.

"All right."

I climbed up the ladder, passed through the trapdoor in the floor of the porch of the main room, and found a good limb to sit on. The three children were pleased. I moved carefully after them through the branches, glad that we had a tree house where I could escape from the world where Eduardo Alvarez had lived and died.

Zee called to me from the balcony, inviting me to join her for a little something. The balcony was a big people's place where children were not allowed. The rule had its benefits. While Zee and I sat there, sipping Luksusowa on the rocks and nibbling on crackers and bluefish pâté, I told her what I'd heard from Sergeant Sylvester and the guys on the pier.

"No surprise, I guess," she said. "But it makes me glad that you're going to find out what really happened."

We looked in silence out toward Nantucket Sound, where the sails were white against the blue water and under the blue sky. The colors reminded me of those in paintings of the Virgin Mary.

"Hey, Pa!" It was Joshua's voice coming out of the beech tree.

"What?"

"When you finish your little something, will you come back and play with us some more before Jim has to go home?"

"Sure."

I had returned to the tree when Zee called to me and said that Brady Coyne was on the phone. I told

46

the kids that I'd be back and swung down to the ground on the rope hung for that purpose.

Brady, unable to get a reservation on Cape Air, was coming to the Vineyard the next day but figured the boat strike might strand him in Woods Hole. I told him I'd try to find somebody to bring him across and that I'd call him back.

After I'd wasted more than an hour trying to do that, Zee said, "Why don't you just take the *Shirley J.* over and bring him back yourself? Take the kids with you, so I can shoot with Manny without having any distractions. We'll stick Brady in the guest room and loan him a car and take him fishing when he's through doing whatever work he's going to be doing."

I had planned to start asking questions the next morning, but the thought of a good sail was very appealing. I hesitated.

"The boat needs exercising," said Zee, eyeing me with wifely sagacity.

And Eduardo Alvarez was already dead, and he'd stay that way whether I learned why tomorrow morning, or later, or never.

"You can talk about the case with Brady on the way home," said Zee. "He may have some ideas that will help you."

Good old Zee, giving me reasons to do what she knew I wanted to do anyway.

I called Brady, told him I'd pick him up in Woods Hole at noon, and went back to the tree house. When Joshua and Diana heard my sailing plans, they invited themselves to join me. Jim looked sad, so I invited him too, if it was okay with his folks. Only Zee, who would be shooting with Manny, would be missing from our merry band.

I took Jim home and arranged to pick him up again in the morning.

"You're sure he won't be a bother?" said Mrs. Duarte.

"If he gives me any trouble," I said, looking down at him, "I'll toss him overboard."

"Fine," she said.

At eight the next morning, I made sure that all of our life vests were on securely, then hoisted the *Shirley J.*'s big mainsail and cast her off her stake between the yacht club and the Reading Room. We eased out of Edgartown harbor, pushed by a light west wind, passed the lighthouse, and reached for East Chop on a port tack. The wind rose a bit with the sun and carried us over a mild sea toward the mainland.

I helped the children handle the tiller and showed them how to change the set of the sail just a bit when we could see Woods Hole on the far side of Vineyard Sound. The tide was perfect for our purposes, falling and helping us on our way, then slowly flattening out as we fetched Woods Hole. The sound was alive with boats.

Brady Coyne, overnight case in his hand, was waiting for us. He put his bag on the dock and caught the line I threw. He got into the life vest I tossed to him, and a few moments later we were headed back to the island, with the wind on our starboard beam and a now-rising tide pushing us home.

"'A capital ship on an ocean trip was the *Walloping Window Blind*,'" chanted Brady to the children. "'No wind that blew dismayed the crew or troubled the captain's mind.'"

They liked the poem so much that they asked him to recite the whole thing. To my surprise, he could and did.

"I thought all you read were law books and fishing magazines," I said when the clapping stopped.

"Shows what you know," said Brady. "What's the news with the strike? I hear somebody got blown up on a boat. You know anything about that?"

"Not much, but I hope to know more soon. You want to take the helm?"

"Sure." He took the tiller.

"Just clear the point of West Chop," I said, pointing ahead.

"Aye, Captain."

He sailed a course making a straight wake, and as he did I told him about the job I'd taken and the people I'd talked to. He listened without interruption, and I had the impression, not for the first time, that Brady had some sort of storage unit in his brain where he kept everything he heard just in case he might need to remember it sometime.

"Well," he said when I was done, "you've got the names of some people who might be able to help you. That's a start."

"It's not much."

"No," he said. "It's not."

Off West Chop we were smothered a bit by the highlands, but the sail still pulled, and then it filled again when we crossed the entrance to Vineyard Haven harbor. The water was crowded with boats, large and small, heading to and from the mainland. A big one, the *Neptune,* with four cars on her deck, bounced us with her wake. We fetched East Chop, then hauled in the sheet just a bit for the long reach to Edgartown.

"You know any more about why Larry Bucyck wants to see you?" I asked Brady.

"No more than I knew when I talked to you on the phone," he said.

"It'll ruin my reputation if anybody finds out I'm a friend of Larry Bucyck's lawyer," I said.

"Who said we were friends?" said Brady.

Off the Chappy cliffs we came about and began tacking into Edgartown harbor. The rising tide helped, and we scooted between Chappy Point and the town dock with no problems. A half hour later the *Shirley J.* was back on her stake, sail furled, and we were all ashore on Collins Beach. I chained the dinghy, the *Millennium Falcon,* to the bulwark, so it wouldn't be stolen by gentlemen yachtsmen trying to get back to their boats in the wee, small hours, and we all climbed into the Land Cruiser and headed out of town.

"A successful sail," said Brady, articulating the adage that any sail that gets you home is a successful one.

We returned Jim to his mother and went on to the Jackson house.

Zee gave Brady a kiss. "Put your gear in the guest room," she said. "You know where it is."

Brady shook his head. "Thanks," he said, "but my

client wants me to stay with him, so I guess that's what I better do."

She dropped her car keys in his shirt pocket and gave the pocket a pat. "If you change your mind, cocktails will be served at the usual time."

"You sure you won't need your car?"

"It's yours for the duration," she said, "as long as the duration isn't too long."

"I don't think it will be," Brady said.

"If your client throws you out of the house," she said, "our guest room is yours."

"Thanks, both of you." He kissed her cheek and shook my hand. "I'll keep in touch."

He got into Zee's Jeep and drove away. We watched until he was out of sight.

"How about you?" said Zee. "Do you have any plans for the rest of the day?"

"Somewhere the sun is over the yardarm," I said. "Why don't I make a couple of drinks, and while we sip them you can tell me about your morning shooting practice. Any new thoughts about trying out for the Olympics?"

"No new ones," she said, "but I liked the Feinwerkbau. I'll get us some nibblies while you fix the drinks. The balcony awaits."

Chapter Four

Brady

I left the Jacksons' house a little before five in Zee's sporty little red Jeep Wrangler, heading west on the Edgartown–West Tisbury Road. J.W. said it would take about twenty minutes to get to Menemsha.

I found myself smiling at J.W.'s and Zee's casual generosity. Whenever I was on the island, they always had a bed for me, no matter how spur-of-the-moment my visit might be. They called their guest room "Brady's Room," though I suspected they also called it "Uncle Charlie's Room" and "Cousin Tilda's Room," depending on who might be sleeping there. And they always made one of their cars available to me. They would've been insulted if I ever brought my own vehicle over on the ferry or rented one. They also made sure a spare house key dangled from the key chain along with the car key. Not only was their *casa* my *casa*, but their refrigerator and shower and TV set and computer were mine, too.

Plus, no matter what they had going on in their lives, if I was on the island, one or both of them would drop everything to take me fishing.

I did my best to match their hospitality. Once or

twice in the winter, J.W. and Zee found a babysitter for the kids, came to America, and took in a B.S.O. concert. I drove to Woods Hole to pick them up, and they spent the night with Evie and me. And in the summer I finagled six Red Sox tickets, and Evie and I treated the Jackson family to a game at Fenway. We gave the grown-ups our guest room and put the kids in my office with sleeping bags.

J.W. and Zee seemed happy with the bottle of Grey Goose vodka I'd remembered to bring. I gave Joshua a book about animal tracks and Diana a CD of bird-songs, and they smiled and said, Thank you, Uncle Brady.

I was hoping I could take care of Larry Bucyck's mysterious business quickly and then spend a little time with the Jacksons.

According to Larry, it had been five years since I'd been there, but as I approached Menemsha, it all started to look familiar, and after I crossed Middle Road, I recognized the left turn that would take me to his shack in the woods. In my memory, it was a dusty little country roadway with a few modest homes tucked back behind the trees. Now it had been straightened and widened and black-topped. Progress.

Four or five big new houses perched uncomfortably in clearings close to the road where there had been a scrubby oak-and-pine forest the last time I was there, cookie-cutter McMansions with three-car garages and professionally landscaped lawns and gardens. You might expect to see aesthetically challenged homes such as these in some cluster development in Acton or Westwood, but not in bucolic Menemsha out at the far end of Martha's Vineyard. Next thing you knew, there'd be Wal-Marts and Circuit Cities and multiplex theaters all over the island.

A hundred yards past the last McMansion, I spotted the ruts angling off to the left. Larry's driveway. Bushes crowded close along both sides, and knee-high weeds grew among the rocks in the ruts. It looked like nobody had driven a vehicle up Larry Bucyck's driveway for years. I was happy to be in Zee's Wrangler, with its high clearance and four-wheel drive.

As I turned onto the ruts, I noticed a giant stack of rocks in the woods. When I looked again, I realized it was a stone sculpture, an objet d'art. It stood there like an eight-foot-tall sentinel guarding the entry to Larry's property, and I was compelled to stop the car so I could absorb it. Its base was a waist-high boulder the shape of a crude flat-topped pyramid. A chunky, weather-beaten boulder at least three feet square was balanced atop the pyramid, and on top of that was a flat rock about five feet wide. The head was a smaller roundish boulder the size of a deformed beach ball.

It represented—to me, at least—a woman. A primitive, Easter Island woman, dignified and powerful and elegant. It was obviously man-made—by Larry Bucyck, I assumed—but it fit so naturally into the landscape that it looked as if it had been there since before history.

Larry had mentioned something about a stone sculpture. This was it. Awesome.

A little farther down the driveway I spotted another rock assemblage in the woods. This one represented a squat animal of some kind. A hippo, maybe, or some kind of dinosaur. Two square rocks side by side with one enormous rectangular boulder balanced atop them. I couldn't begin to estimate how much the hippo's body weighed or to guess how it had been lifted atop its legs. It was the size of a small sofa.

The roadway curved around to the right, and Larry Bucyck's little house sat in a small clearing in the woods. Several other stone sculptures stood guard around it. A few of them were nothing more than two or three big boulders balanced atop another one like snowmen, deceptively simple structures that compelled me to notice the shapes and colors of the rocks and the way eons of weather had etched designs into them. Others suggested animals and ships.

I pulled into what passed for a front yard—an area of beaten-down grass where about a dozen Rhode Island Red chickens were pecking gravel. A brown-black-and-white dog with floppy ears snoozed on his side in a patch of afternoon sunshine. An old balloon-tire bicycle with a rusty wire basket on the handlebars leaned against the side of the house.

When I got out of the Jeep, some of the hens came over to check me out. The dog lifted his head, looked at me, then dropped it back onto his paws and closed his droopy eyes.

Since I'd been there last, Larry had added a small lean-to–shaped room onto the side of what I remembered as a square, one-room shack. Otherwise, it hadn't changed. Vertical planks for walls, a few mismatched windows, a weathered oak door, an aluminum stovepipe sticking out of the roof.

It was bigger than Thoreau's hut on the banks of Walden Pond, fourteen or fifteen feet square. But its purpose—to simplify, simplify, to enable Larry to "front only the essential facts of life"—was the same. Thoreau wrote philosophy and stuck it out for a little more than two years at Walden. Larry Bucyck built rock sculptures. He had lived here in the woods of Menemsha for about fifteen years.

The scent of salt air was strong, and I remembered that the ground sloped away behind the house so that you could see Menemsha Pond, just a few hundred yards away, and off to the right, Vineyard Sound.

If you were determined to become a hermit, you could do worse than hole up here.

I stood there for a minute, then cleared my throat and said, "Hey, Larry? You here?"

When there was no response, I knocked on the door and called Larry's name again. I waited there for a minute, then went over to one of the windows and pressed my face against the glass. The inside of Larry's house was one dimly lit room—a sink with a hand pump and what appeared to be an icebox at one end, a square table with a kerosene lantern on it, three mismatched wooden chairs, a couple of stuffed chairs, several bookcases bulging with books and magazines and loose papers, and one narrow bed.

Larry wasn't inside.

I remembered that the outhouse was out back. Maybe that's where he was. I headed for the rear of the house. Three or four of the chickens followed me.

I turned the corner and paused there, admiring the view and looking around for Larry—and that's when something slammed against the backs of my knees. My legs felt as if they'd been chopped off, and I toppled forward onto the ground.

Then something round and hard jammed into my kidneys.

"Don't move," growled a voice, "or I'll blow a hole in you."

"Aw, Larry, Jesus," I said. "It's me."

"Brady?" he said.

"Like you weren't expecting me? Cripes. What did you do to my legs? Feels like you cut me off at the knees with a machete or something."

I felt his hand on my shoulder. He helped me to roll over and sit up. "Your legs'll be okay," he said. "I paralyzed the tendons, that's all."

"Paralyzed," I said. "Excellent. I think you crippled me for life."

"Naw. I coulda, but I didn't. It's a trick somebody showed me. Those tendons behind your knees, you can paralyze them, what I did, but it only lasts a minute. I'm sorry, you know? But you'll be okay. I was afraid you were somebody coming after me." He was holding what appeared to be a walking stick. It was a four-foot length of inch-thick sapling with the twigs cut off, an excellent weapon for knee-tendon whacking. Judging by the bark, it was from an oak tree. He put it to his shoulder, pointed it at me, grinned, and said, "Bang, bang. You're dead."

"Oh, great," I said. "So you got the drop on me with a stick." I sat there with my arms wrapped around my knees and looked up at him.

Larry Bucyck seemed taller and skinnier and more

creased and wrinkled than last time I'd seen him—
which, of course, is what happens to people as they
get older. His hairline had receded quite a bit. His
scraggly beard and the long hair that he'd pulled back
into a ponytail were now more gray than blond. It was
hard to see the pink-cheeked, broad-shouldered young
major-league pitcher in this Larry Bucyck. Now he just
looked like a sinewy old hippie in baggy jeans and a
dirty T-shirt.

"So is this how you normally greet your friends?"
I said. "Loyal, concerned friends who come all the
way from America because you told them you had a
problem and needed their help? You try to disable
them?"

"Aw, hell, Brady. Really, man. I said I was sorry. I
guess I'm a little edgy these days."

"Edgy? That what you call it?"

"Nervous, that's all."

"Full-blown paranoid," I said. "Certifiably psy-
chopathic, if you ask me. You gonna tell me why?"

He held his hand down to me. "Come on. Stand
up. Walk around a little, your legs'll feel better."

I took his hand and hoisted myself to my feet.

"Go on, walk around," Larry said. "Stretch 'em out."

I did, and pretty soon my legs didn't hurt anymore.
Larry was watching me. "Better, right?"

I nodded. "They were even better before you hit me."

He smiled, stepped toward me, wrapped both arms
around my shoulders, and hugged me hard. "Man,"
he said, "I'm glad you're here."

I returned his hug, then stepped back from him.
"So why don't you tell me what it's all about, you're

glad I'm here, urgent phone calls, whacking people behind their knees."

"You hungry yet?" he said. "Dinner's about ready. Raked the quahogs this morning, low tide right at dawn, couldn't be fresher, soaked 'em, shucked 'em, washed 'em, cut up the potatoes and onions and everything, had the chowder simmering all afternoon, man."

He pointed his walking stick at a steaming black kettle that was nestled in a bed of coals near the rear corner of the house. I went over, pried the cover off with a stick, and took a sniff.

"Yum," I said to Larry. "Saliva is dribbling off my chin. I could eat anytime."

"As soon as I hung up yesterday," Larry said, "I remembered the ferry strike. I don't pay much attention to the news. I mean, I avoid it if I can. But I should've remembered that. I felt terrible, asking you to come down here, no ferry."

"I got a ride on a catboat," I said. "It was fun. I never would've done that if you hadn't called."

He smiled. "Aw, you're just saying that."

"I wouldn't say it if I didn't mean it."

"Right. Brady No Bullshit Coyne."

"That's me," I said. "So you gonna tell me what this is all about?"

"I got some pigs," he said. "Wannna go see my pigs?"

"No," I said. "I want to know what kind of trouble you think you're in, what you want to show me, what I can do for you."

He nodded. "Yeah, I don't blame you. They're just

pigs, I guess. I call them Pig One, Pig Two, Pig Three, like that. I was afraid if I gave them people names, I'd never be able to slaughter them. I built a sty for them downwind in the woods. Want some wine?"

I was beginning to remember how Larry's mind worked. When he was fresh out of college, a hot-shot pitcher with a major-league contract and a pretty wife, he was smart and articulate and funny. Reporters loved him. But after living alone for all these years, avoiding human intercourse, his social skills had atrophied to the point where you could never be sure if he even heard what you said, and the easiest thing was to just go with his mind's peculiar flow.

"Wine," I said, "would be nice."

"You stay here, have a seat, stir the pot," he said, waving his hand at the black kettle.

I went over and sat on a rock beside the cast-iron kettle. It was resting on a bed of red coals mixed with baseball-sized rocks. I guessed Larry had built a big hardwood fire there, and as it burned down to coals, the rocks themselves became red-hot. They would hold their heat for a long time, providing perfect simmering conditions for a vat of quahog chowder.

I picked up the long-handled wooden spoon that sat in it and gave it a stir, and that released a new cloud of aroma.

A few minutes later Larry came back with two jelly glasses three-quarters filled with a cloudy greenish-yellow liquid. He handed one of them to me, then sat on a rock beside me.

I sniffed the wine, then looked up at him with my eyebrows arched.

"Apple and pear and rose hips," he said. "Made it myself. It's really good. Take a swig."

I put the glass to my lips and let a little slide into my mouth. Tears instantly sprang to my eyes, and I had all I could do to resist the urge to spit it out. Larry's wine tasted like Liquid Drano.

"Wow," I said.

"Yeah," Larry said, "it's pretty strong. It's got more alcohol in it than regular wine. Robust, I call it." He tilted up his glass, poured about a third of it into his mouth, rolled it from cheek to cheek, swallowed it, and smiled. "Nice, huh?"

"I've had moonshine that went down smoother than this," I said. "Jesus." I put the glass down. "Come on, Larry. Let's have it. What's so important, I had to hitch a ride on a catboat to come down here to meet with you?"

"Did you see my sculptures?"

"Hard to miss them. They're magnificent. Stunning."

He grinned. "Yeah? You think so? Really?"

I nodded. "I really do. I'm Brady No Bullshit Coyne, remember? I don't like your wine, but I'm very impressed with your sculptures. What kind of machines did you use to build them, anyway?"

"Machines? Gas-powered machines, you mean? Like backhoes or something?" He shook his head. "No machines. No way. Machines would violate the woods, contradict the spirit of my sculptures." He smiled. "Levers and pulleys and human muscles. That's it for machines."

"Does somebody help you, at least? Those boulders must weigh tons."

"Don't need help." He tapped his head with his forefinger. "Just need to figure them out. Levers and pulleys and muscles and time. That's it."

"How much time?"

He spread his hands as if time didn't matter. "You can't rush it. You can't think about how long it will take or how hard it will be. I never pay attention to time. The sun rises and sets, the tide comes in and goes out, the moon grows and shrinks, the seasons come and go. That's all you need to know about time. Takes three seasons to grow a sculpture, I guess. Start in the springtime after the winter heaves up the rocks, finish in the fall. That's usually how it goes. One sculpture a year. Looking at the rocks takes a long time, seeing what's in 'em, figuring which ones belong together, understanding what they mean, what they want, what their destiny is, then visualizing how they'll look. You can't rush that. Then bringing them together, rigging the pulleys, all that." He grinned. "I got all the time in the world."

Well, I wanted to say, *I don't, so let's get on with why you dragged me down here that sounded so urgent on the telephone.*

But Larry wasn't going to let me push him. He'd tell me his story when the time was right. To him, this was just another form of building sculptures. You couldn't rush it, or it wouldn't come out right.

I found myself feeling oddly envious of Larry Bucyck, who'd made a life for himself that was the polar opposite of mine, a life with no deadlines or obligations, no worries about money or relationships, dependent on nobody, nobody dependent on him. Eat, sleep, build sculptures, rake quahogs according to the earth's clock. Not so bad.

We sat on the rocks around the kettle behind Larry's house. He stirred the chowder and I gazed down at Menemsha Pond, where the cottages and houses and docks that crowded its banks were beginning to show their lights. Beyond the pond, the sun was sinking into the sound, and we didn't say much. Larry had made it clear that he'd tell me what he had to tell me when he was ready.

I tried another sip of his wine, and this time I was ready for it, and it wasn't so bad. It numbed my mouth and burned all the way down, leaving a faint aftertaste of fruit and rubbing alcohol.

When Larry noticed my empty glass, he grabbed it and started to stand up.

"No," I said. "No more. Please."

"I got plenty," he said.

"One glass of that stuff was an adventure," I said. "Two would be sheer folly."

Larry made his quahog chowder the way my grandmother used to, with a thin milk broth, lots of fresh-from-the-mud-flats chopped-up quahogs, plenty of potato and onion and crispy salt pork, coarse-ground black pepper. He served it in big wooden bowls he'd carved himself, with a loaf of round bread that he'd baked in an outdoor Dutch oven.

It was all delicious, and by the time I finished eating I understood that Larry had figured out how to live the life he'd chosen.

I'd always assumed he'd gone to the woods in Menemsha to escape the unbearable pressures and pains of baseball notoriety. Now I understood that he'd been seeking rather than escaping all along, whether he knew it or not, and it seemed to me that he'd found what he was looking for.

We sat in Larry's backyard eating bread and chowder, and afterward we sipped some kind of herbal tea and watched the moon rise over the ocean. Larry didn't seem inclined to talk, and I gave up trying to push it.

It was fully dark when Larry stood up, said, "Come on," and started walking down the long wooded slope toward Menemsha Pond.

We followed a meandering trail that might have been created by deer. The moon and stars of the August night sky lit our way. I remembered how pervasive smog and ambient city light obscured the sky over Boston. Down here on Martha's Vineyard the air was pure and the lights were few. It was a Montana sky, big and clean. You could see for light-years into it.

After about five minutes we emerged from the woods at a band of shoulder-high marsh grass on the bank of the pond.

Larry put his hand on my arm and pointed off to the left. "This way," he whispered.

We skulked through the woods along the rim of the pond until we found ourselves hiding in a clump of rhododendrons alongside a house. A short wooden dock extended from the front of the house into the pond. It was dark.

We appeared to be about halfway around the east side of the pond. A point of land extended into the pond about fifty yards or so off to our right. Farther off to the right it narrowed and opened to the ocean. Off to our left it opened up into a big round pond a mile or more in diameter.

"Now what?" I said.

"Now we wait," he said. "Watch over there." He jerked his thumb at the point of land to our right. A cottage of some kind, a summer house, it looked like, sat just inside it, and another dock extended from it into the pond. Orange light glowed from a couple of windows. "You'll see."

The salty breeze was sharp, and after a while I found myself shivering in spite of my fleece jacket. Larry wore just a flannel shirt, but he didn't seem to notice the night chill.

He crouched there, gazing over at the cottage and the dock, and I had no choice but to crouch and gaze with him. I saw nothing. No boat was tied to the dock, and I detected no sign that anybody occupied the cottage except for the lights in the windows.

We'd been hiding there for at least an hour when I poked him and said, "Listen, I—"

He slapped my shoulder and hissed, "Shh."

We waited some more. The moon moved across the sky, and the breeze lay down, and my legs cramped up, and I began to shiver in the nighttime chill.

Larry was infinitely patient. Maybe it was easier,

knowing what the hell he was waiting for, but I had the impression that he was prepared to spend the night out there kneeling on the mulch in the rhododendrons.

I guessed it was well past midnight when he touched my shoulder and said, "It's not going to happen. Let's go."

We crept back along the rim of the pond to Larry's deer trail, then followed it up the long wooded slope to his house.

We went inside. His dog, which had been lying in the dust beside the door, lumbered to his feet and followed us. He had short legs, long ears, and soulful eyes. Mostly basset, with a sprinkling of other DNA mixed in.

"What's your dog's name?" I said.

"Rocket," said Larry.

"Because he runs fast?"

He smiled. "Not hardly. Named him after Roger Clemens. He was kinda my hero."

"Your teammate back then?"

He nodded. "Best pitcher I ever saw."

Rocket waddled over and curled up in a corner.

Larry lit a couple of kerosene lamps. "How about some wine?" he said.

"That stuff," I said, "is not wine."

"It's good, though, huh?"

"Actually," I said, "I wouldn't mind having a little. Warm me up."

He poured two jelly glasses full, handed one to me, put the wine jug on the table, then stoked up his woodstove.

Pretty soon, between Larry's moonshine wine and the woodstove, my chill was gone.

I leaned across the table and narrowed my eyes at him. "Okay," I said. "No more bullshit, no more evasion, no more changing the subject. I want you to tell me what I'm doing down here, whether it embarrasses you or not."

He took a long pull from his wineglass, then set it on the table. "I'm not embarrassed," he said. "I'm scared, is what I am. I haven't been scared since I quit baseball. I'd forgotten what a crappy feeling it is."

I started to speak, but he held up his hand. "If they catch me," he said, "they'll kill me. I can't prove that to you, but it's what I believe. It's how I feel. I'm scared to death. That's why I whacked the back of your knees. This isn't me, Brady. I stopped being scared as soon as I stopped worrying about where my fastball was going to end up. I don't hurt people. I don't believe in it. But I hit you. More wine?"

I shrugged, and he topped off my jelly glass.

He refilled his own glass full from the earthenware jug. "The other night," he said, "the night I called you? Um, when was that?"

"You called yesterday," I said. "That was Thursday."

"Okay," he said. "This happened Wednesday, then. High tide was around midnight. I was down at the pond fishing. Out on the end of the dock where we just were, right next to that house we were looking at. Guy named Mumford, I think his name is, owns it. The one we were watching. He's a rich doctor of some kind, only comes down in the summer. I like to fish off that dock where we were, next to Mumford's place. It's a great spot for flounder, the way the currents curl in there. The flounder move into the pond this time of year, and from the end of the dock you can catch a mess of 'em just dropping a hand line, nice dinner-plate size. Clams or mussels for bait. So I'm out there on the dock, got my little kerosene lantern beside me, nice night, sky full of stars, big full moon, flounder biting good, and then I see this big boat coming through the jetties into the pond. Oh, must've been sixty, sixty-five feet long. I didn't think too much about it, lots of rich people, big boats around here, but then, what got my attention, soon as this boat passes through the cut it doused its lights. I could barely hear its engines, they're so quiet, just burbling. Even so, I didn't think too much about it. The flounder were biting good and it was none of my business. But still, it was unusual, you know?" Larry arched his eyebrows at me.

I nodded and waited for him to continue.

He splashed more wine into our glasses. I didn't bother to object.

"I'm not sure why," he said, "but when that boat turned off its lights, I blew out my lantern. It seemed like it was going to pass right in front of me where I was sitting there at the end of the dock, so without thinking about it I kind of crouched down behind a piling. There was something sneaky about the boat, evil, almost, going slow and quiet like that, no lights, and it made me nervous. I could see that there were some men on the deck. They seemed to be looking around, kind of studying everything, watchful, suspicious, you know? It was pretty obvious they didn't want anybody to see them, and that made me duck my head down even lower."

"Did you catch the name of the boat?" I said.

He shook his head. "Never got a look at the transom."

"Make or model?"

"I don't know much about boats," he said. "All I know is, this one was white, and it was a big fancy one. Had those gizmos twirling on top of the cabin. Radar, I guess, and lots of antennae and stuff."

"Okay," I said. "So what happened?"

"Well, like I said, the boat kind of spooked me. It wasn't just the fact that it was running without lights, which if the Coast Guard ever caught them would be a giant fine. That was strange. But there was something else I couldn't put my finger on. Those guys on the deck, maybe. All watchful and tense. I don't know. So anyway, the boat turns on its searchlight, pans around the shoreline, then curves around and pulls up to Dr. Mumford's dock. Then some other people come down from the cottage onto the dock with flashlights, and I caught a few quick glimpses of those men. I could see that they were wearing dark turtleneck jerseys and blue jeans and black watch caps, and a couple of them had machine guns slung over their shoulders. They were talking into walkie-talkies or cell phones or something. I could hear the mumble of their voices across the water from their dock to the one I was on, but couldn't make out any words. Couldn't even tell if they were speaking English, but—"

"Whoa," I said. "Back up. Machine guns?"

He nodded. "Those small ones. Uzis, maybe? Let me finish. So they tied off at Dr. Mumford's dock and offloaded some wooden crates from the boat and lugged them to a van that was parked there at the end of the dock with its lights on and motor running."

"Any idea what was in those crates?"

He shook his head. "They were, I don't know, three or four feet long, and they looked to be pretty heavy. It took two men to carry one of them."

"How many crates?"

He shrugged. "Six or eight. Maybe more. I didn't count."

"What about the van? Any writing on it?"

"Like I said, it was just moonlight and some flashlights. There might've been some kind of logo on the side, but I'm not sure. I couldn't tell you the make or model, either."

"So what happened?"

"The longer I kneeled there behind the piling, the scareder I got. I just wanted to get the hell out of there, but I wanted to see what they were doing, too. After they finished unloading those crates, some of the men stood around talking. I could hear their voices across the water, but I couldn't tell what they were saying. And then the van drove away and the men got back on the boat, and it backed away from the dock, still not showing any lights." Larry looked at me. "Then I did something stupid."

"They saw you?" I said.

"The boat started to turn," he said, "and they were going to pass right in front of me, and I guess I panicked. I—I ran, and almost instantly there's a shout and then this big searchlight from the boat goes on, sweeping across the water toward me, and, Jesus, I realize they've spotted me. Their light's panning around, and I'm running down that dock, seems like it's about a mile long, and then they've got me in their beam and I'm waiting for them to start shooting their Uzis at me, but they don't, and then I'm off the dock and zigzagging across the yard, trying to get behind the house and into the woods, and a couple times the searchlight catches me and they yell some more, but I can't tell what they're saying, not that I care. Couldn't even tell if it was English. I just keep going, running as fast as I can, waiting for them to shoot me. But they don't shoot, and I realize, they don't want anyone to hear gunshots, and they're out there on their boat and I'm on land, and if I just keep running they'll never catch me. So that's what I did. I ran all the way home. And they didn't catch me."

"And you're all right," I said.

"They saw me," he said. "They know what I look like."

"How well could they have seen you?"

"That spotlight, it was like I was on a stage. They probably had binoculars. I think they saw me pretty good."

"You're saying you think they might recognize you?"

He nodded. "That's what I'm afraid of. Not many people look like me."

I looked at him, imagined him running down the dock. Tall, skinny, with his scruffy beard and that gray-blond ponytail trailing behind him. He was probably right. "That was two nights ago, huh?" I said.

"Don't tell me not to be scared," he said.

"All I'm saying is, if they were going to try to catch up with you, they probably would've done it by now."

"I went back last night," he said. "After I called you."

"You're that scared, but you went back?"

"I didn't go out on the dock. I hid in the bushes, like we did. I just wanted to see if they came back again."

"Did they?"

He nodded. "It was the same thing as before. They pulled up to the dock in front of Dr. Mumford's place, and the van was there, and they offloaded more boxes."

"Did you notice anything different?"

He shook his head.

"So you brought me down here because you wanted me to see this boat offloading big wooden crates at night."

"And because I'm scared," he said. "They saw me. They know I saw them. They had machine guns."

"But they didn't show up tonight," I said. "So maybe whatever they were doing, they're finished. Maybe they're gone, and you won't have to worry about them anymore."

Larry looked down at the table and shook his head. "Yeah, maybe I overreacted. Maybe I shouldn't've bothered you. Maybe it's nothing."

"No," I said, "it's something. Of course it's something."

"I keep thinking I should tell somebody," said Larry. "Except if I do, they'll know who told. Me. The guy they caught in their searchlight. They had guns, Brady."

I took a sip of wine, blinked away the rush of tears in my eyes, took another sip, then said, "You called me, and here I am. So what do you want me to do?"

He looked up at me and shrugged. "I don't know."

"We've got to report it."

He shook his head. "Not me, man. I'm staying out of it."

"You want me to handle it. That your idea?"

"You're a lawyer."

"Meaning, you're my client, whatever you tell me is privileged. Right?"

"That's what I was thinking," he said. "Yes. I mean, you can report what I told you. Just leave me out of it."

I smiled. "Okay, so let's see. I go to, say, the Coast Guard station here in Menemsha, and I say, 'I'm a lawyer, and this client of mine, he saw this big boat come into the pond, and there were men with guns, and they were offloading some big wooden crates.' What do you think the Coast Guard people would say to me?"

Larry nodded. "First thing they'd say, I guess, would be, Who is this client? What you're telling us, it's nothing but hearsay. Get your client in here so we can cross-examine him and get the story firsthand." He reached across the table and put his hand on my wrist. "See, Brady? That's why I wanted to show it to you. So you could see it for yourself. So it wouldn't be secondhand."

"Relieve you of all responsibility, huh?"

He nodded. "You put it that way, yeah, I guess so. So I'm telling you, you can't mention me. If I tell you not to tell anybody where you heard what you heard, that's what you've gotta do, right?"

I nodded. "If you insist, yes. You're my client. Whatever you tell me is privileged."

"I didn't move down here to get involved," Larry said. "All I want is to be left alone."

"If you really felt that way," I said, "you wouldn't have dragged me down here. You think you've seen something shady and dangerous, and you can't ignore it."

"I guess you're right," he said. "I couldn't ignore it. So I told you. I did my civic duty. So will you do it?"

"Me?" I shook my head. "Oh no. Not me. Us. Whether you like it or not, we're going to handle this together."

He shook his head. "Aw, man . . ."

"You and me, Larry."

"Not if I don't want to. And I don't. I don't want to. You can't make me."

"You want to be responsible for somebody getting blown up or something? Is your—your anonymity, or whatever you call it, your privacy—is that worth it?"

He looked at me, then shrugged. "Yeah, I guess I knew you were gonna say that. Okay, then. What are *we* going to do?"

"Right now," I said, "we're going to go to sleep. It's the middle of the night, and that wine has reached my brain."

Larry gave me a crooked smile. "Mine, too. Whew."

"Tomorrow night," I said, "we'll go back to the pond, hide in the bushes. I'll bring my cell phone. If that boat comes in, we'll call the Coast Guard."

"What if they don't show up?"

"We'll go to the Coast Guard anyway, tell them your story."

"You could go back to the pond without me," said Larry. "I showed you how to get there."

"Maybe I could. But I'm not going to. It's gonna be you and me."

"You don't understand," he said. "I need my life to be simple. I need my privacy. I can't—"

"Think of it this way," I said. "If I go there without you, and if they spot me and catch me and shoot me, how will you feel?"

"Oh, man," he said. "I just wish to hell I'd never gone flounder fishing that night."

"We'll take care of it in the morning," I said. "Right now, I've got to go to sleep."

"You take the bed." He pointed his chin at the bed. It wasn't much bigger than a cot, but it had what looked like a clean blanket and a plumped-up pillow on it.

"What about you?" I said. "I can't take your only bed."

"I sleep outside in the hammock in the summer."

"Will you feel, um, safe, sleeping outside?"

He smiled. "Rocket will be with me. He's not much of a watchdog, but he'll howl like crazy if he hears noises in the night. You ever hear a basset howl?"

I smiled. "Doesn't it get a little chilly for sleeping outside this time of year?"

"That's how I like it." He stood up, staggered, and braced his hand against the wall. "Wow. My wine's pretty good, huh?"

I stood up, too. When the room began to spin, I sat down again. "Your wine," I said, "is positively lethal."

He grinned.

I stood up again, more carefully this time, and after a moment the room righted itself.

Larry and I went outside and peed in the yard. The sky was bottomless and full of stars, and the air was chilly.

"Sure you'll be all right," I said, "sleeping outdoors?"

"I'm used to it." Larry grinned. "All that wine, I bet I could sleep through a nor'easter."

After we zipped up, he said, "I don't want to talk to anybody, Brady. Do I have to?"

"I'll be with you," I said. "It'll be okay."

He nodded. "Okay," he said. "I trust you." He wrapped his arms around me and hugged me hard. "Thanks, man."

I patted his back. "It's what lawyers are for."

Then I staggered inside and went to bed.

Chapter Five

J.W.

Father Georgio Zapata headed one of the dozen or so small churches on the island that offered religious services to the growing Vineyard population of people of Portuguese and Latino descent, many of them Brazilian. They, like the practitioners of every ethnic or religious group of which I was aware, apparently couldn't agree about what constituted the True Faith and therefore worshipped at a lot of different churches, varying from Protestant evangelical ones to others preaching forms of ultraconservative Catholicism. As a Baptist friend once told me, "If you have four Baptists, you have at least three churches."

Zapata's church was reportedly an institution of his own making, combining elements from various more traditional forms of Christian worship, chiefly Roman Catholicism. I presumed he'd taken his title as Father from the latter.

Gossip had it that Zapata had been born in Brazil but, like many South Americans, had only arrived in the United States after wandering and working, and in his case preaching, his way through Central America and Mexico. In any case, he led two services on Sun-

79

days, one in Portuguese in the morning and one in Spanish in the evening, thereby saving his different congregations from the dangers of nodding off while listening to sermons in languages they didn't understand. It was a wise idea, I thought, remembering the Bible story of the young man named Eutychus who, when listening to Paul preach, had gone to sleep and fallen out of a third-floor window and been killed, thus becoming the first person officially recorded as bored to death by a sermon. For this I had personally canonized him, making him St. Eutychus.

When he wasn't leading his flock, Father Zapata ran a company called Zapata Landscaping and was doing good business. He owned half a dozen trucks and a couple of backhoes adorned with the company logo, and he had several crews of workers armed with the hand tools they needed to establish and care for gardens, lawns, hedges, trees, and shrubs.

Since it was Saturday, I caught up with him overseeing the work at a big new house not far from the Katama airport. He was a medium-sized man who appeared to be in his thirties. He wore a billed Red Sox cap and a white shirt over khaki work pants. He was calling out some orders in Portuguese when I approached, but switched immediately to only slightly accented English when I asked if he was Father Zapata. He was one of those people whose hands moved when they talked, rising, falling, constantly gesturing. I'd often wondered if such people could speak at all if they had to keep their hands in their pockets.

"I am Georgio Zapata," he said, and he put out one of those bronzed hands.

I took it. He had a good grip, but not one of those that intentionally tests the hand it meets.

I gave him my name and said, "Any relation to Emiliano?"

He smiled and shook his head. "Not that I know of, though I wouldn't mind if I was."

"Do you share his views about politics and economics?"

He spread those talkative hands. "Emiliano fought for the poor, and they are my people as well. I try to lift them up even though Jesus said they will always be among us. My sermons are mostly along the lines of loving God and following the golden rule."

"It's a better rule than most," I said. "I've been asked to investigate the death of Eduardo Alvarez. Since I don't know much about him, and since he was one of your parishioners, I hoped to talk with you about the sort of man he was."

Zapata's friendly smile lingered on his face. "He was an ordinary man, like all of us. He will be greatly missed."

"His wife described him as almost a saint."

Zapata's voice was kind. "I have known many men and women, but no saints."

I said, "It's popularly believed that Eduardo killed himself by accident when he blew up the engine of the *Trident*. His wife says that's impossible because he didn't believe in violence and would never have done such a thing. What do you think?"

He put his hands on his chest. "Our Savior tells us to judge not, that we be not judged."

"That's probably good advice," I said, "but I'd still

like your thoughts about Eduardo. You don't have to judge him. Just describe him. Was he as gentle as his wife says he was? Or was he capable of violence?"

Zapata looked around the yard at his workmen, then brought his eyes back to mine. "Even Christ grew angry at the money changers."

"I can refer to scripture, too, and the devil can quote it," I said a little impatiently, "but I'm asking about Eduardo Alvarez."

He held up a hand. "Peace, Mr. Jackson. Peace. All I mean to say is that even the best of us are capable of almost any act if the circumstances are right. Eduardo was probably no different. But if you'll grant me that caveat, I will say that he was the very last person I would have thought of as a potential bomber. He supported the union out of loyalty, but he hated the anger and violence that pervaded the strike. He wanted the strike to end before anyone got hurt."

"Ironic."

"Yes. I never heard him say a bad word about anyone on either side of the issue."

I didn't know what I expected to learn from Zapata, but whatever it was, I hadn't gotten much that was new. I asked, "Do you have any idea what he might have been doing in the engine room of the *Trident*?"

"I do not." His hands opened to show they held nothing.

"Do you know of any friend who might have led him to do something he otherwise would never have done? Some more passionate partisan, perhaps."

Zapata shook his head. "My people rejoice in their feelings, but few of them have close emotional ties with the boat line. They're concerned about the strike because it may make their lives more difficult, but no more or less than other people on the island who have the same concerns."

"Is there anyone in your congregation who might know why Eduardo was on the docks that night and not at work at the restaurant where he was supposed to be?"

He was silent for a moment, then said, "No, I can't think of any such person. Perhaps you should make inquiries at the restaurant."

"I plan to do that." I scribbled my name and phone number on a piece of paper and gave it to him. "Well, thanks for your time. If you think of anything, please let me know. Gloria Alvarez hates these rumors about her husband."

He shook my hand. "I will. You are doing a good thing. It is a blessing for those who mourn to have one who comforts them."

"That's a twist on the beatitude," I said. "Besides, I haven't comforted anyone yet."

"You're trying," he replied. "God gives you credit for trying."

"That's good," I said.

I'm leery of anyone who presumes to know God's desires, and Zapata seemed to read my mind. "It's called faith," he said, smiling and pointing a forefinger toward the sky.

It was mid-morning, but not too soon to visit the Wheelhouse, since the restaurant served breakfast, lunch, and dinner. Most tourists were not yet up and about, so I figured I might even find a parking place.

On Martha's Vineyard, certain locations attract restaurants that go out of business within a couple of years only to be replaced by other restaurants that go out of business a couple of years later. According to my friend John Skye, who is a professor of things medieval at Weststock College, a lot of people who love food are sure that they would find bliss in opening a restaurant and running it the way it should be run. The problem, he says, probably correctly, is that a love of food and cooking is not a guarantee of a successful restaurant any more than a love of books is a guarantee of a successful bookstore. What any business takes is a good business mind, an unimaginable amount of hard work, and a lot of luck.

The Wheelhouse was the latest restaurant incarnation on a site on Edgartown's upper Main Street, not far from Cannon Ball Park, so-called because it features stacks of cannon balls much too large for the cannons situated beside them. There had been other restaurants in the building before it became the Wheelhouse, and there would probably be others to come, because it looked like a wonderful site in spite of the historical evidence that it was not.

I parked in the restaurant's almost-empty lot and went inside.

The place was halfway between breakfast and lunch, and the only people there were cooks in the kitchen and workers setting things up for the noon crowd they hoped would come. I asked to see the manager and was directed to her office.

She turned out to be a woman whose face I'd seen around town. She was about my age and had reading glasses on her nose. She looked a bit harried but had time to stand up from her desk and give me a smile and a handshake.

I gave her my name and thanked her for seeing me, since obviously she was busy.

"I'm Nellie Gray," she said, sitting back down. She waved at the piles of menus, orders, and food and restaurant magazines that cluttered the room. "Forgive the mess. What can I do for you?"

I told her the nature of my investigation and ended my speech by saying, "Eduardo Alvarez was supposed to be working for you last Wednesday night, when he was killed. I'm hoping that you or someone else who was here can tell me why he wasn't here."

She tightened her lips and shook her head. "I wish he had come to work here that night, because then he'd still be alive. I liked him. He was a hard worker and until that night had been absolutely dependable. He didn't call in to say he wasn't coming. He just never showed up. That happens sometimes, especially this time of year when some college kid doesn't see any need to tell you he's leaving."

I nodded. "The scuttle is that they're kids who want a vacation before going back to school and who don't plan to come back next year looking for a job."

"That's right." She signed something and absently tapped her pen on her desk. "They're mostly pretty good kids, but they're thoughtless. But I didn't take Eduardo to be that type. He had a wife and daughter, and he was serious about taking care of them. Do you know what time he got killed? I know it was Wednesday night, but I haven't heard just when. I've wondered if maybe he planned to come to work but died before he could."

"When was he supposed to come on duty?"

"At ten. He helped bus tables until we closed at midnight, then he was on the crew that cleaned up and got things squared away for breakfast."

"How long had he worked here?"

"A couple of weeks. When did the strike start, exactly? I forget. Three weeks ago? Anyway, he came looking for work just a few days later."

"Did he ever talk about the strike?" I said.

"Only to say he wished it was over. I told him I was kind of glad it wasn't, because I liked having him work for me. We both knew he'd go back to the boats as soon as he could."

"Any other strikers work here?"

"Only one," she said. "Norm Frazier. But I could use a couple more if they're as dependable as Eduardo."

Honest, dependable, hardworking Eduardo. Every boss's dream employee, a perfect husband, a friend to all mankind.

"Did he have any particular friends here?" I asked. "Anyone he might have confided in?"

"He seemed to like Norm. I guess they worked together on the ferries. Here they acted like they enjoyed their jobs and each other. You know what I mean? Some people just do the work, some people do it but don't like it, and there are a few who do it and make it seem like fun. Eduardo and Norm were two of that kind. After the customers were all gone, the two of them bustled around whistling like the Seven Dwarfs." She paused. "Come to think of it, Norm wasn't here Wednesday night, either, because it was his night off."

"I should talk with him, too, I think. Maybe the two of them were together."

I wished her luck with her restaurant as I left. History suggested that she'd need it.

It was a bit early to hit the Fireside, but I drove to Oak Bluffs anyway, taking the road along the barrier beach between Nantucket Sound and Sengekontacket Pond where, at one spot, I could see our house on the far side of the pond. Above me, the pale blue sky arched from horizon to horizon, and beyond the sound I could see the hazy line that was Cape Cod.

The parking places on the sound side of the highway were rapidly filling with cars as young families lugged children, umbrellas, blankets, coolers, and toys to the beach only a few yards from the road. It was the best beach on the island for small children, because it was so close to the parking spots, and because the wind was generally offshore, the waves were small, and the water shallow and warm. We called it Mothers' Beach because it was so popular with young moms, many of whom sported Mothers' Tans. Because the sun was behind them as they sat watching their offspring play in or near the water, their backs and the fronts of their thighs were brown but their bellies and calves remained pale. You could spot a young mom quite easily by her two-toned tan.

When their children got old enough, the moms could take their eyes off them long enough to turn their pale parts to the sun, so after that you had to identify them by their hair. Moms wore their hair short, whereas non-moms often wore theirs long. Zee, mom though she was, wore hers long anyway. On her pillow it looked like a blue-black halo.

Men were raking for quahogs in the pond, fishermen were casting from the stone jetties, and kids were diving off the big bridge into the channel as they had done for as long as I could remember. I'd done it myself when I'd been a kid, and it wouldn't be long until Joshua and Diana would be doing it. Adults were always worried that some kid would hit a boat as it passed under the bridge, but I'd never heard of that happening.

It looked like what it was: summer on Martha's Vineyard.

In Oak Bluffs I eased through mobs of pedestrians, passed the crowded little harbor, and continued on to the state-police headquarters. I parked in back of the office, went inside, and found Officer Olive Otero at the desk reading reports. Olive and I had once been fire and ice, but we had managed to leave that behind us, much to the relief of her boss, Dom Agganis.

"Now, let me guess," said Olive, pushing her reading glasses up into her hair. "You've been hired to figure out who blew up the *Trident,* and you're here to learn if we already know who done it and if we'll tell you so you can tell your employer and collect a bonus for being quick."

"Close, but no cigar," I said. "I've been asked by Eduardo Alvarez's wife and, worse yet, by my own wife, to clear Eduardo's name. The ladies are positive that Eduardo would never do anything violent. And there isn't any bonus."

"Ah, so if I can assure you that Eduardo absolutely, positively had nothing to do with the explosion, you'll take that information back to the widow and to Zee and you'll go away and leave me alone?"

"Sounds good. It's a deal."

"Well," she said, "I can't do it, because we're still investigating, and Eduardo is still what they call a person of interest." She stretched and looked down at the papers on her desk. "If that's all you wanted, I've got quite a bit of work here."

"I've talked to half a dozen people who'll swear Eduardo sits at the right hand of God."

"We've heard that, too," said Olive, putting her specs back on her nose, "but there are people who expect King Arthur to return when Britain needs him."

"I don't suppose you have anyone else on your list of suspects."

"Nobody we're ready to identify to you."

"Where's Dom?" I said. "Maybe he'll be more talkative."

She laughed. "Don't bet the farm on that fantasy. Anyway, he's out earning his pay. Up-island, someplace, I think."

"I figured he'd be nosing around the docks in Vineyard Haven."

She shook her head. "This isn't the only crime we have on Martha's Vineyard, you know. Maybe they didn't have cops in the original Eden, but we need them here in this one. Come to think of it, if they'd had one guarding the orchard, Eve might not have stolen that apple."

"Oh, I don't know," I said. "She'd probably have

slipped the guard one for himself just so she could have one of her own. You know how women are."

"I know more about it than you do, for sure," she said, "although that's not saying much. If you learn anything that might get Eduardo off the suspect list, let us know. He'll be one less guy for us to investigate. Now, if you'll just be on your way, I can get back to these important papers." She wiggled her fingers good-bye, and I left.

I was no smarter than when I'd gone in. Maybe I should try prayer and meditation or fasting. If I had a bo tree, maybe I could sit under it and resist temptations until I achieved enlightenment.

I hoped that Brady was having better luck with his client's problems than I was having with mine.

It was still an hour before noon, but it was a warm day and I felt like having a beer or two, so I drove back into town, where, to my surprise, I found a parking place in the Fireside parking lot, off Kennebec Ave. Some of the cars already there bore bumper and window stickers proclaiming their owners as union men and their cause as just.

I went past the trash barrels and into the bar through the back door. It was semidark inside as usual, and the smells of beer, booze, bodies, and pub food filled the air, as usual. There were a couple of dozen customers lounging at tables, in booths, and on the stools in front of the bar. They looked a bit rougher than the usual college and tourist crowd, and conversation, for the most part, had to do with hostile observations about the strike and the August swoon of the Red Sox. When I entered, the voices slowed, and eyes turned toward me.

The only people I recognized were Jake the bartender and Bonzo, my gentle, dim-witted friend, who was man-of-all-work in the Fireside, where he labored on the cusp of his mental skills, serving beer from the bar and food from the kitchen, wiping tables, cleaning the floor, and carrying supplies between the basement and the barroom. Long before I met him, it was said, he'd blown out a good brain with an overdose of bad acid and had thereby transformed himself into a sweet, bird-loving, eternal child. I was very fond of him.

Now he waved, and I went right over and took an empty booth.

"Hi, J.W.," said Bonzo. "How you been? I ain't seen you for a while."

"I'm a married man, Bonzo. I don't hang out in bars so much anymore." I asked for a Sam, and he went to the bar and brought it back. I knew better than to offer to buy him one, because Bonzo took his job seriously and never had a beer until closing time.

"Here you go," he said, putting down my glass. "Whatcha doing these days, J.W.? You doing any fishing?" His eyes widened at the thought, because Bonzo loved fishing better than anything except watching and listening to birds and recording their songs, and his schoolteacher mother, who was growing older with a child who never aged. I took Bonzo fishing several times a year, sometimes when I knew no fish would be there, just because he loved to cast his line.

"I'm not doing any fishing right now," I said. "I'm

trying to learn about the man who was killed in that explosion on the boat in Vineyard Haven. I see that some of the men in the union are here, and I want to talk with any of them who knew Eduardo Alvarez. Do you know if he was ever in here?"

The happy look went away from Bonzo's face. "Oh, I heard about that explosion, J.W. That was bad. You know what it made me think?"

"What?"

"It made me think of that saying that only the good die young. Because Eduardo was young and he was good, too. You ever hear that saying, J.W.?"

"I've heard it, Bonzo. Are you telling me that Eduardo came into this bar? Did you talk with him?"

Bonzo's head nodded like a bobble head. "Oh, sure. We was friends. He was friends with lots of people, and I was one of them. Almost everybody was his friend." He waved a thin-wristed hand in a gesture that took in most of the room. Then the hand stopped, and I followed its line to a man at the bar who was looking at us with an unfriendly face. "Except, maybe Steve, there," said Bonzo, lowering his voice and dropping his arm. "Steve and Eduardo used to argue and almost fight."

"Almost?"

"Oh, Eduardo would never fight," said Bonzo, apparently surprised that I didn't understand that obvious characteristic. "He'd just put up his hands and move back, and then somebody would always step between them, and Steve might hit that guy before the other guys would stop him and give him a beer and quiet him down." He put his face close to mine.

"Once, though, the police had to come and take Steve and another guy away because they wouldn't stop fighting."

Whiskey warriors are commonplace, unfortunately. If you give certain normally mild people enough alcohol to get drunk, they become nasty. On the other hand, if you get some normally obnoxious people drunk, they might become sentimental and burst into song. *In vino veritas.*

I looked at Steve and found him staring at me beneath frowning brows. I brought my eyes back to Bonzo. "What were they fighting about?" I asked.

"Oh, about the strike. You know, there's some guys who want it to stay peaceful and others who want to get tougher about it."

"Is that what Eduardo and Steve argued about?"

Bonzo's head bobbed some more. "Yeah. I'll tell you something, J.W. We don't mind people arguing when they keep their voices down, you know what I mean? But we don't like it when they get mad and loud, and we don't like fights at all. It's bad for business."

I finished my beer. It had tasted good enough to have another one, and Bonzo said he'd be glad to get it. I watched him go to the bar and saw Steve's big hand grab his shirt when he got there. Steve's voice reached across the room. "You talking about me, you half-wit?"

Bonzo was his height but half his weight. He pushed at Steve's hand. "I'm just getting a beer for my friend. Lemme go."

Jake, the bartender, moved closer. "Now take it easy, Steve," he said. Other voices said the same.

But Steve's hand didn't let go. He gave Bonzo a shake. "Fuck your friend. You keep your mouth shut about what you hear, you brainless idiot, or I'll punch you even sillier than you already are."

I was halfway to the bar before I realized I'd left the booth.

Steve, however, had seen me from the start, and he was smiling. He shoved Bonzo away so hard that he'd have fallen if a couple of men hadn't caught him as he stumbled back.

"Bonzo's not quite your size," I said to Steve, trying to control a little flicker of primeval red madness that was rising in the blackness of my psyche. I looked at Bonzo. "You okay, Bonzo?"

He nodded. "I'm okay, J.W."

I stopped myself two yards from Steve and took a deep breath. "All right," I said. "It's over."

"The hell it is," said Steve, coming toward me.

I stepped back, willing down that feral fire within me. "You've already been in jail once," I said. "That should be enough."

Steve's eyes were full of fury. "I'll be in jail, but you'll be in the hospital, you fuck!" He came after me as I backed away, then with surprising speed he kicked toward my crotch.

I turned and caught the blow on my thigh. A spear of pain pierced my leg, and a red film fell over my eyes, turning the world crimson. I caught his foot with both hands, twisted as hard as I could, and heard his ankle bones grind and crack. I heard his scream as I twisted harder then threw him back onto the floor. As he went down, I went after him, knock-

ing aside his defending arms and slamming his head
on the floor.

My hands were hard around his throat when
Bonzo's head was suddenly between my face and
Steve's, looking up at me while his thin hands pushed
vainly against my chest, and I heard his voice, saying,
"No, no, J.W.! No, no! Stop! Stop! Don't hurt him
anymore! Don't!"

Slowly the red veil fell from my eyes, and I saw
that Bonzo had thrown himself on his back between
us and was making himself a barrier between Steve
and me.

Steve was coughing and sucking in huge gulps of
air. I took my hands away and saw Bonzo smile up at
me as he patted me the way you pat a dog for obeying
a command.

"That's good, J.W., that's good," he said, scrambling to his feet and pulling on my shoulders. "Here,
let's go back to your booth and I'll get you that beer."

I got up. On the floor, Steve was moaning. Around
me men were wearing frightened faces. I felt my
fangs become teeth again, my claws become hands. I
looked at Jake, who was still behind the bar. "You'd
better call an ambulance," I told him.

Jake nodded and reached for the phone.

Bonzo led me back to my booth. "You okay now,
J.W.?"

My hands were shaking. "I'm okay," I said.

He brought me a Sam. "You got to try never to get
mad," he said.

"I know."

I drank some beer.

By and by a couple of cops came in with two EMTs.

"What happened here?" asked a cop.

"Steve, here, was dancing on a table," said one of the guys at the bar. "He fell off."

"Yeah," said another man. "That's what happened."

Heads nodded all around the room.

The second cop leaned over Steve. "You're too old to be dancing on tables, Steve. Look what you've done to yourself."

Steve gritted his teeth. "I guess it could have been worse. I could have broken my neck."

The cop scribbled on his report pad. "You know what they say. If you're gonna dance, don't drink. If you're gonna drink, don't dance."

Steve groaned. "I'll try to remember that."

Our eyes met as they carried him out of the room. I had another name to put on my list of people I wanted to talk to.

Chapter Six

Brady

I woke up sometime in the middle of the night. It took me a minute to remember where I was and why my head hurt and my stomach was jumpy. The darkness outside the window in Larry Bucyck's little house was a couple of shades lighter than the darkness inside. I guessed I'd only been asleep for an hour or so. A lot of alcohol, for me, always means a rough night of sleeping.

Living in the city, I wasn't used to the quiet of the Vineyard woods. The only sound was the almost sub-audible hiss of the Vineyard breeze sifting through the trees. The silence was almost spooky.

I lay there staring up into the darkness, imagining Evie's sleek body next to mine and wondering what the hell Larry had gotten me into, and after a while, I went back to sleep.

The next time I opened my eyes, gray light was seeping in through the windows. The sun had not yet cracked the eastern horizon, but it soon would.

I rolled over, but it was no use. I was awake. I got

up, shut my eyes against a sudden wave of dizziness, and went outside to pee. The first rays of morning sunshine were just touching the treetops, and the air was full of birdsong.

I went back inside and got dressed, then prowled around Larry's kitchen area for coffee. After Larry's wine, I really needed coffee.

All I came up with was a plastic container with a few Lipton tea bags in it. It would take gallons of tea to give me the caffeine I needed. There was no substitute for morning coffee, and Larry didn't have any.

I went out back. Larry's hammock hung between a pair of oak trees off to the side of the yard. He was lying there with his arms crossed over his chest like a corpse, and if he hadn't been snoring, I might've thought he was dead. Like Poor Jud, he looked peaceful and serene, and I decided not to wake him up yet.

Rocket was lying directly under Larry's hammock. When he lifted his head and looked at me, I snapped my fingers, and he got up and followed me back into the house. I found a piece of paper and a pencil, and wrote, "Seven o'clock. Looking for coffee. Back in a while. Brady."

Then Rocket and I went outside. When I got into Zee's Wrangler, Rocket sat there on the ground and looked at me.

"You want to come?" I said to him.

He stood up and wagged his tail.

I reached over and opened the passenger door, and he clambered in. I guessed if Larry woke up before we got back, he'd see that my car was gone and would figure out that Rocket was with me.

I drove out the dirt roads to the main road, then through Menemsha and Chilmark without any luck, and I ended up going all the way to Edgartown before I found an open gas station with a coffee urn. I got an extra-large, black. I thought about buying one for Larry, but I figured if he drank coffee, he'd've had some in his house. He probably preferred tea, or more likely some vile homemade concoction made from roots and twigs and dirt.

I bought a doughnut, too, and shared it with Rocket as we headed back to Larry's house.

By the time I got there, I figured I'd been gone a little over an hour. The sun had fully risen, and I'd drunk some of my coffee, and it had turned into a bright new day, full of hope and promise after all.

I parked in the front yard, and Rocket followed me into the house, his purpose transparently obvious. I found a bag of dog food in a cabinet and an empty bowl on the floor beside a water dish. I dumped a few cups of dogfood into the bowl, added a little water, and put it on the floor.

Rocket gobbled it down.

The note I'd left for Larry was right where I'd put it. I assumed he hadn't yet come inside. I didn't know what his sleeping habits were, or how tolerant he was of that awful wine of his, but we hadn't gotten to bed until after two in the morning. There was no reason to wake him up.

So I went out into the front yard, found a rock in a patch of sunlight to sit on, and finished my coffee.

An hour or so later, when Larry still hadn't appeared, I went around back to wake him up.

I went over to the hammock to shake him awake, but Larry was not in the hammock.

I stood there for a minute, looking around. I did not spot him. "Hey," I called. "Hey, Larry?"

No answer.

I waited a minute, then called again.

What the hell?

My first thought was that while I was out trying to track down coffee, Larry had gone off to buy bagels or muffins for us. But surely he would have left a note when he found me gone. Anyway, his bicycle was still leaning against the side of the house, exactly where it had been when I arrived the previous afternoon.

It took me a minute, but then I got it. Larry had chickened out. He had decided not to go to the police or the Coast Guard with me to report the ominous boat with the Uzi-toting men aboard. He was hoping that if he wasn't around, I'd do it without him.

Okay, he was scared. I understood that. I'd probably be scared, too, if I'd seen what he claimed he saw, and if those men with Uzis had spotted me.

But, damn it, he'd called me, begged me to come down here to help him. There were a million things I'd rather be doing, like sipping morning coffee and reading the Saturday *Globe* and watching the chickadees in the feeders in my walled-in patio garden on Beacon Hill with Evie and my own dog for company.

Instead, here I was in the woods on the far end of Martha's Vineyard, and I had to drive all the way to Edgartown for my morning coffee.

I scanned the woods that surrounded the little clearing in Larry's backyard. I imagined him lurking behind a tree, watching me, waiting to see what I was going to do.

"If you're out there," I said loudly, "you better show yourself." I paused. "Damn it, Larry. You are pissing me off. I swear I'm gonna wring your scrawny neck."

Nothing happened.

"If you think I'm going to talk to the police without you," I said, "you can forget about it. No way. We made a deal."

No response.

"Larry," I said, "God damn it, I had to hitch a ride on a fucking catboat to get here. What the hell is wrong with you?"

There was no movement in the woods, and I was beginning to doubt if Larry was hearing what I was saying.

"I'm warning you, man." I wasn't quite yelling. But almost. "This is it. I'm ready to pack up and go home, and I promise you, if you try to call me again, ever, for anything, I don't care what, I'll hang up on you."

I blew out a breath. If Larry was lurking in the woods, he wasn't going to show himself, no matter what I said.

Maybe he had gone for muffins. Maybe he always took a long walk in the morning. Maybe . . .

Whatever. I'd wait for a while. If Larry didn't come back, I'd go talk to J.W. and see if he wanted to give me a catboat ride back to Woods Hole.

It didn't take my thoughts long to shift from anger to worry. I didn't really know Larry very well. He certainly wasn't the same man he'd been when he was a big-time athlete. I didn't quite know what to make of his story, what he'd really seen in the darkness that night and what his imagination had embellished for him, but I did believe he was afraid.

Maybe he hadn't just chickened out. Maybe something had happened to him.

I waited around while the sun rose in the sky and the air grew warm. I thought about Evie. When we were apart, we usually talked before bedtime. Whoever was away called to say good night, I love you, all is well.

Between Larry's storytelling and his wine, I'd forgotten.

I took my cell phone out of my pocket and pressed the On button. When the screen lit up, it read: "New message."

Oh, shit. Evie, no doubt. Very few people have my cell phone number. She gave the thing to me for occasions exactly like this one, to encourage me to call and reassure her that I was okay when I was off on some quest.

I accessed voicemail, hit Send, and was told I had one new message. It had been delivered at twelve thirty-seven that morning. A little after midnight, while Larry and I were lurking around Menemsha Pond.

"Hey," said Evie's recorded voice. "Are you okay? Call me, will you?"

No "I love you." Just "Call me."

She was pissed.

I called our home number. Evie didn't answer. In the shower, maybe. Or maybe she'd hooked up with one of her girlfriends for a day of shopping.

Or maybe she was standing there holding the telephone in her hand, seeing on the caller ID window that it was from me, and giving it the finger.

"Hi, babe," I said when our voicemail invited me to leave a message. "It's your wayward boy, somewhat hungover here on Saturday morning after a night of drinking Larry Bucyck's homemade wine, which by comparison makes me yearn for a tall, cool glass of rubbing alcohol. Had an uneventful ride over on J.W.'s catboat. He and Zee send their love. Having an interesting visit with Larry. I'll tell you all about it. Anyway, I wanted you to know I'm fine. Sorry I didn't have a chance to call last night. It was thoughtless of me, though I do have an excuse. I'll try you later on. Hope you're having a good day. Love you."

I doubted if any of that would mollify Evie. I should have called her. She expected me to and would worry if I didn't. She wouldn't've minded if I'd called late and awakened her.

I waited around for another hour or so. When there was still no sign of Larry Bucyck, I filled Rocket's bowl with fresh water and left it by the front door. Then I climbed into Zee's Wrangler and headed back to the Jackson abode.

J.W. would know what to do.

His Land Cruiser wasn't there when I pulled into their driveway, but Zee was inside. She told me that J.W. had gone off to find some people he needed to talk to, and if she knew her husband, I'd have a good chance of finding him at one of his watering holes. "Try the Fireside," she said. "If he's not there, I bet he's been there and somebody can tell you where he was headed when he left."

Zee offered to feed me, which I declined, but I did accept a big travel mug full of black coffee, which kept me company as I drove to the Fireside. J.W. had taken me there several times before. I'd always found it a friendly place, but this time after I had found a place to park and was walking to the door, I saw a police cruiser and an emergency vehicle out front. A small crowd had gathered on the sidewalk to watch the EMTs load a man into their wagon.

Inside the restaurant, I spotted J.W. sipping a beer at a table and talking with his friend Bonzo. I went over to their table and said, "Hey."

J.W. turned and arched his eyebrows at me. "Hey yourself."

I slid in beside him.

"You remember Bonzo?" he said.

"Of course." I shook hands with Bonzo. "How's it going?"

Bonzo smiled. "Very good, Mr. Coyne. Thank you."

J.W. was frowning at me. "Everything okay?"

"Well," I said, "Larry Bucyck seems to have disappeared, for one thing. What about you? I saw an ambulance out front. I doubt it's a coincidence. You in here, an injured body out there."

He smiled. "Guy fell off a table, that's all. You want to talk about Larry Bucyck?"

I nodded. "I do. I could use some perspective. And maybe some advice."

"Okay," he said. "You want a beer?"

I held up the mug of coffee Zee had given me, which I'd brought into the restaurant without thinking. "I'm good."

Bonzo stood up. "I got work to do," he said, "and I bet you've got things to talk about." He shook hands with both of us and wandered away.

I told J.W. about Larry's encounter with the Uzi-toting men on the boat, how they'd come sneaking into Menemsha Pond in the middle of the night and offloaded mysterious wooden crates into a van, and how they'd caught Larry in their searchlight.

"Uzis?" said J.W.

I shrugged. "Larry wouldn't know an Uzi from a garden rake. Some kind of nasty weapon."

"You believe this story?"

I shrugged. "Larry believes it. I know he's afraid. I'm not sure what he actually saw, or how much his imagination has colored it. He saw something, all right. Could've been some fishermen unloading their gear, I suppose."

"Without running lights?"

I shrugged. "If, in fact, that's what Larry saw."

"I wonder what was in those crates," J.W. said.

"Nothing good, I wager," I said. "Nothing legal."

"You're probably right. And that was Larry's conclusion, too, I gather."

"He's really scared," I said. "I made him agree to go to the police or the Coast Guard or somebody with me this morning, but when I got back from fetching coffee, he was gone."

"He was there when you woke up?"

"Snoring away in his hammock."

"But gone when you got back from your coffee run."

I nodded.

"You think something happened to him?"

"That's what worries me. At first I thought he'd just chickened out, decided he didn't want to talk to any authorities. He's a very shy, private guy, living like Thoreau down there in the Menemsha woods. He says he just wants to be left alone. But the more I think about it, yeah. I'm worried about him. I do believe something might've happened to him."

J.W. nodded. "Sure you don't want a beer? You could use a beer."

"I got coffee," I said. "I'm all set."

He nodded. "Some of us dig alcohol, some prefer caffeine. You in your way, me in mine. Tell me more about this guy Bucyck. He sounds a little . . ." J.W. waved his hand.

"I got nothing against alcohol," I said. "Drank quite a bit of it last night, in fact. And yeah, Larry is a little . . ." I waved my hand, imitating J.W.

I told J.W. about my evening with Larry Bucyck, the way he'd chosen to live, his stone sculptures, his excellent quahog chowder, and his vile homemade wine, our midnight walk down to the pond where he'd seen the boat come in.

"Except," J.W. said, "the boat didn't come in."

"No boat," I said. "It was like he was telling me, I can show you right where it happened, which proves I'm telling the truth, so now you've got to believe me."

J.W. chuckled. "I keep remembering the hard-throwing right-hander who couldn't find the plate that night against the Angels," he said. "Hard to reconcile that kid with this nutty old hippie you're describing."

"What were you like when you were twenty-one, twenty-two?"

He nodded. "Valid point."

J.W. drained his beer glass, pushed back his chair, and stood up. "Sounds like we better go check it out, then."

"I can't ask you to do that," I said. "You've got—"

"Did you ask?" he said. "I didn't hear you ask. This is my idea. Let's go. I'll follow you."

We went outside. J.W. got into his Land Cruiser, and I climbed into Zee's red Wrangler, and we headed for Menemsha.

When we came to the dirt ruts that led to Larry's house, I stopped. J.W. stopped behind me, got out, came up to my window, and pointed into the woods. "That has to be one of those sculptures you mentioned."

I nodded. "He says he moved those rocks without machinery. Levers and pulleys and planning and time, he said."

J.W. blew out a quick breath. "Impressive work. I like it a lot. It's like I can almost see it breathe."

"I agree," I said. "I think creating them is a Zen thing for Larry."

"It's a Zen thing for me, too," J.W. said, "just contemplating it."

J.W. went back to his car, and we drove up the driveway and parked in the dooryard.

J.W. and I got out of our vehicles. I opened the

door to the house and looked inside. Larry wasn't there, but I said, "Hey, Larry," anyway.

He didn't answer, of course.

We went around back. I half expected to see Larry cooking something in his big kettle, or chopping wood or moving rocks around, or snoring in his hammock, but he wasn't doing any of those things.

I didn't see Rocket, either.

J.W. meandered over to the outhouse on the edge of the woods. The door hung ajar. He poked his head inside, then turned, looked at me, and shook his head. He came back to where I was standing. "You hear that?" he said.

"What?"

"Howling. Hear it?"

I listened, and then I heard it, off in the distance.

"That must be Rocket," I said. "Larry's hound."

"And that odor," said J.W.

I sniffed the air. "Pigs," I said. "Larry said he had some pigs. I didn't smell anything yesterday."

"The wind's shifted a few degrees," J.W. said. "It's more westerly today. It was out of the south yesterday, as you no doubt noticed when we sailed in it."

I didn't tell him that I'd paid no attention whatsoever to the direction of the wind, landlubbing sailor that I was.

"Let's go see the pigs," he said. "It's in that direction. Where the howling is coming from."

It wasn't hard to follow our noses along the pathway that wound down the hillside to the pigsty, which we found tucked in a shady area under a couple of big oak trees. Larry had cobbled together a pen and a lean-to–style shelter. The fence was about four feet high, made from random-sized planks of wood nailed to posts made out of six-inch-thick tree trunks. The shelter had a tin roof.

The odor was overpowering, and Rocket was sitting outside the fence. When he saw us, he stopped baying and came over to us.

There were five pigs, oinking and grunting and rooting around in the pig-knee-deep muck. They were enormous pinkish creatures, and when J.W. and I leaned our elbows on the fence, a couple of them waddled over and looked up at us out of their squinty, intelligent eyes.

"Sorry, fellas," I said. "No food."

Then J.W. said, "Oh-oh."

I turned to him. "What?"

He pointed toward the far side of the pen, where one of the pigs was digging his nose in the mud.

It took me a minute to recognize what I was seeing sticking up out of the mud.

It was a hand and part of an arm. The elbow was at a funny angle.

When the pig moved, I saw the rest of the mud-covered body sprawled on his belly. His face was buried in the muck, but I recognized the ponytail.

"Jesus," I said. "It's Larry."

J.W. put one leg over the fence. When I started to follow him, he said, "You stay there."

"He's dead," I said.

He nodded. "I want to be sure," he said. "If so, we should leave him for the police. No sense both of us getting stinky. I'll do it."

I watched as J.W. climbed over the fence and began to slog over to where Larry lay in the muck. The pigs stood back and watched him. When he got over there, he gave the pig that was rooting around Larry's body a gentle kick in the ribs, and it moved away.

J.W. squatted down and lifted Larry's face out of the mud. He bent close to him and pressed his fingers against Larry's throat.

A minute later he looked over at me and shook his head.

He lowered Larry's head back into the mud, came back to where I was waiting, and climbed out of the pigpen.

He stood there frowning at me.

"What?" I said.

He shook his head. "Nothing. He's dead, that's all."

"Could you tell how he died?"

"No. He wasn't breathing. No pulse. That's all I know. He's all coated with mud."

"Like he went in to feed his pigs and they attacked him?"

J.W. shrugged. "I don't know if pigs do that."

"Or he slipped in the mud and . . . and drowned in it?"

"I don't know."

I blew out a breath. "He was murdered, wasn't he? That's what happened, isn't it? Somebody killed him."

J.W. patted my shoulder. "Take it easy, man. We don't know anything."

I was shaking my head. "I really didn't take him seriously," I said. "I was humoring him. And now . . ."

"I don't see how you can blame yourself for this," said J.W.

"The man was truly frightened. Now he's truly dead."

"That doesn't make it your fault. You got your cell phone on you?"

I took my phone out of my pocket and handed it to J.W. "Who are you gonna call?"

"State cops. Dom Agganis, if I can reach him. Or Olive Otero. It would be a pretty good joke if Olive had to go sloshing around in a pigsty."

"I feel funny," I said, "leaving Larry's body there in the mud."

"The cops should see him where we found him," he said.

I nodded. "I know that." I looked at J.W., and I couldn't help it. I smiled. His feet and legs and arms were caked with wet pig muck. He had mud on his face and in his hair.

"What?" he said.

"You don't smell so good. Zee won't let you in the house."

"We got an outdoor shower."

Rocket and I stayed there beside the pigpen watching over Larry Bucyck's body while J.W. wandered away with my cell phone. The pigs apparently had lost interest. They were ignoring Larry's corpse.

J.W. came back in a minute. He gave me the phone. "They want one of us to go back up to the, um, Larry's house and wait for them there, and one of us to stay here, keep an eye on the body. You better go. I might scare them away. Take the dog with you."

I nodded. "You are quite scary."

"Keep the phone turned on. If they get lost, they'll call."

"You gonna be all right?"

He smiled. "As long as I stay here, nobody will know how bad I smell."

It took about half an hour for them to arrive. When they did, it was a full-blown cavalcade—state-police cruiser, two unmarked sedans, a Chilmark PD cruiser, and an emergency wagon. They pulled into Larry's front yard and parked randomly.

Dom Agganis, whom I'd met a few times previously, got out of the passenger side of one of the unmarked sedans. He came over to me. "Where is it?" he said.

"Down the hill behind the house. I'll take you there."

I led him down the path to the pigsty. Rocket came along with us. The rest of them—Olive Otero was one of them, and the others, I assumed, were forensics experts and people from the coroner's office—followed along single file behind us. The occupants of the Chilmark cruiser remained behind.

When we got there, Agganis turned to me and said, "You stay here." He went over to talk to J.W.

Olive Otero touched my arm. "Let's go over there." She led me through the grove of trees to the edge of the clearing and gestured at a couple of boulders. "Sit down."

I sat, and Rocket sprawled on the ground next to

me. From there, I couldn't see what was going on at the pigsty.

Olive sat beside me. She gave Rocket a pat on his head, then took a notebook out of her pocket. She arched her eyebrows at me. "Why don't you tell me about it?"

"What do you want to know?"

She shrugged. "Everything. Why you're here. Everything you know about Mr. Bucyck. How you and Jackson found him."

"It's a long story."

"Don't leave anything out."

"Do you know who Larry Bucyck is?" I said.

"Dead, is all I know," she said.

So I told her Larry's whole story, from his brief career as a Red Sox pitcher to his flight to the Vineyard to his years as a hermit. I told her how he called me on Thursday and insisted I come down to help him. I told her how it was important to him that I was his lawyer so that whatever he had to tell me would be privileged.

"Now he's dead," she said.

"Yes. So now I'm telling you his story. If he was alive, I wouldn't."

"I don't think any of that would qualify as privileged information," she said.

I shrugged. "You're probably right. I wouldn't've told you anyway without his permission. Whatever. Now the question is moot."

"So what happened today?" she said.

"I don't know. When I woke up this morning, he

was sleeping in his hammock. I drove to Edgartown for coffee—the dog came with me—and when we got back, Larry wasn't in his hammock and we couldn't find him. After a while, I went and got J.W. We heard Rocket howling and found Larry there." I pointed in the direction of the sty. "J.W. climbed in. Larry was dead. So we called you."

"How come J.W. climbed in there instead of you?"

"He said he didn't mind getting dirty."

Olive looked sideways at me, then shrugged. "Okay. Let's go over that again."

She made me tell it all over again, except this time she kept interrupting me with questions. A few times I found myself contradicting myself, confusing times and sequences, mixing up elements of the stories Larry had told me. Olive seemed to find it interesting that we'd drunk quite a bit of moonshine wine before bed, and that gave me the idea that after Rocket and I went to Edgartown for coffee, Larry might've rolled out of his hammock and wandered down to the sty, hungover and unsteady on his feet, to visit his pigs. Maybe he went into the sty to feed them or something, and he slipped and fell in the mud and panicked, and the pigs came over, poking and prodding him with their snouts, smothering his face in the smelly muck.

I shook my head. It sounded pretty far-fetched, and I didn't share the scenario with Olive Otero.

After a while, Dom Agganis came over. His legs were caked with wet pig muck.

Olive got up and went to talk with him. Then she headed off in the direction of the pigsty.

Agganis sat on the boulder beside me. "How you doing, Mr. Coyne?"

"I'm all right."

"We're going to have to go over the whole thing again," he said. "Okay?"

"How did Larry die?"

"I'm the one who's going to ask the questions," he said, not unkindly. "If you don't mind."

"I mean," I said, "was he murdered, or what?"

He narrowed his eyes at me for a minute, then nodded. "One shot in the back of the head. Small caliber. No exit wound."

"Executed," I said.

He shrugged. "Shot dead, for sure. Now you talk to me."

So I told Dom Agganis what I'd just told Olive Otero twice, and he took notes in a notebook that looked identical to the one Olive used. When I finished, he made me go over it again, asking his own questions, a few of which were ones that Olive hadn't asked. He kept circling back to the story that Larry had told me about the boat with its lights off unloading wooden crates in Menemsha Pond and the men with Uzis Larry thought he'd seen.

All I could do was repeat what Larry had told to me. I told Agganis that I didn't think Larry was entirely trustworthy, that he was unstable and paranoid and depressed, had been for years, and normally I would have assumed that he'd imagined, or exaggerated or distorted, all or parts of his story.

But now he had been murdered, and that lent his story a lot of instant credibility.

While I was talking to Dom Agganis, J.W. appeared. "How long you going to keep him?" he said to Agganis, jerking his head at me.

"A while. I don't know."

"What about me?"

"We don't need you anymore right now." He smiled. "Why don't you go get a shower."

J.W. nodded. "I'm going to head back, then," he said to me. "I've got places to go, people to see. You'll be at our house for dinner."

He made it a statement, not a question or an invitation.

I looked at Agganis, and he nodded.

"Great," I said to J.W. "I suspect by then a martini would come in handy."

"Be gentle with him," J.W. said to Agganis. Then he turned and trudged up the hill to where his Land Cruiser was parked.

By the time I'd finished talking with Agganis, I had given him about five versions of the previous twenty-four hours of my life.

Finally, he said, "Okay."

"Okay what?"

"We're not done," he said. "But okay for now."

"You're not done?"

"No. You'll need to be available."

"Available. How long?"

He shrugged. "Until we get a handle on this case."

"I plan to go back to America tomorrow," I said. "I've got a law practice to run."

"I'll write you an excuse," he said. "Unless something miraculous happens, you won't be leaving the island tomorrow, even if you did manage to find a ride back to the mainland."

I looked at him. "You making a suspect out of me?"

He shook his head. "You know how it works, Mr. Coyne."

"Yeah, yeah. Everybody's a suspect."

"I assume you have an interest in this case," he said.

"Of course I do."

"Then don't argue with me."

Chapter Seven

J.W.

I don't often find dead bodies in pigpens, and I was glad when Dom Agganis and Olive Otero were through with me.

When I got to Larry Bucyck's house, I used his hand pump and a bucket to wash the worst of the mud off, glad that I was wearing summer shorts so that most of the muck was on my skin and easily removed. Still, I smelled like something other than a rose as I drove home.

There, before I collected a towel and headed for the outdoor shower, I found a note from Zee informing me that she and the kids had gone to the beach with a friend and her children, who were about the ages of Joshua and Diana. Smart Zee, lying on the beach while I was wading in a pigsty.

While I showered and got into cleaner clothes, I thought about poor Larry Bucyck, and then I thought about myself.

When I was a kid I'd heard of people seeing red, but I'd always thought it was just a manner of speaking, a way of saying you were angry. Then, one day when I was grown, when fear and fury and pain possessed me in some confrontation, that red film had fallen in front of my eyes and turned the whole world scarlet, and I had to be pulled off a man before I killed him. Afterward, I'd been so frightened by the experience that I'd promised never to become angry again.

But once or twice since then, in spite of my vow, the red curtain had fallen and I'd gone mad. The beast within me had broken free, and only luck had prevented me from committing homicide. When I thought about it, it seemed to me that the madness was caused by intense rage, that the rage was caused by fear, and that the fear was caused by pain or some other assault on what I held most dear. In this case, it had been Steve's roughhousing of Bonzo, followed by the pain of Steve's kick. It didn't seem to take much.

I wondered who Larry Bucyck had frightened so badly? Was his killer some monster who got off on killing? Or was his murder what the cops sometimes think of as a rational killing, one that is logical, given the morality of crime? A killing to prevent someone from talking, to protect a secret, to eliminate a rival, or to protect a loved one, or a territory, or a friend.

Dostoyevsky thought that there was little difference between murderers and the rest of us. In my case, I thought there was none at all. I didn't like it.

Clean and shiny on the outside, at least, I went out to the truck and felt the midday sun pour down on me. It made me feel better, if not good. Nature is never spent.

I drove to the hospital and went into the Emergency Room. Zee was at the beach, but nurse Terry Grace gave me the information I needed.

"Your man is back there resting," she said, "with a cast on his leg. He took quite a tumble."

"I'd like to see him."

"He's sedated," Terry said, "so let me take a peek and see how he's doing. His wife is on her way, and after she gets here we'll probably send him home. Ankles are pretty complicated, and he broke a couple of bones. They say he was dancing on a table and fell off. Well, he won't be doing any more dancing for a while, but I guess he'll be all right."

"I'll wait," I said, and sat down in a chair.

I was looking at the cartoons in a months-old *New Yorker* when Terry stuck her head around the corner of the waiting room and said, "You can see him now, J.W., but he may still float in and out of fuzziness."

"Anybody with him?"

"No. But like I said, his wife is on her way."

I followed her back to a bed surrounded by white curtains.

Steve's eyes widened when Terry said, "You've got a visitor."

She went away, and I looked at the new cast on his leg, then put out a hand and touched it. I had the impression that he'd have pulled it back out of my reach if he'd been able to, but of course he wasn't. "What is it that you didn't want Bonzo to tell me?" I asked.

"Nothing."

"I'm sorry we got tangled up back there."

"Not as sorry as I am."

"Your wife is on her way," I said. "They say you'll be okay."

"Good," he said. "I want out of here. I don't like hospitals. People die in them all the time."

I gave the old saw a small smile. "What is it you didn't want Bonzo to tell me, Steve? It wasn't nothing. It was something."

"I told you. It was nothing."

Stubborn Steve.

"If I don't get it from you," I said, "I'll be annoyed, but I'll get it from someone else."

But he was obstinate. "I tell you, it was nothing. There wasn't anything he might tell. I was drunk. It was the beer talking."

"You weren't drunk then and you're not drunk now." His good ankle was under a sheet. I touched it lightly and he jerked his leg back.

"Lemme alone!"

I leaned over him. "You can tell me now or tell the police later. A man is dead. Maybe you know something about that. The cops will come and ask you questions, and then they'll ask some more, and then they'll start backtracking you. They'll find out things you never thought anybody could find out. You don't want the cops on your case, believe me."

"Leave me alone, damn it."

Although they'd given him some kind of painkiller, the memory of his hurt was fresh, and his stubbornness diminished before it.

"Last chance," I said. "I'm losing my patience. You don't want that to happen. As I just said, if I don't get it from you now, I'll get it from somebody else, and you'll get the cops."

"All right, all right," he said. "No cops. I don't need no more cops in my life."

Nobody does. I leaned over him. "What did Bonzo see? What does he know?"

He wiped a hand across his lips. "You keep this to yourself, damn it."

"I'll decide that." I looked at him with narrow eyes. Tough guy.

"I got a wife and kids," he whined. "I don't want nothing happening to them."

"I'll keep that in mind. You keep in mind that you already have a broken ankle and won't be working for a while, strike or no strike. You can try for two, if you want."

"Christ," he whined, "they'll do more than break my leg if they feel like it!"

"Who?"

"I don't know! I don't know! I can't tell you what I don't know."

"Tell me what you do know. What Bonzo knows."

It came out hard and slow. "He seen me talking with Harry."

"So what? Who's Harry?"

"Harry Doyle. Works for Bob Mortison."

"So?"

"So Mortison owns the *Neptune*."

"So?"

"Mortison is hauling more cars and passengers back and forth to Woods Hole than almost anybody else. He's got the *Neptune* and he owns a couple of them barges, too. How's it gonna look to the guys in the union if I'm hanging around with a strike buster like Harry? They'll break my other goddamned leg!"

"Why were you talking to Harry?"

There was fear in his face. His eyes flicked toward the curtains I'd come through, and his voice got small. "I knew Harry over in New Bedford when we was kids, before he came here and started working for Mortison. He and me ran a little on the wild side and did some rough jobs over there before I wised up and got married and got into the union."

He paused for a moment and shut his eyes. When he looked at me again, I saw pain in them. "Harry came looking for me last week, found me down on the docks, and wanted me to do a job with him. Said he knew the strike was costing me money, but he had some for me if I gave him a hand. I asked him what the job was, and he got cozy. I asked him if it's legit work, and he said it wouldn't be any skin off my nose. Then I look up and there's this idiot Bonzo staring right at me, and he's with Ed Alvarez. The dummy's got a pizza box in his hands. It's noon, see, and they've got lunch from Giordano's. Gonna eat out in the sunshine, I guess. Bonzo gives us that dizzy look of his and says, 'Hi, you guys. Whatcha talking about?' We tell them to fuck off, and they do, but it's too late. They seen us talking."

"So what?" I was getting my lines memorized.

"So this. Once when we was kids in New Bedford, Harry and me got hired to do some damage to some boats. Nothing big, and we never got caught, but I don't do that stuff anymore, and I got to thinking that Harry had something like that in mind, so I told him thanks but no thanks, I didn't want his job. Then, when the *Trident* blows up, I figure I was right."

"You think that Harry Doyle blew up the *Trident*?"

He yawned but tried to keep focused. "I don't know for sure, and I can't prove nothing, but I wouldn't be surprised. The thing is, Alvarez knew who Harry works for and what kind of guys him and his boss are, and he found me later and said he didn't think it was a good idea for me to hang around with Harry because Bob Mortison would love it if the strike never got settled, and if anything bad happened, I might be nailed for it. Moralistic prick. I told him to go fuck himself, but he said he was gonna keep an eye on Harry to make sure that I didn't get mixed up with him and that there wasn't going to be any dirty work that would make the union look bad."

The painkillers seemed to be working on him. His eyes were getting heavy, and his voice was woolly.

I shook his shoulder as his consciousness slid away. "Are you saying that Harry Doyle might have been with Alvarez when the *Trident* blew up, and that Bob Mortison might have been behind it?"

But Steve only mumbled something and sank deeper into his bed. I'd get no more from him, and I couldn't be sure that I'd gotten anything at all except suspicions.

As I left, a woman about Steve's age was coming toward the bed. She had a worried face. Terry Grace was with her.

"I think he's asleep," I said to Terry, and walked on to the front desk, where I borrowed their phone book. There were several Doyles listed, but only one Harold. There was also one Mortison, Robert.

If I was a spy, I don't think I'd hide out with an alias and become an expert on secret codes and sneak around taking pictures and trying to get people to tell me secrets. I'd get a room with a refrigerator full of beer, a telephone, and a computer. I'd get a subscription to the *New York Times* or maybe the *Boston Globe* and do all my intelligence collecting from my easy chair.

But I'm not a spy, so I wrote down the phone numbers and addresses, offered thanks for the use of the phone book, and went out to my truck.

Doyle lived in Vineyard Haven, and Mortison lived in Edgartown. Vineyard Haven was closest, so I drove to Doyle's place, which turned out to be a second-story apartment in a building on one of the little dirt roads out near the Misty Meadows golf course. The first floor of the building was apparently a storage area for somebody who did heating and air conditioning, or so it seemed to me when I peeked through a cobwebby window beside a padlocked double door. Nobody was there to tell me about the renter upstairs.

I went upstairs and knocked, then peeked through a smudgy door window. Nobody was there, either. Harry Doyle was probably at work. I wiggled the doorknob. Locked.

Zero for one.

I got back in the truck and drove to Edgartown.

Bob Mortison lived higher off the hog than did Harry Doyle. Not surprising, since he owned a fishing boat and barges. His house was one of the big ones down on Slough Cove Road in Katama, across the way from the farm and not too far from Slough Cove itself, where my father used to take me oystering on Thanksgiving when I was a kid and we went down to spend a chilly holiday in our old fishing camp. Mortison's house wasn't one of the mansions that were being built all over the Vineyard, but it was big enough.

There was a two-car garage beside the house and a forest green Mercedes sedan parked in front of it. I parked on the far side of the car and walked to the house along a brick walk lined with flowers. The lawn was neatly mowed and trimmed. The door knocker was a brass dolphin. I used him or her to rap on the door.

After a bit, a woman opened the door and smiled at me. "Yes?" Behind her, somewhere, soap opera voices were speaking of lovers who couldn't be trusted.

She was fifty or so and was softening around the edges. A week at a decent spa would melt off those extra inches, probably. She was wearing comfortable summer clothes—loose pastel purple knee-length shorts and a pastel blue blouse decorated with a pastel pink flower growing on a pastel green stem with pastel green leaves. Very Lilly Pulitzer.

"My name is Jackson," I said, returning the woman's smile. "Are you Mrs. Mortison?"

"Yes, I am." She seemed to have one ear dedicated to me and the other to her television drama.

Over her shoulder I could see a living room featuring overstuffed furniture, small tables with doilies on them, and a fireplace whose mantel was adorned with framed photographs of healthy people who looked a lot alike. The most prominent of these pictures featured a broad-faced man standing at the stern of a large fishing boat with the name *Neptune* scrolled across the transom. Her husband, Captain Robert Mortison, I presumed. Almost as large was a photo of the same man with his arm around the shoulders of a younger man with similar features. The men were grinning, and in the background was a palm tree bending over a jungle shack of some sort. Dad and son on a Caribbean holiday?

"Is your husband at home? I'd like to talk with him."

"Oh, dear. I'm afraid not. Bob is almost never home these days. He's working all the time. It's the steamship strike, you know. Bob is ferrying people and cars and freight night and day. I hardly ever see him." She laughed.

"I'm sure you'll be glad when the strike is over and you have him home again," I said. "Still, I'm also sure he's glad to be making good money. Fishing is a tough way to make a living, and fishermen have to make it when they can."

"That's certainly true. But you know how we wives are. We like to have our husbands home with us as often as possible. Ha, ha."

"I won't keep you," I said, nodding agreeably. "Maybe you can help me. Do you know a man named Harry Doyle? I'm told he works for your husband."

Her smile dimmed, then disappeared. "Harry Doyle? Yes, he works for Bob, and he's been here to the house once or twice. I hope you're not his friend, because to be frank, I don't really care for him. I don't know why Bob keeps him on, in fact, but I don't interfere with Bob's business, so my opinion doesn't count."

"I'm not his friend," I said. "What is it about him that you dislike?"

"I just don't like him. I didn't like him the first time I saw him. Call it woman's intuition." She raised her chin.

I thought of Dr. Fell. "What does he do for your husband?" I asked.

Her smile was long gone. "I'm afraid I can't tell you. I really don't know much about business. I was one of those stay-at-home mothers raising the children. Now they're gone, and I'm learning to play tennis to fill the time. Bob doesn't talk much about his work except to complain about the price of fish and the cost of doing business."

I glanced around at the house and grounds. "He seems to be doing very well."

The smile came back small. "Yes, but don't ask me how. To hear him tell it, you'd think we were about to go to the poorhouse."

The television voices behind her lifted into a spat.

"Well," I said, "thank you for your time. I'll try to catch up with your husband in Vineyard Haven."

She was turning back toward the television set as she shut the door.

I drove to our house and found no one home. It was a perfect beach day, and my family was taking advantage of it while I was driving around talking with strangers about a case that until very recently had been of no personal interest to me. Dumbness is its own reward.

Visitors to our house are usually surprised to discover that I keep a set of lock picks on the living room coffee table, along with a couple of practice locks. I got the picks at a yard sale long ago from a widow who was selling her deceased husband's goods and didn't know what the picks were. At the time I'd wondered what he really did when he supposedly was doing legitimate work. Over the years since, I'd gotten better at picking, but I was far from a master. Now I took the picks and a pair of latex gloves, returned to the truck, and drove back to Harry Doyle's street. I parked about a block from his apartment and walked the rest of the way.

There was still nobody around. I climbed up to Doyle's door, knocked, waited, peeked through the dirty window again and saw no one. I looked around and still saw nobody, so I put the gloves on my hands and put the picks to Doyle's lock. It was a cheap one and didn't put up much of a fight. Inside, I shut the door behind me and walked around looking the place over. It was a four-room apartment: small living room, small bedroom, small kitchen and dining area, small bathroom, all in need of housekeeping.

There was no sign of any roommate living there. All of the clothes were the same size. One dirty plate was on the table, and one dirty coffee cup was in the sink. There was nothing to indicate that Doyle had friends or family: no photographs, no mementos of good times together, no old letters in the drawer of his bedside table. There was a religious pamphlet in the drawer, but I didn't think God was a relative.

There was a magazine rack beside the sagging chair

that faced the television set. It held a news magazine, one of those army surplus catalogs, a book of Sudoku puzzles, mostly done wrong, and copies of island and mainland newspapers. One of the papers was folded to a story about ex-President Joe Callahan possibly coming to the island to serve as a mediator between union and management. I wondered if Doyle wanted him to come or wanted him to stay away, since he and his boss were making good money off the strike.

I peeked under the seat of the chair and under the mattress on the bed, looking for anything of interest. Nothing. I poked around the kitchen. Nothing. I looked at the ice cube trays. Did Doyle have diamonds hidden in the ice? I didn't think so.

His checkbook was on the bedside table. It showed a small balance and regular deposits. Bob Mortison paid him pretty well, and Doyle spent it pretty fast.

Doyle didn't have a computer. Interesting. He was the only person I knew of who didn't. Even I had a computer.

Beside his bed was a thin book about survival in a country gone corrupt. The United States was the country, and the book was full of tips about how to make counterfeit money, make explosives out of soap, survive interrogations and worse, live off the land using homemade traps and weapons, live in a city without money, and make $40,000 a year as a musician without a contract.

I leafed through the last part, hoping for instructions, but I found none and decided not to go that route. I didn't see any musical instruments in the apartment.

I heard an engine, felt my guilty heart jump, and moved quickly to the front door. A truck had pulled into the yard. Words and an emblem on its door identified it as the property of a registered local heating contractor. The door opened and a man in shorts and a shirt with the same emblem over its pocket got out and walked toward the building. He was whistling.

I inched the door open and listened. Below me, there was a click as the padlock on the double door opened, then the sound of the door itself sliding open. The whistling disappeared inside and I eased through Doyle's door and shut and locked it behind me, then soft-footed my way down the stairs and up the dirt driveway.

When I got to my truck, I was panting. I was getting too old for this sort of thing.

I looked at my watch. Time to do something useful for a change. I drove home, woked some chicken breasts, went out to the garden and picked vegetables, and made a big chicken salad for supper. We still had some homemade white bread in the breadbox. Between the bread and the salad, the Jacksons and Brady Coyne would eat well that evening.

I took a Sam Adams up onto the balcony and drank it, thinking about what I'd seen and done that day. By and by a neighbor's car came down our driveway and emptied out my wife and children. While they took turns washing off sand in the outdoor shower, I went down and collected cheese, crackers, and smoked bluefish pâté on a platter, made two vodkas on ice with olives—green for me, black for Zee—and put them on the platter, then took the platter back up onto the balcony.

By the time Zee joined me, her long, blue-black hair still damp from the shower and her tanned skin shining, I was well into the nibblies.

We exchanged a kiss.

"Well," I said, "how was your day?"

"Excellent. And yours?"

"I made little progress, but I didn't lose any ground."

"You had no ground to lose."

"There is some bad news and some good news."

"Tell me."

"I've prepared supper," I said. "That's the good news."

"Indeed it is. Tell me about the rest of your day, including the bad news."

So I did. Not everything, though. Not the part about the red haze. That was passed over lightly as a shoving match. Finding Larry Bucyck was the bad news.

When I was through, Zee said, "What do you think?"

"I'm not sure. Somebody executed Bucyck, but I don't know anything about that. My focus is Eduardo Alvarez's death. What I want to do is talk with Doyle and Mortison."

She frowned. "Maybe I shouldn't have talked you into taking that job. Why don't you just give their names to Dom Agganis and let him deal with them."

Sensible advice, but I said, "Dom has Bucyck on his plate."

"Brady has him on his plate, too."

"Maybe he'll know something when we see him,"

I said. "He'll be staying here tonight, and you can play Grand Inquisitor."

"I'm glad he's coming," she said. "Maybe we can do some fishing before he goes home. He can't do anything more for his friend."

"The fishing is a good idea," I said. But I didn't think Brady Coyne would be abandoning Bucyck, even though he was dead. I figured he'd be around for a while.

Chapter Eight

Brady

Ten or fifteen minutes after J.W. left, state-police officer Dom Agganis led me back up the hill to Larry Bucyck's house. We got there just in time to see the emergency wagon pull away and go bumping down the driveway—carrying Larry's body, I assumed.

"Can I go now?" I said to Agganis.

He turned to me and smiled. "Nope."

"What now?"

"Now we head over to the police station so we get your story on tape."

"How many times do I have to tell it?"

"Which version?"

"Look," I said, "I haven't rehearsed it, you know? My old friend, my client, we found his dead body in a pigsty and you tell me he was executed. It's all kind of spinning around in my head."

"Good thing, too," said Agganis. "I don't trust pat stories. But we've got to get it on tape, and it's going to take a little while. You might as well get used to it."

"You could at least say you're sorry."

He smiled. "I'm truly sorry about your friend. I'm not sorry I have to interview you some more." He touched my arm, steered me over to the Chilmark PD cruiser, and opened the back door. "Get in, please, Mr. Coyne."

"Chilmark?" I said. "We're in Menemsha, aren't we?"

"Chilmark and Menemsha," he said. "One police force. Same jurisdiction. The village of Menemsha is part of the township of Chilmark. Get in, now."

I bent over and began to slide in. Agganis guided me with his hand on top of my head as if I were a criminal.

I sat on the backseat and looked out at him. "What about my car?" I said. "Zee's car, I mean."

"Someone will drive it over to the station for you. Got the keys?"

"They're in the ignition."

He nodded and shut the door. Then he went to the front window and spoke to the uniformed officer behind the wheel for a minute.

The cop in the passenger seat half turned and looked back at me through the wire mesh. "Bucyck was dead in pig muck?"

I nodded. "You knew Larry?"

"Sure. Everybody does. Did. I don't mean *know* him. He was too strange to know. But everybody knew who he was. I don't think he had any what you'd call friends, but he was kind of a legend around here. Looney old sonofabitch, some kind of hermit, living in the woods, no electricity or anything. Totally harmless, of course. Used to pitch for the Sox, for God's sake."

"Yeah, well," I said, "he's dead now."

The cop shrugged and turned around. We were bouncing slowly down the driveway. I spotted a couple of Larry's rock sculptures in the woods. Now they were monuments. There wouldn't be any more of them.

There was a buzz from up front, and the cop behind the wheel put a cell phone to his ear. "Radko," he said. He listened for a minute, then said, "No shit? Tomorrow? So that probably means . . ." He paused. "Everybody, huh?" Another pause. "When tomorrow, do you know?" He blew out an exasperated breath. "Well, fuck, you know? It's gotta be Sunday, of course. I was gonna have a cookout. Already invited the neighbors over . . . Yeah, sure. I hear you." Radko snapped his phone shut and tilted his head toward his partner. "It's happening sometime tomorrow, they think."

"It's really happening, huh?" said the other cop. "I figured it was just gossip."

"It's in all the papers," said Radko.

"That's what I mean. Rumors. They were just reporting rumors. That's what newspapers do. They don't know anything. I never thought he'd come back."

"Well, he's coming back, all right. Private plane, and it's gonna be sometime tomorrow. If they know exactly when, they're not saying. So everybody's on duty, in case you were planning anything, like a cookout."

"I was maybe gonna go fishing is all," said the cop. "Since you didn't invite me to your cookout."

"It was supposed to be for the neighbors," said Radko. "People with kids. A family thing. No cops.

You can forget about fishing tomorrow. I hear the stripers've been biting pretty good at Lobsterville, though, huh?"

"Yeah, well fuck it, I guess."

We drove the rest of the way in silence, and after about ten minutes we pulled up in front of a little wood-frame building with weathered cedar-shake shingles and white trim. It had a bell tower and a brick chimney. I thought it once might have been an elementary schoolhouse, but the sign indicated that it was the Chilmark police station.

The two cops led me inside and put me in a big square room with a few rectangular oak tables and tall windows. I would have taken it for a fourth-grade classroom, except the windows were covered with thick wire mesh.

Radko told me to sit at one of the tables. "You want some water or something?"

"Coffee would be good."

He shrugged and left the room. The other cop stood at the doorway and ignored me.

A few minutes later Dom Agganis and Olive Otero came in. Olive set a mug of coffee in front of me. They both sat across from me.

Agganis put a tape recorder on the table. He spoke into it, played it back, nodded, then said, "It's Saturday, August 23, um, two twenty-seven P.M. We're at the Chilmark police station. State-police officers Agganis and Otero interviewing Mr. Brady Coyne regarding the Larry Bucyck homicide." He looked at me and nodded. "State your name and occupation for us, please."

"Brady Coyne. I'm a lawyer."

"You were Larry Bucyck's attorney, is that right?"

"That's right."

"Okay, Mr. Coyne," said Agganis. "Let's go over this again. Why don't you start where Larry Bucyck called you at home and just tell us everything. Don't leave anything out."

It was a little after four-thirty when they finally let me go. Agganis told me not to leave the island without checking with him, and I assured him that I'd be staying with the Jacksons and he could always reach me by cell phone. I promised not to talk to the newspapers about Larry's murder.

An officer at the front desk gave me the keys to Zee's Wrangler, and I went outside into the August afternoon. I sat on a bench next to the parking area and lifted my face to the afternoon sunshine. My brain was spinning with scenarios and conjectures and doubts and sadness.

The only thing I knew for certain was that Larry Bucyck had been alive this morning, and now he was dead. I was having You-never-know and Count-your-blessings thoughts.

After a few minutes, I got up and went over to the Wrangler. I started it up and turned onto the road heading to the Jacksons' house in Edgartown.

Then I remembered Rocket, and Larry's hens, and the pigs, too. What would become of them?

So I turned around and drove back to Larry's place in Menemsha.

I half expected the driveway to be barricaded with

yellow crime-scene tape, but it wasn't, nor was Larry's house, nor was there a cop standing guard over it. It looked just the way it had looked when I woke up in the morning. Larry's bicycle still leaned against the wall, and Rocket was snoozing in a patch of sunshine. As if nothing had happened. As if I'd find Larry out back stirring a big kettle of quahog chowder.

Rocket's water dish was empty. I picked it up, went inside, and took the dish to the sink.

I was pumping water when a voice said, "Put your hands on top of your head," and something hard rammed into my kidneys.

I let go of the pump and set down the dish and put my hands on my head. I remembered how Larry had gotten the drop on me with his walking stick. "Is that a piece of wood you're poking me with?"

"Try something and you'll find out." It was a low, growly voice. A woman's voice.

"Look—"

"Who are you?" she said.

"I'm Larry Bucyck's lawyer. From Boston. I stayed with him last night."

"What's your name?"

"Brady Coyne."

"You got ID?"

"Left hip pocket."

"Take it out. Slowly."

I reached back with my left hand, took out my wallet, and held it there.

She took it. "Put your hand back on your head."

I did.

After a moment, she said, "Okay, Mr. Brady Coyne. I bet you can tell me what's been happening here today. Here's your wallet."

I reached behind me, and she put my wallet into my hand. I shoved it back into my pocket. "Somebody murdered Larry," I said.

"Murdered," she whispered.

I nodded. "I'm sorry."

She didn't say anything for a minute. Then she blew out a long slow breath and said, "I was afraid of that."

"You thought somebody was going to murder him?"

"That's not what I meant." She cleared her throat. "I saw all the police cars, and that was my worst-case scenario. Did you do it?"

"The police have been asking me versions of that question all day. The answer is still no. I'm the one who found his body."

"Why'd you come back here?"

"I was worried about the animals," I said. "Can I please take my hands off my head?"

"Just let me think." She didn't say anything for a minute or so. Then the stick, or whatever it was, stopped poking me in the back, and she said, "Okay. I remember your name. Larry used to talk about you. He thought you were a good guy. You can turn around."

I lowered my hands and turned around.

She had taken a couple of steps back from me. She was holding a pump-action shotgun at her hip. Twelve-gauge, I guessed, judging by the size of the bore, which was pointing at my stomach.

141

She was younger than I'd guessed from her voice. Somewhere in her thirties. Quite tall. Taller than me, six-two maybe, with muscular arms and shoulders. She wore snug-fitting jeans and a black tank top and dirty white sneakers. Black hair and unwrinkled skin the color of an old burnished penny.

Her chocolate eyes were glazed with tears.

"I'm sorry about Larry," I said.

She tried to smile. It didn't work very well. "Somebody ought to cry for him, don't you think?"

I nodded. "What's your name?"

"Sedona. Sedona Blaisdell. I live in one of those big butt-ugly houses you passed on the road in."

"A neighbor, then."

She shrugged. She had a wide mouth, even white teeth, and a long thin nose with a bump on the bridge, as if it had once been broken. "I sort of took care of Larry," she said. "He was good to his animals, but he didn't pay much attention to himself. It was our secret. If my husband knew about me coming here . . ." She waved her hand. "I liked him a lot." She stopped and looked up at the sky. "I've been visiting Larry just about every day for the past six years," she said after a minute, "and my husband never notices. He doesn't notice me when I'm there, so I guess he doesn't notice me when I'm not."

"I'd say that was his loss," I said. "Would you mind aiming that thing somewhere else?"

She looked down at the shotgun she was holding and frowned as if she hadn't seen it before. "Sorry." She lowered the muzzle so it was pointing at the floor.

"There were all those worrisome vehicles traipsing in and out, and I had to know what was going on. I figured it wasn't anything good, so I grabbed my husband's gun and snuck through the woods."

"You and Larry were more than just neighbors," I said.

She cocked her head and smiled. "Well, I guess you could say that. You could certainly say we were friends. It wasn't easy being friends with Larry Bucyck. He lived pretty much in his own muddled head. But sometimes we'd talk about baseball. We had that in common."

"You're a baseball fan?"

She shrugged. "I played college hoops on scholarship. We both used to be athletes, that's all. He'd talk about the pressure, how it got so it wasn't any fun. I could relate to that. I mean, he did it for money, I did it for an education." She shrugged. "He was a very sad man. Reason I used to come see him, I worried about him doing something to himself. Then today, seeing all those vehicles, that ambulance . . ."

"I used to worry about that, too," I said. "But I thought he'd made peace with it."

She shook her head. "He could put on a good front. But he was haunted. Look, you don't need to worry about the animals. I'll take care of them till I can figure out what to do with them. I guess I'll take Rocket home with me. My husband won't like it, if he even notices, but the hell with him. Rocket's the sweetest dog."

We went outside. She leaned her shotgun against the

side of the house, and we sat on some rocks. Rocket came over and nuzzled Sedona's leg. She dropped her hand so he could lick it.

"Can you think of anybody who'd want to murder Larry Bucyck?" I said.

"Besides himself, no," she said. "He was about the least offensive person I've ever known. Only thing is . . ." She looked up at the sky and shrugged.

"What?"

"Well, you know how people are about anybody who's different? I've lived with it all my life, this big gangly black girl who could play basketball better than most boys and beat them at arm wrestling, too. People can be cruel, is all I'm saying."

"People were cruel to Larry?"

She nodded. "That's one of the reasons he just tried to stay by himself. He looked different and acted different, and people don't understand somebody who dances to his own tunes, you know? It makes them uncomfortable."

I thought about how Larry had ended up face-down in a pigsty with a bullet in the back of his head. I assumed that his murder was connected to what he apparently witnessed on Menemsha Pond a few nights earlier, but it was possible that some sick mind might consider shooting him and dumping his body in a pigsty the ultimate indignity and fitting justice for somebody whose differences they found intolerable.

"Do you know anybody specific who could do something like that?" I said.

She shrugged. "Let me think about it. Larry has mentioned some things, and I've seen some things. A gang of kids came around last spring and knocked down some of his sculptures. I might be able to find out who they were."

"You should tell the police if you have any ideas."

She looked at me and smiled. "I should. You're right. Thing is, my husband might not understand me being involved in all this." She waved her hand. "Well, the hell with him."

"Or you could tell me," I said. "Looks like I'm going to be down here for a few days. Hang on a minute."

I went into Larry's house, found a pad of paper and a pencil, and wrote down my cell phone number and J.W.'s number.

I went back outside, gave the paper to Sedona, and sat beside her. "The state police are handling the case," I said, "if you decide to talk to them. But you can call me. It might be easier. As I said, I'm a lawyer. I can be discreet."

She took the paper, looked at it, folded it, and shoved it into the hip pocket of her jeans. "Discreet, huh?"

I smiled. "It's about all I'm really good at. It's my main area of expertise. My specialty, you might say. Discretion."

"Oh," she said, "you're way too modest. I bet you're pretty good at a lot of things." She reached over and touched my arm, then lowered her chin and smiled up at me. "Am I right?"

Jesus. I was pretty sure she was flirting with me, and right then, for the first time, it occurred to me that Larry Bucyck, the hermit who slept in a hammock and kept chickens and pigs, and Sedona Blaisdell, who lived in a big McMansion unnoticed and unappreciated by her husband, might've been something more than neighborly friends.

I patted her hand where it rested on my arm, then stood up. "If you're all set with the animals," I said, "I'd better get going. I'm supposed to be at a friend's house for dinner, and the martini hour is upon us."

She stood up, too. "Don't worry about the animals. And look. If you need to reach me, my number's in the phone book. Blaisdell, S. I've got my own line."

"Sure," I said. "Thanks." I held out my hand to her.

She took it and held on to it for an instant too long.

I smiled, and she smiled, both of us awkwardly, as if we weren't sure what, if anything, had passed between us, and then I climbed into Zee's red Wrangler and got the hell away from there.

Once I got out onto South Road heading for the Jackson abode, I fished my cell phone from my pocket and called home.

Evie answered on the first ring. She didn't say, "Hello," or, "Hi, honey," reading my number off her phone's caller-ID window.

What she said was, "Are you okay?"

"Didn't you get my message?" I said. "I called this morning. I said I was okay."

"I heard what you said. Hearing your voice, I figured you were alive. That was a relief."

"You're mad because I didn't call last night," I said. "I'm sorry."

"Yes, you said you were sorry. When are you coming home?"

"Are you?"

"Am I what?"

"Mad at me," I said.

"I guess so. Sure. I'm mad. I lay awake half the night, scenarios whirling in my head. Completely unnecessary and thoughtless. So when will you be home?"

"I don't know."

She paused. "What does that mean?"

"Look, babe—"

"Brady," she said, "what the hell is going on down there?"

"I don't want you to worry—"

"Too late for that. I'm already worried. If you don't tell me what's happening, I'll imagine the very worst possible thing. Nothing you could tell me would make me worry more."

I blew out a breath. "Larry was murdered."

Evie didn't say anything.

"Honey?"

"I didn't imagine anything that bad," she said softly. "Now you've got to tell me the truth. Are you in danger?"

"Me? No. Of course not. Don't worry about that. What happened to Larry has nothing to do with me. Okay?"

"Really? Promise?"

I crossed my fingers. "Promise."

"Good," she said. "Okay."

"The police say I've got to hang around for a couple more days, though."

"Can you tell me what happened? I mean, Larry wanted you down there, and when you get there he's murdered. What's it all about, anyway?"

"It's a really long story, honey. No matter how I'd tell it, it's still a long, bad story. I'll tell you all about it when I see you."

"Well, okay," she said. "I really just want you to be safe and come home."

"I'll be there as soon as I possibly can," I said. "Believe me. If J.W. won't give me a ride on his catboat, I'll swim. I'll let you know as soon as I know."

"You better keep in touch."

"I will. I promise."

She didn't say anything for a minute. Then she said, "I like it better when you're here."

"Me, too."

"Give my love to J.W. and Zee and the kids."

"I will."

"Some for you, too."

I found myself smiling. "I love you, too."

"You better," she said.

I pulled into the Jacksons' driveway fifteen minutes later. When I got out of the car, I looked up at the balcony and saw J.W.'s arm wave. "Come on up," he yelled.

Joshua and Diana were playing in their tree house. They called, "Hi, Uncle Brady," to me, and I said, "Hi, kids," to them.

"Wanna come play with us?" said Diana.

148

"Later, maybe," I said. "Your mom and dad need me right now."

"He means he wants a martini," said Joshua to Diana.

Smart kid.

I went up onto the balcony. Zee and J.W. were sipping from martini glasses.

J.W. held up his glass. "Ready for one of these?"

"At least one," I said.

Zee handed her glass to him. "Refill," she said.

J.W. took the martini glasses into the house, and a minute later he returned. He handed a full glass to me. I sat down, put my feet up on the balcony railing, and gazed out over the salt pond to the ocean beyond, where white gulls were wheeling in the afternoon breeze and white sails were inching across the blue water.

I took a long sip of martini and sighed. "That's much better."

J.W. reached over and poked my leg. "Zee was saying how she ran into Coop this afternoon," he said, "and he told her he found a school of bonito chasing bait off East Beach yesterday. Isn't that right, hon?"

"That's right," said Zee. "His clients threw flies at them but couldn't catch any. Coop said they didn't know how to cast a fly in the wind. He said competent anglers might've had better luck."

I took this as a hint that they didn't want to talk about murder, which struck me as a sound policy for any family cocktail hour.

So we sipped martinis and talked about fishing, and

149

after a while the subject switched to the Red Sox, and by the time we'd trooped downstairs and called in the kids for dinner, our conversation, punctuated by occasional comfortable silences, had touched on migrating seabirds, Beethoven, Hemingway, skunks, and Errol Flynn.

Dinner was an excellent chicken salad with home-baked bread. Afterward J.W. brewed a pot of coffee, then wandered outside with the kids. I helped Zee clean up in the kitchen while I waited for the coffeemaker to do its job.

"J.W. told me about your friend," she said. "I'm very sorry."

"Larry was a sad, unstable man," I said, "but I'm pretty sure he wanted to live."

"Any idea who did it?"

"No. He told me about seeing a suspicious boat sneaking into Menemsha Pond at midnight earlier this week. He thought they were doing something illegal, and he said they caught him in their spotlight. I wondered if he made it up, or exaggerated it. Larry wasn't that well balanced. He seemed paranoid."

"Well," Zee said, "since he ended up getting murdered, that would suggest his story was real, wouldn't it?"

I nodded. "It surely would. Although I met a friend of his this afternoon, a neighbor woman who apparently watched out for him, who said that intolerant bigots sometimes harassed and bullied him. She also has a husband who might be jealous of the attention she paid to Larry, although she didn't suggest anything like that."

Zee was loading dishes in the dishwasher. Without looking up, she said, "All bigots are intolerant, aren't they? By definition?"

I smiled. "I guess you're right."

"You don't think that's what happened, do you?" Zee said.

"No," I said. "I think it had something to do with what he saw the other night."

"I suppose you're going to try to figure it out, huh?"

"I feel like I should do something."

"And while you're at it, you'll probably want J.W. to join you."

"I haven't talked to him about that."

"Except you brought him with you this afternoon," she said, "and he saw the body and waded in the pig muck. You don't for a minute think he isn't interested."

"Oh, I'm sure J.W.'s interested," I said. "But he's already got something he's working on."

"Maybe he could use some help with that," she said. "Quid pro quo, the two of you."

I nodded. "I already thought of that."

When we finished cleaning up, Zee called the kids in, and all three of them came, including J.W. I poured us some coffee, and J.W. and I took our mugs up to the balcony while Zee helped Joshua and Diana get ready for bed.

"You want to tell me more about what you're working on?" I said to J.W.

"Sure. Maybe you've got some thoughts."

He proceeded to bring me up to date about the man who got killed in the boat explosion and the var-

151

ious people he was talking to and those that he was trying to track down. He concluded by telling me—rather proudly, I thought—about picking the lock and prowling around the apartment of a man named Harry Doyle.

"Breaking and entering," I said.

"Damn near got caught, too," he said. "It got the adrenaline flowing, I can tell you that."

"I'd say you're doing what any competent sleuth would do," I said. "Kicking the bushes and seeing if anything flies out."

"That's about it," he said. "I want to find out more about Doyle and Mortison, and I'm not done with this guy Steve. But so far I'm kind of stumped."

We sat there sipping coffee and watching the darkness fall over the island.

"This afternoon I overheard some cops talking," I said after a few minutes. "It sounded like they're mobilizing all the police on the island. One of them was complaining about having to cancel a neighborhood cookout. Something's up. Whatever it is, it's happening tomorrow."

"There are rumors that Joe Callahan is coming to the island to try to settle the strike," said J.W.

"The ex-prez," I said. "That would account for it, all right. You know him, don't you?"

He shrugged. "His daughter. One summer when they were vacationing here. She's a young woman now. I don't know him really. Met him a couple times, but it's not like we're buddies."

Zee joined us on the balcony. "So what're you two Sam Spades hatching? Going sleuthing, are we?"

J.W. turned to me. "Want to?"

"Want to what?"

"Go see if we can spot the boat that Larry Bucyck said he saw?"

"Why not," I said. "Doing something always beats sitting around thinking unpleasant thoughts." I turned to Zee. "Okay with you?"

She shrugged. "Doesn't matter. I'd much rather know what you were really up to than have you pretend you're going fishing because you think I'd worry if I knew you were sleuthing."

"Who?" said J.W. "Us?"

Zee rolled her eyes.

He turned to me. "We could go fishing."

"Let's go sleuthing," I said.

"Okay, then," he said. "Come with me."

We went inside, and I followed J.W. through the house to his office.

I sat on the sofa. He looked through some stuff in one of the bookshelves, said "Aha," and came over and sat beside me. He unfolded a road map of Martha's Vineyard on the coffee table.

"This is where Larry lived," he said, jabbing at the map with a pencil. "Show me exactly where he said he saw that boat."

He handed me the pencil, and I used the eraser end to trace the general path that Larry and I had taken from his house through the woods to Menemsha Pond. "We walked along the shoreline here—it's all reedy and muddy—and hid behind some rhododendrons right about here. There's a point of land maybe fifty yards off to the right, and just inside it is a cottage where he said that boat docked. About here." I pointed with the pencil. "Mumford. That's who Larry said owns the place. Some doctor who Larry said only comes down in the summer."

"Mumford," mumbled J.W. "Don't know him." He stood up and went over to a closet, rummaged around for a while, then emerged with an armload of stuff, which he dumped onto the sofa beside me. "Dark windbreaker for you, dark windbreaker for me," he said, sorting through it. "Dark Red Sox cap for you, one for me."

He draped a pair of binoculars around his neck and stuck a flashlight in his pocket. He gave me a flashlight, too. Then he handed me a big Leatherman tool, which had heavy wire cutters and pliers and a knife blade, not to mention screwdrivers and bottle openers and other useful implements that all folded together cleverly.

"Don't know what good the binocs are going to do," I said. "It's nighttime, you know."

"The binoculars are infrared," he said. "Got 'em at the Army-Navy store."

"Cool," I said.

I put the flashlight and Leatherman in my pants pockets.

"What else do we need?" he said.

"Depends on how many weeks we plan to stay," I said. "Stove? Tent?"

"Yeah," he said without smiling. "Funny." He glanced at his watch. "Ready to go?"

It was around nine-thirty. "Larry said the boat came in around midnight."

"A midnight rendezvous with the van at the dock," said J.W. "Sounds about right to me."

"I didn't really believe him," I said.

"Larry?"

I nodded.

"Why would he make up something like that?"

"I just figured he saw something and sort of expanded and distorted it," I said. "Larry lived alone for a long time. I didn't really trust his grasp of reality."

"It was enough for him to call you in Boston and ask you down here," said J.W. "And apparently it was convincing enough for you to agree."

"His fear was convincing," I said.

"I'd say a bullet in the head is pretty convincing, wouldn't you?"

I nodded. "I don't doubt his story anymore. I just feel bad that I doubted him. Maybe if I'd taken him more seriously, if . . ."

"Don't blame yourself," said J.W. "It's not your fault."

"Nice try," I said. "Thanks."

J.W. stood up. "Let's figure out who killed him. That'll make you feel better."

We went in J.W.'s Land Cruiser. He followed South Road to Menemsha, and when we came to the intersection with Middle Road, he went left. A short way later he took a right turn onto a narrow secondary road that ended at the pond.

We got out, pushed through some bushes, and found a spot on a little rise about fifty feet from the shoreline. Dr. Mumford's place was a hundred yards or so off to our right.

We crouched there behind the bushes. J.W. lifted his binoculars, panned along the shoreline, then grunted. "Look there." His voice was a soft whisper. He pointed. "See?"

"Yes. There's a boat docked there. And a light in the house."

He handed me the binoculars.

I raised them to my eyes. In the greenish night-vision light, I could see the boat and the dock and the house quite clearly. Lights glowed from the house's windows.

I panned the length of the boat, which was moored against the dock.

"I can't make out the boat's name," I said. "The transom's facing the wrong way. Looks like an ordinary boat to me. It's where Larry and I were looking the other night. But he said the boat he saw was a sixty-, sixty-five-footer. That one's maybe forty."

"Larry probably exaggerated," said J.W. "Or he wasn't a very good judge of boat lengths. Or maybe he saw a different boat. What else do you see?"

"Nothing. I—wait." I squinted through the binoculars. Things were pretty shadowy and dim, even with the night-vision binoculars, but after a minute I spotted a figure standing on the dock. He was wearing dark clothing, and he was holding something.

"There's someone on the dock," I said. "It's hard to see . . . I'm not sure, but . . ." I handed the binoculars to him.

He peered through the binoculars. "If I'm not mistaken, that's a weapon in that guy's hands. It looks like an Uzi."

"Jesus," I whispered.

"You nervous?"

"Shouldn't I be?"

"Of course," said J.W. "It'd be stupid not to be."

"I guess I'm pretty smart, then," I said. "Time to leave?"

"Nah," J.W. said. "Not yet."

Chapter Nine

J.W.

The house was on a point of land thrusting out from the east shore of Menemsha Pond. A boat was tied to a dock on the outermost part of the point of land, giving the armed man on the dock a good view of all the pond and the shore to the north and south.

He couldn't see through underbrush, though, so we kept that between us and him as we crept toward the house beside its starlit driveway. It was possible, even probable, that he wasn't the only guard on duty, so we moved slowly and noiselessly, stopping often.

This paid off when, during one of our stops, a light flared briefly ahead of us as a man lit a cigarette. The red dot at the end of the cigarette lingered after the flare of his lighter went out. I didn't think his boss would be pleased by his carelessness, but it's been said that it's harder to give up nicotine than heroin. Could be.

I thought about our options. There were three: sneak past the guard, disable the guard, or go home.

I felt Brady touch my shoulder and heard his whispered voice in my ear. "I have a nice-sized rock in my

159

hand. If you can get him looking the other way I may be able to smash him on the head. I almost never hit people with rocks unless they try to hit me first, but I can make an exception in this case."

I wished I had a fishing rod. If I had one, I could walk along the driveway pretending to be looking for a good spot to cast and, when challenged, could act startled and then embarrassed about being on private land and hope that the smoker would keep his gun pointed at the ground and turn his back to Brady just long enough to get himself whacked with Brady's rock.

But I didn't have a fishing rod, so I decided to be a half-drunk stranger looking for my rented but misplaced house. After whispering this plan to Brady, I retreated a few yards, stepped out onto the starlit driveway, and started shuffling toward the house, mumbling and staggering as I went.

Ahead of me, the red dot of the cigarette dropped straight down and disappeared, presumably ground out by a shod foot. I pretended to trip and muttered a curse, then staggered on. Suddenly a light was in my face. I blinked at it and put up a hand to hide my eyes.

"Hold it right there," said a voice from behind the light.

But I lurched on a few more steps, then said with a slur, "Is that you, George? Where the hell is the house?"

My steps took me past the torch, so that its holder had to turn to grab my arm. "I said to hold it, buddy. I mean it. Not another step."

I swayed and peered at the light. "George?"

"I'm not George, buddy," said the guy, "and you're walking down the wrong road. This is a private driveway. Let me see some ID."

"ID, ID." I patted various pockets. "Don't be mad, George. You know me. Whatcha want ID for? Where is it? I know I got it somewhere. Maybe I lost it. Damn."

"You just stand right there," said the voice. "I'm gonna call somebody to come and get you."

I put confusion into my own voice. "You don't have to call anybody, George. All you got to do is tell me where my damned house is."

"You're too drunk to know what you're doing, buddy," said the voice. "And I'm not George."

As he spoke those words, I heard a thud, and then the flashlight fell to the ground, rapidly followed by a body. Brady's shoes stepped into the light of the fallen flashlight, and his hand reached down and covered most of the lens, creating a dimmer, smaller light. This he used to look at the guard.

"Well, well," he whispered. "Old George here has himself an Uzi and a radio."

"Thanks to you, he didn't use either one," I whispered back.

I put my ear to the sentry's chest and heard his heart thumping steadily.

He moaned, then, and moved a hand. I looked at his head and saw no blood. "I don't think you damaged him too much," I said, "so let's wrap him up and gag him before he comes to."

Using his belt and bootlaces, we trussed him up,

gagged him with his own handkerchief, and dragged him into the bushes. Then I put his radio into my pocket and gave the Uzi to Brady, who slung it over his shoulder and doused the flashlight.

Ahead of us was the front yard of the house, and parked there were a dozen cars. Conscious of the fact that where there were two guards, there might be three or four or more, we moved very carefully to the edge of the yard. Above us, the summer stars glittered in the sky and cast a silver sheen over the scene before us.

We crouched in the shadow of an oak and watched and listened but spied no other guard.

"You want to sneak up to the house and look in a window?" asked Brady in a whisper. "Maybe you'll recognize somebody."

It wasn't my idea of a splendid thought, but we'd come a long way, and going just a little farther didn't seem any more irrational than anything we'd already done.

"All right," I whispered back. "While I'm doing that, you stand guard. If somebody spots you, yell 'Police,' then cut and run. I'll be right on your heels."

"And what if somebody spots you?"

"I'll be out of here like a greyhound. You'll have to run fast to get in front of me."

"What I'll do," said Brady, patting his Uzi, "is cut loose into the air with this thing. Then, while the guards are scrambling for cover, we can get away."

I hoped it wouldn't come to that. I wanted to get away without causing any more excitement than we already had.

I slid away from him and moved toward the house. It was a big summer place with porches on all four sides and balconies above the porches. Two big chimneys were dark against the sky.

I thought that if I wanted to conduct a well-guarded meeting, I'd post a man or two on the porches and balconies, and I'd have some others circulating to make sure no one intruded on the company inside. So I crouched beside a hydrangea bush and watched, but saw nothing. Maybe I was wrong. Maybe the host thought a couple of guards, one on the dock by the boat and one on the driveway, were enough.

I waited a few minutes longer, then slipped across the lawn, up onto the porch, and over to a lighted window. I could feel my heart beating, and my breathing sounded loud enough to wake the gods. I inhaled deeply and peered in the window.

I was looking at a large, comfortable room with a fireplace at the far end. There were a dozen men seated in chairs facing a large map of the Vineyard that was mounted in front of a book-lined wall. Save for one man who was using a laser pointer to illustrate something on the map, and whose face was turned in my direction, the others all had their backs toward me.

The man with the pointer was unknown to me. No surprise there. There are 100,000 people on Martha's Vineyard in the summertime, and I don't know almost all of them. It was Dr. Mumford's house, so maybe it was Dr. Mumford. I didn't know what kind of a doctor Dr. Mumford was, but judging by his house and his boat, he was a rich one. The man's hair was white and he wore old-fashioned wire-rimmed glasses. His clothes were Vineyard casual chic. I couldn't see his feet, but I was willing to bet that he wore boat shoes or sandals without socks, just like me.

I know a woman who, in St. Paul, Minnesota, had once had a stranger come up to her and say, "Weren't you in Nottingham, England, a year ago? I thought I recognized the back of your head." The woman with the identifiable head had been surprised by the stranger's identification talents.

I could have used that stranger's genius now, because as I looked at the backs of the heads facing the speaker, I didn't recognize a single one. Then one head turned slightly, and I caught a brief glimpse of a face that was somehow familiar. But the face turned away before I could attach a name to it, and I had one of those lightning fast psychological moments wherein countless images and recollections whip through your mind so fast that fact and fiction, art and reality, become inseparable and indistinguishable, and I wasn't sure whether I'd seen the face in fact or in some photograph or film.

The man with the pointer was pointing first here, then there, on the map. Was he some sort of real estate tycoon, indicating choice locations for development? If so, it was an odd hour for an investors' conference. The pointer lingered down near Deep Bottom Road, then here and there in the state forest—at the end of Otis Bassett Road, I noticed, and out by the forest headquarters. It danced for a while on the airport business park and then near the road to Scrubby Neck Farm.

So much for the real estate theory. Two of the spots of interest to the man with the pointer were on state land that was beyond the reach of even the most wealthy and connected developers.

Pointer Man tapped the map again and made a sweeping circle that touched the various areas of interest to him. I wished I had one of those gadgets that allow you to hear what's going on inside a room. This one was well insulated, and I couldn't hear a thing.

Then I heard the scrape of footsteps coming around the pond-side corner of the house, and a voice said, "Hey! What the hell are you doing there?"

I straightened, pointed a finger at him, and said, "Police. Hold it right there. Don't say a word. Put your hands on your head. You're under arrest." I pulled George's radio from my pocket, looked out into the dark shrubbery beyond the lawn and waved my imaginary officers toward the house. "All right, men," I said into the radio, "I've been spotted. Come on in." I looked back at the man who had discovered me. "You stay right where you are."

I turned and walked to the front of the house and brayed, "Johnson, call in the cruisers. Block the driveway. Don't let anyone leave."

I stepped around the corner, jumped off the porch, and ran across the front lawn past the parked cars.

Brady was there, a dim shape in the starlight. Behind me, I heard the thud of running feet on the porch.

"Run!" I said to Brady, showing him how to do it as I passed him and raced away along the driveway.

A shout came from the house, and I heard Brady's feet pounding along behind me. My hundred-yard-dash days were far behind me, and it wasn't long before my chest was heaving. From the direction of the house, floodlights suddenly went on, and then my shadow was racing along in front of me. The road was a ribbon of moonlight over the purple moor. Good grief, what was Alfred Noyes doing in my mind at a time like this?

How far to the Land Cruiser?

My breath was coming in great heaves.

Then, just as I rounded a bend in the driveway and left the white house lights behind me, I heard a car engine roar into life. They were coming after us in a vehicle and were sure to catch us. I ran on anyway, because there didn't seem to be enough undergrowth to hide in beside the driveway.

Brady's feet matched the rhythm of my own, and we weren't far from the Land Cruiser, but behind us the car was coming fast, and I knew we'd never outrun it.

Then I no longer heard Brady's pounding footsteps. I threw a backward glance and saw him kneeling in the center of the driveway just as the lights from the pursuing car swung around the bend behind us. He had the Uzi in both hands, and as the car lights centered upon him, he pulled the trigger, sending a stream of bullets low into the front of the car, shattering the headlights and flattening tires. The car swerved and plowed into some bushes, and I wondered if he'd killed anybody. Then, before I could move, Brady was up and running past me.

"Run!" he said, showing me how to do it.

I followed him away from the shouts and curses behind us until we reached the Land Cruiser. Brady threw the Uzi into the bushes and piled into the car. I got in behind the wheel, fumbled the ignition key into its slot, and finally got it started, and a minute later we were on our way back down-island, headed toward Chilmark center.

When I got my breathing back more or less to normal, I said, "I didn't know you were a machine gunner."

"It was a required course at Yale Law School," said Brady. "Court Options 101."

"Were you aiming at the driver?"

"No. At the lights and tires. What do you think? If I aimed at the driver, I'd've hit the driver. But if those guys were the ones who murdered Larry Bucyck—and I bet they were—I wouldn't weep if a stray bullet did hit one or two of them."

"The trouble is, we don't know if they were."

I felt his glance. "Who do you think they were? Sunday School teachers holding a midnight prayer meeting? Larry spotted a boat here, complete with an armed guard who saw him, too. And you know what happened to Larry. And these guards had guns, too. Do you think that's just a coincidence?"

No, I didn't think that and said so. I looked in the rearview mirror. There'd been a lot of cars in that yard, and Brady had only stopped one of them. I saw no lights behind me, but that could change.

We passed the Chilmark police station, where no lights shone in the windows. Ahead was the intersection at Beetlebung Corner, giving us three road options: South Road, Middle Road, and Menemsha Cross Road. Ordinarily I'd have felt fairly confident about shaking a tail there, because normally nobody can follow you three ways at the same time, but in this case there were enough bad guys to follow every road, so instead of taking any of them, I drove up Menemsha Cross Road for a few hundred yards, then turned around and parked, facing the intersection again.

"I presume you have a plan," said Brady, a hopeful note in his voice.

"It's not much of a plan, but it is a plan," I said. "This old truck will never outrun any of those cars we saw at the house, so if they come after us, I plan to go down-island behind them instead of in front of them. As soon as we see lights coming along that road we just followed and getting close to the intersection, we're going to make believe we're coming from Menemsha and heading for Edgartown. If we time it right, we'll get to the intersection just after they do, and then we'll just waddle on down South Road and watch their taillights disappear in the distance."

"Are you full of confidence?" asked Brady.

"If we fail," I said, "you could shoot them all, if you still had your Uzi. Maybe you chucked it too soon."

"I never had any secret desire to shoot an Uzi," said Brady. "I'm glad to be rid of it. I have a pistol in my office. Locked in a safe. That's enough gun for me."

"Too bad you don't have it here," I said. "But if things go right, we won't need it."

Beyond the Chilmark Store, headlights flickered as a half dozen cars came rapidly along the road, following one another in close succession. I put the Land Cruiser in gear and began to move slowly forward, until I gained normal driving speed. By the time the lead car reached the intersection, we were still some distance away. The stream of cars split into three groups of two cars. Each pair took a different road. The two that turned our way moved slowly, as though curious about our identity, but I passed them blithely and followed their brethren down South Road.

"Too easy?" asked Brady.

"Maybe not. They knew they were looking for a car, but they didn't know what kind."

"There's one thing they know they're looking for."

"What?"

"Me," he said. "Larry didn't have much to tell them before they killed him, but he surely told them everything he could think of, and that definitely included me showing up and him telling me everything he'd seen. They'll think that I'm the only one who knows something's rotten in Denmark."

"Not after tonight," I said. "When they find that guard you coshed on the head, he'll tell them that at least two guys were there. He got a good look at my face and the guard at the house saw me."

Our headlights picked up a deer that was ambling casually across the road and into the woods on the other side. A good reason for driving slowly on Martha's Vineyard. Every year about two hundred deer are killed by island hunters, and about the same number by island drivers. Maybe the two search cars in front of us had been moving too fast to miss their deer. Maybe we'd find them wrecked beside the road and could stop and administer first aid.

We didn't.

"I feel sort of like that deer," said Brady. "In the headlights."

It was after midnight, not a good time to intrude upon people. On the other hand, serious skullduggery was afoot, and it was no time to be excessively civil.

"I think we need to tell Dom Agganis about what just happened," I said. "He won't be happy to be rousted out of bed, but we just tangled with guys with assault weapons, and he'll want to know about that. If he knows, and they know he knows, you'll be off the hook."

"You know him better than I do," said Brady. "This island isn't my bailiwick."

"What would you do if this happened up your way, in America?"

"I'd go right to the state police," said Brady.

Great minds.

On either side of the starlit highway the dark trees came out of the night and passed behind us. Was the wind a torrent of darkness? Was Zee waiting, plaiting a dark red love knot into her long black hair?

In West Tisbury we turned toward Edgartown, having seen no more of the two cars that had preceded us along South Road. We passed the old millpond and Cynthia Riggs's bed-and-breakfast, where she catered to writers and artists because they'd understand when she disappeared to do her own writing. We passed Joshua Slocum's last house and then the airport where, if he actually came, ex-President Joe Callahan would land in hopes of mediating the Steamship Authority strike to a happy conclusion.

Beyond the airport we took a left, crossed the four-way stop at the Edgartown–Vineyard Haven Road, and drove into Oak Bluffs, where Sergeant Dom Agganis lived on a side street that led off Barnes Road down toward the lagoon.

"I thought the state cops lived upstairs above the station on Temahigan Avenue," said Brady, as I turned off Barnes.

"Only the summer cops," I said. "Dom has his own place."

His own place was a newish modified Cape with a farm porch stretching across the front. A breezeway hooked the house to his two-car garage, and his yard was neat, with a freshly mowed lawn and well-kept flower beds beside the walk that led from the driveway to the porch, and hydrangeas and azaleas in front of the porch. Behind the house, I knew from previous visits, was a veranda and another lawn that fell away down the slope to the water, where there was a short dock to which was tied a nice, twenty-five-foot fishing boat with a cuddy cabin. All in all, not the sort of place you'd associate with a guy as big and tough as Dom Agganis.

I pulled into the driveway, and we got out and looked at the house. It was dark.

"You knock," said Brady, as we walked to the front door. "You know him better than I do."

A light came on when we stepped onto the porch, and I saw the motion sensor above the door. I used the bronze knocker, then stood back where I could be seen through the peephole in the door.

By and by the door opened, and Dom, dark-jawed beneath the beginnings of a heavy beard, stared at me. "This better be good," he growled.

"I think it is," I said. "I am fully aware that in these days of Homeland Security I'm taking a chance by waking up a possibly trigger-happy minion of the law in the middle of the night."

"Get inside before you wake up the neighbors and they call the cops." Dom stood aside and we went in. "Sit," he said, waving at chairs in the living room and taking one for himself. Archie Bunker's chair. Every man has his Archie Bunker chair. "Now, what is it?" he asked. "Not even you would come here for no reason."

We sat and told him about our adventure, leaving out nothing.

He listened in silence, his eyes weary but increasingly bright. When we were through, he looked at Brady. "Do you think you hit anybody with that Uzi?"

Brady shook his head. "I aimed low, for the lights."

Dom nodded. "Okay. But it's still against the law to possess an automatic weapon or to fire a gun close to a house. Where's the Uzi?"

"I tossed it."

"Great. If we had it here, it'd be evidence that you two aren't crazy." He narrowed his eyes. "Are you?"

"Are we what?" I said.

"Crazy."

"No," I said. "This has to be connected to what

happened to Larry Bucyck. We were checking out his story, and it checked out."

Dom looked at Brady. "Dr. Mumford's house, you say. You're sure?"

"That's what Larry Bucyck told me," said Brady.

Dom tapped a sausage-sized finger on the arm of his chair, then stood up. "Wait here." He went out of the room. He was gone for about twenty minutes. When he came back, he said, "You two can go home now. I suggest that you stay there."

I was tired, so his suggestion seemed like a good one. Still, I was curious. "What's happening?" I asked.

"None of your business," growled Dom. "Thanks a lot, and good-bye."

I guessed that he was sending people up to Chilmark to find out what was going on. One man had already been killed there, and if our report of men wandering around with machine guns was correct, he had more trouble than he needed. The strike was causing enough problems by itself.

He led us to the door and waved us out. As we passed him, he said, "You're sure you've told me everything? You haven't left anything out?"

"You know it all," I said.

We drove away and were turning down my long sandy driveway when Brady said, "I just remembered one thing you didn't tell him."

"What was that?"

"You didn't tell him about the places that interested the guy with the pointer."

Rats. It was true.

"We'll look at your map," Brady said. "I'd like to see what he seemed to be pointing at."

"We'll check it out," I said, "and then we'll have something more useful to tell Dom."

I love maps and charts. Besides, Zee and I needed good island maps to find yard sales on Saturday mornings. A lot of what I know about the Vineyard is the result of following roads I previously knew nothing about to yard sales. It's surprising what you'll sometimes find at the end of such roads—not only lone houses, but sometimes whole communities that you never knew existed.

We stopped beside Zee's little red Jeep and went into the house through the screened porch. The cats, Oliver Underfoot and Velcro, came out of the bedroom, stretched, and said hello. Seeing them, I felt even wearier, but I got the big Vineyard map and spread it out on the kitchen table. We bent over it.

"Here's one spot," I said, putting a finger on it. "And here's another." I moved my finger from site to site, telling Brady of my failed real estate theory as I touched state forest lands.

"You didn't really think those guys were talking about real estate, did you?" asked Brady. "At midnight, surrounded by armed guards?"

"No," I said, "but nothing else made any sense to me, and it still doesn't."

We were speaking quietly so as not to wake Zee and the children. The cats rubbed on our legs in a friendly fashion.

"I don't know the Vineyard well enough to know anything about these sites," said Brady. "Do you?"

"No. I've lived here for a long time, but I haven't seen most of the island." It was true. Martha's Vineyard is only 20 miles long, but its land mass is somewhere around 130 square miles, and I don't know anyone who's seen all of it, or even most of it.

"Why don't you mark these places," said Brady, "so I'll know where they are in case you get run over by a truck?"

I got a pen and marked the spots as best I could remember them. They appeared to be totally random locations. My thinking, however, was fuzzy, and getting fuzzier by the minute.

"There," I said when I'd marked the last site. "Do you see anything I don't see?"

He stared down at the map and shook his head. "Nope. But there must be some significance to these places. They're all more or less in the center part of the island. Nothing up in Aquinnah or on Chappy or next to any of the town centers."

"Mostly in West Tisbury and Edgartown," I agreed, "and mostly away from the main roads." I yawned.

"Can you find these spots?" he asked.

I studied the map. "I can get close to them, but I can't guarantee that I can find them. The guy with the pointer just indicated the general areas. He wasn't precise and it all happened fast, so I don't know exactly what he was pointing at."

"I think we should try to find out." Brady straightened and looked at me. "Don't you think you should call Dom about this?"

I told Brady I didn't think Dom would be happy to hear from me again at this hour of the morning, but given the circumstances, I probably should try. I went to the phone.

But no one answered. I left a message on his answering machine, then called the state-police station. He wasn't there either, but a sleepy-sounding young summer cop was, so I told him about the map and the man with the pointer and asked him to get the information to his boss.

He said he would.

I hung up and looked at Brady. I was suddenly tired to the core. "I need some sleep," I said. "My brain is mush. A couple of hours in bed are all I need, but I need them badly."

Brady was staring at the map. "Something's happening fast," he said. "I can feel it in my bones." Then he looked up at me and said, "Go get some rest. I think you may need it before this day is out."

"Yes."

He was still looking at the map as I went to the bedroom where Zee was sleeping and, I hoped, dreaming sweeter dreams than mine.

Chapter Ten

Brady

After J.W. trundled off to bed, I remained sitting there in the living room staring at his map of Martha's Vineyard spread out on the coffee table. I knew I was supposed to be tired. It was two in the morning, and I'd been awake since sunrise. But I felt jittery and jangly and a bit light-headed. Adrenaline was still coursing through my veins, which is what happens when people chase you in a car and you shoot out their headlights with an Uzi.

J.W. hadn't seemed the least bit jangled. I suppose if you've been a soldier and a cop you handle things better than you would if all you've ever been is a lawyer and a trout fisherman. Anyway, he had Zee to play spoons with. Curling up with the woman you loved could unjangle a man pretty fast.

I looked at J.W.'s map, trying to see some kind of pattern. I wished I'd sneaked up to the window in Dr. Mumford's house so I could've seen the map on the wall and the men that J.W. had seen. As it was, I had only his descriptions.

The circles J.W. had drawn on his map appeared utterly random. Some were close to the ocean, some were quite a distance inland. About the only logic I saw in the pattern was that all of the circles appeared more or less in the middle parts of the island, and none seemed to encompass a populated area. They did not include roads or neighborhoods or villages. A close look at J.W.'s map revealed that there were more unpopulated areas on Martha's Vineyard than one might conclude by driving around.

Well, it was no longer our problem. We'd done our duty. We'd rousted State Police Sergeant Dom Agganis in the middle of the night and dumped it all on him.

J.W. still had his ongoing investigation of the death of the man who got blown up on a boat. But as for me, I'd come here to see what I could do for Larry Bucyck, and I guess I did a poor job of it, because now he was dead. I no longer had any reason to linger on the Vineyard, and I certainly had no desire ever again to shoot an Uzi at people who were chasing me. Maybe tomorrow Agganis would let me go home, and maybe I could talk J.W. into giving me a catboat ride back to Woods Hole.

Maybe tomorrow night at this time I'd be playing spoons with Evie.

I yawned. That was a good sign. Maybe I'd get some sleep after all.

I turned off the lights in the living room, brushed my teeth and splashed water on my face in the bathroom, then went to the guest room, which doubled as J.W.'s office, and crawled into bed. Closed my eyes. Took a deep breath. Let it out slowly. Instructed my limbs to relax, one by one. Tried to blank my mind . . .

No such luck. My brain whirred and jumped with

images and memory flashes. Waking up at dawn in Larry Bucyck's little house. Larry snoozing in his hammock out back. Taking Rocket, his mostly basset, on a coffee run. Back at Larry's house, his hammock empty, looking and yelling, getting no answer. Then searching with J.W., finding Larry face-down in the pig muck, a bullet hole in the back of his head. Being interrogated, Dom Agganis and Olive Otero forcing me to tell and retell my story. Sedona Blaisdell getting the drop on me with her shotgun. Creeping around in the dark, peering through J.W.'s green-tinted night-vision binoculars. Smashing a rock down on a man's head, picking up his Uzi. Being chased by a vehicle, running away, running faster than I thought I could run, but not fast enough. Turning, kneeling, and firing the Uzi at the car. Running some more, tossing the weapon in the bushes, then eluding capture in J.W.'s ancient Toyota Land Cruiser. Pounding on Dom Agganis's door, then seeing the skepticism on his face . . .

I looked at my watch. It was 2:35 A.M. I was wide awake.

J.W.'s computer sat right there on his desk. I was tempted to turn it on and join an online game of Texas Hold'em, except getting out of bed felt like too much of an effort.

I thought about calling Evie. It would've been nice to hear her sleepy, sexy voice. She'd tell me she loved me. She could talk me down from this adrenaline high. Her voice would relax me and soothe me and enable me to drift off to sleep. She wouldn't mind if I awakened her in the middle of the night. She liked it when I needed her.

I imagined her in our bed in our townhouse on Beacon Hill in Boston, hugging her pillow, sleeping on her belly, snoring softly, with Henry, our Brittany, curled against her hip, snoring, too. I imagined me, sneaking into our dark bedroom, slipping out of my clothes and creeping under the covers, where Evie kept it warm and fragrant, and Evie groaning and twitching, rolling onto her side, hooking her long smooth leg over my hip, slithering her arm around my chest, sliding her body on top of me, the whole bare length of her covering the naked length of me, moving on me, her mouth pressing against the side of my neck murmuring, "You're back. Mm. I'm glad you're back . . . ."

A thumping noise dragged me up from the depths of a dreamless sleep. It was J.W. pounding on my door. "Hey, wake up, Brady," he was saying. "Rise and shine. Greet the day."

"What the hell time is it?" I mumbled.

"Little after seven. Olive Otero's here. Let's go. The coffee's all made."

I moaned and stretched and forced myself to crawl out of bed. I went into the bathroom and took a long steamy shower. It didn't help much. I still felt groggy and hungover. An overdose of adrenaline will do that as surely as a couple of martinis.

I got dressed, staggered out to the kitchen, poured myself a mugful of black coffee, and took it into the living room. Olive Otero was sitting on the sofa sipping from her own mug of coffee. J.W. was sitting in his favorite easy chair across from her. They appeared to be glaring at each other.

I sat on the sofa beside Olive. "What's going on?" I said.

"We got a little problem," said J.W.

"Not so little," said Olive.

"It's Dr. Mumford," said J.W.

"It's not Dr. Mumford," said Olive. "That's the problem. There is no Dr. Mumford."

"Except," said J.W., "I saw him. Dr. Mumford."

"Wait a minute," I said. "Slow down. I have no idea what you're talking about."

"Well," said J.W. "It's—"

"No, listen," said Olive. "I don't know what you guys are trying to pull, but you wake up Dom Agganis in the middle of the night with some crazy story about Uzis and suspicious characters and sneaky midnight meetings, and you tell him it's at some house on Menemsha Pond owned by some nonexistent doctor named Mumford, I call that a big problem. Dom is furious. He stayed up half the night trying to figure out who the hell this Dr. Mumford is and where he lives so he could do his duty and check out your yarn, and finally he figured out that there was no such person. He was ready to come pounding on your door at four this morning, and if you hadn't had young kids and an innocent wife living here, that's what he would've done. Instead, he waited till seven and sent me." She turned to me and fixed me with a glare that could have frozen the Indian Ocean. "And you," she said. "Every time you show up on our island some-

181

thing happens. Something bad. If I had my way, you would be declared persona non grata. You'd be banned for life."

I blinked at her, then turned to J.W. "That guy with the pointer. Wasn't he . . . ?"

He shrugged. "I saw a white-haired man in that house last night. He was in charge of the meeting, pointing a red laser light at a map. He looked sort of kindly and intelligent, like he might be a doctor. It was you, actually, who said his name was Dr. Mumford."

"Actually," I said, "it was Larry Bucyck who told me that the house belonged to somebody named Mumford. A doctor, Larry said. A summer person. That's what he told me."

"Point is," said J.W. to Olive, "whatever his name is, we saw what we saw. The house, the midnight meeting, the men with guns, the map . . ."

"So you guys are sticking to your story?" said Olive.

J.W. looked at me, and then we both looked at her. "It's not a story," he said.

"We can show you the house," I said. "There'll be a vehicle there with bullet holes in it. We'll find that Uzi. I can show you where I threw it into the bushes."

Olive Otero was shaking her head. "Nothing but trouble," she muttered. "As if there wasn't enough going on around here these days."

"Look," I said. "You know Larry Bucyck was murdered. I explained to you guys about a dozen times yesterday how he dragged me down here because of what he told me he saw the other night when he was fishing on Menemsha Pond, and how it frightened him. So doesn't it make sense that what J.W. and I saw last night was pretty much what Larry was talking about? Those people who chased us in their cars had to be the people who killed Larry. Right? They would've killed us, too, if J.W. hadn't cleverly eluded them. Surely you can see that."

"It was you who shot out their headlights," said J.W. "Otherwise we would've been dead before we ever got to the Land Cruiser."

"You were the one who pulled the wool over that guard's eyes," I said, "pretending to be drunk. You would've fooled me."

"Yeah," said J.W., "but you were the one who snuck up on him and conked him on the head."

"Now we've got a damn mutual admiration society," grumbled Olive. "You're heroes, both of you, okay?" She blew out a long breath, then stood up. "I guess you'd better show me where this mysterious Dr. Mumford lives, then. Let's get this out of the way. I've got a busy day ahead of me. Come on."

"I can give you directions," said J.W.

Olive turned and glared at him. "You're coming with me. Both of you."

He held up both hands, palms out. "Okay, okay."

I detoured to the kitchen to refill my coffee mug, and then the three of us went out to the driveway where a state-police cruiser was waiting with its motor running and a uniformed trooper sitting behind the wheel.

Olive slid into the passenger seat beside the trooper.

J.W. and I climbed into the backseat.

Olive half turned in her seat. "Okay," she said. "How do we get there?"

J.W. gave the directions, and twenty minutes or so later we were creeping down the narrow roadway to Menemsha Pond.

I realized I'd only been there those two times, first with Larry and then with J.W., both times at night. Everything looked different in the daylight. Nothing was familiar. I never would've been able to find it, or recognize it if I managed to stumble upon it.

But after a few minutes, J.W. said, "There. That's the place. Dr. Mumford's house."

The trooper pulled the cruiser into the driveway, and then the general layout began to look right. I thought I recognized the bushes where I'd hidden, and the place where I'd smacked the guard on the head with the rock, and the window J.W. had peeked into.

A silver-colored Lincoln Town Car was parked in the turnaround in front. No bullet holes in its grille.

The lawn in front of the house sloped down to the pond. A long dock extended into the water. The boat moored there was a center-console runabout, maybe sixteen feet long. The name on its transom was *Penelope L.*

No sign of a forty-footer guarded by men with Uzis.

"You sure this is the place?" said Olive from the front seat.

"This is it," said J.W.

She opened the car door. "Come on, then. Let's get this straightened out once and for all."

J.W. and I piled out of the cruiser, and the three of us went to the front door. Olive rang the bell, and a minute later the door opened.

Standing there was a little white-haired man wearing chino pants and a green golf shirt. He had a newspaper in his hand and an uncertain smile on his face. "Can I help you?" he said.

"Dr. Mumford?" said Olive.

He frowned. "No . . ." Then he blinked. "You mean Lundsberg? That's me. Nathan Lundsberg. Dr. Lundsberg, in fact. I am a doctor. Semiretired now." He looked from Olive to J.W. to me. "So what can I do for you folks so early this morning? Won't you come in?"

"Thank you," said Olive quickly.

The man stepped aside and Olive went in.

J.W. leaned close to me and whispered, "That's him." Then he followed Olive, and I followed J.W., into the house.

Dr. Lundsberg led us into the living room, which was on the pond side of the house. The front was mostly glass. There was a fieldstone fireplace and a scattering of leather chairs, with two big sofas arranged so that those who sat on them could watch the ducks and terns on Menemsha Pond.

Dr. Lundsberg asked if we wanted coffee, and before I could say, Yes, Olive said, No, thank you.

Lundsberg took one of the leather chairs. Olive and J.W. and I introduced ourselves to him, then arranged ourselves on the two sofas.

"You're a police officer?" Lundsberg said to Olive.

She smiled pleasantly. "I am."

"And you, gentlemen?" he said to J.W. and me.

"We're just friends of Officer Otero," said J.W.

The doctor frowned for a moment, then shrugged. "You haven't told me how I can help you."

"You have a beautiful place," said Olive.

185

He smiled. "I spend way too little time down here, I'm afraid. Soon I will retire completely. Then I think I'll try living here year-round."

"Is that your boat?" she said. "The *Penelope L*?"

He nodded. "It's just right for putting around the pond, running over to Edgartown or Vineyard Haven. I like to do a little fishing. The stripers come into the pond on the tide."

"Do you own another boat?"

"No," he said. "Is there something about my boat? Is that why you're here?"

"We're looking for a bigger boat," said Olive. "Something around forty feet."

Dr. Lundsberg shrugged.

"I was told it was docked here," she said.

"A forty-footer?"

She nodded.

"When?"

"Last night."

"I'm sorry," he said, "but whoever told you that was mistaken. Occasionally I have visitors who come in their boats. But I had no visitors last night, and in any case, I don't even know anybody who owns a forty-foot boat."

"Are there other people here?"

"Now, you mean? Here in the house?"

Olive nodded. "Yes."

Lundsberg shook his head. "My wife passed on several years ago. Since then, I've been alone."

"So there's nobody else here?" said Olive.

"No. Just me, I'm afraid."

"We heard you had a party last night."

He frowned. "A party, you say?"

"A gathering. A meeting, maybe. Late. Around midnight."

"I'm sorry," he said, "but whoever told you that was mistaken. I was here alone. Just me. In bed by ten. I'm not good for much at night anymore. I retire early and rise early."

"Did you hear any shooting?"

"Shooting? Like guns, you mean?"

"Yes," said Olive.

He smiled. "Goodness, no. That's what I love about this place. It's quiet. The neighbors are very friendly, but they don't live close enough to bother me. Perhaps this party you're referring to, and that boat, and the shooting, maybe it was all happening at some other house on the pond. I wouldn't know anything about it if that were the case."

"We were told it was here," said Olive.

"Were you told that by the same person who thought my name was . . . what did you say?"

"Mumford," said Olive.

Lundsberg spread his hands. "Well, there you have it. Maybe somebody named Mumford was visiting one of my neighbors."

Olive nodded. "You're probably right. We were misinformed. It was probably somebody else around here." She gave me and J.W. a quick frown, a little warning not to interfere, and then she stood up. "I'm sorry we bothered you on a Sunday morning, Doctor."

Lundsberg stood up. "It was no bother. I'm sorry I couldn't help you. I'll keep my ears open, and if I hear anything . . ."

Olive plucked a business card from her pocket and handed it to him. "I'd appreciate it. Just give me a call."

He took the card, glanced at it, and put it on the coffee table. "I will. Of course."

We all walked out of the house. Dr. Lundsberg followed us to the cruiser, where the uniformed trooper was leaning against the door gazing out at the pond. We shook hands with Lundsberg, piled in, and backed out of the driveway.

The doctor stood in his driveway watching us with a hand raised in a little wave.

"That's him," J.W. said to Olive. "Lundsberg is the man I saw last night."

Olive turned and looked at him. "You sure?"

He nodded. "Yes."

At the end of the driveway, J.W. said, "Go that way."

The trooper turned onto the road so that he was following the route J.W. and I had taken when we were running away from the car that chased us.

"Where was it you dumped the Uzi?" he said to me.

I pointed. "Right up there, I think."

"Stop here," said J.W.

We stopped, and all four of us got out.

I stood there trying to visualize it—J.W. and I zigzagging down the road in the darkness, the car's headlights coming up fast behind us, catching us in their beams, me stopping, kneeling, and letting off a volley of shots at the grille and headlights, the car, suddenly darkened, swerving off the road and into the bushes.

"I was right about there," I said, pointing fifteen or twenty feet up the road. "I knelt there, on the side, let off some shots, then turned and ran. I tossed the gun up there." I pointed again at some underbrush alongside the road.

Olive went to where I remembered kneeling in the roadway when I shot the Uzi at the car. The trooper joined her. Both of them bent over at the waist and began pacing around, peering hard at the ground.

"Looking for cartridge casings?" said J.W.

Olive grunted.

J.W. and I joined them.

After about ten minutes, Olive said, "There's nothing. So where do you claim you threw the Uzi?"

"I don't claim it," I said. "I did it." I walked up the roadway, trying to remember. "Somewhere along here," I said. "It was on this side of the road, I'm sure of that."

The four of us poked and probed at the bushes and weeds alongside the road until it became quite evident that no Uzi was there.

"This is a big fat waste of time," said Olive. "Let's go."

"Somebody cleaned it up," I said. "We're not making this up."

"Maybe, maybe not," said Olive. "If we'd found just one empty cartridge in the road, I'd believe you. But there is not one shred of evidence that this is anything but some fantasy you two guys have concocted."

"You know us better than that," said J.W.

She shrugged. "I thought I did."

"Why would we concoct a fantasy like that?"

"You tell me."

"Mumford," he said. "That's how Larry Bucyck heard Lundsberg's name. Mumford, Lundsberg."

"Not that close," Olive said.

"Well," said J.W., "Mumford or not, I'm telling you that Lundsberg is the very man I saw pointing his laser light at the map last night in that very living room where we just were."

Olive didn't say anything.

"I know Larry wasn't that reliable," I said. "But the point is, he told me his story, how he'd seen a big boat similar to the one we saw last night come into the pond and tie up right there, on that same dock, and he told me how he got caught in their spotlight. And then he brought me here the other night, to this house. And then he got murdered. That was no fantasy. You know that. And then last night I brought J.W. here, and we saw what we saw."

"Well," said Olive, "I'll tell Sergeant Agganis what we found out—or what we didn't find out—and he can decide what he wants to do. Now let's get out of here."

We got into the cruiser and headed back to Edgartown. Olive didn't say anything, and neither did J.W. or I. Even when they dropped us off back at J.W.'s house, she didn't say anything.

J.W. and I stood in his driveway and watched the cruiser back out and pull away.

"She's not that happy," I said.

"Neither am I," he said.

"Lundsberg covered it all up."

"He and his cohorts," said J.W. "I got a glimpse of a face last night that looked familiar. Wish I could place it, but damned if I can."

We went inside. Zee and the kids were at the table eating their breakfast cereal. J.W. went around and gave them all a kiss.

"Where've you guys been?" said Zee.

"It's a long story," said J.W. "I'll tell you later, okay?"

She shrugged. "I imagine it's connected to the long story you're going to tell me about where you were until two A.M. last night."

"It is," said J.W. He poured himself a mugful of coffee.

So did I. "Now what?" I said to him.

"Follow me."

I followed him into my bedroom. Guest room by night, J.W.'s office by day. He sat at the desk and switched on his computer.

I pulled a chair up beside him. "What're you doing?"

"Googling Dr. Nathan Lundsberg," he mumbled.

I watched the screen. Pretty soon a list popped up, URLs to click on, each with a two- or three-line annotation. J.W. scrolled through the list, then clicked, and another list popped up, and so forth through several pages of lists. Scanning the annotations, it appeared that we'd found two Dr. Nathan Lundsbergs. One of them, Dr. Nathan Lundsberg, Jr., was not our man. This one, based on the years of his college and graduate-school degrees, was around forty years old. He had a Ph.D. in mathematics from Purdue University and was a professor at Oregon State.

He'd written some scholarly articles and had coauthored a textbook.

The other Dr. Nathan Lundsberg appeared far more abundantly on the Google list. He was our white-haired man of Menemsha, which J.W. verified by finding a fairly recent photograph of him. Lundsberg was born in 1932, the only son of wealthy parents, earned his MD from Harvard, and embarked on a career as a specialist in public health. He'd served on the NIH and was a member of the Surgeon General's staff during the Reagan administration. For the past twenty years he'd apparently been out of both public service and private practice. Instead, he'd spearheaded the creation and funding of health clinics in the villages of Nicaragua and Guatemala and Haiti. He'd appeared at public functions with Presidents Jimmy Carter and the first George Bush and Bill Clinton and Joe Callahan, plus numerous governors and senators. He'd lobbied both the United States Congress and private foundations for policies and for money. He'd given graduation speeches at universities. He'd received a dozen honorary degrees and had an endowed chair named for him at the Harvard Medical School. He'd written op-ed articles for *The New York Times* and the *Washington Post* on the subject of children's health in Central America. He'd written a book called *It Takes More than a Village*.

Dr. Nathan Lundsberg was eminent as hell. He had devoted his life to doing good works. I felt ignorant, never having heard of him before.

The doctor had a son, Nathan Junior, the math professor, and a daughter, Penelope, an elementary school teacher in Cedar Rapids, Iowa. Lundsberg's wife, Julia, had died thirteen years earlier.

"Named his boat after his daughter," I observed.

"The man's a damn saint," muttered J.W.

"So why's he hanging out with men carrying Uzis?" I said.

"Lemme keep reading," he muttered.

I sat back and let J.W. scroll through more of the stuff that Google found for him.

An hour later he flexed his arms, arched his back, and groaned. "I don't know," he said. "If he's diverting funds from his clinics to accounts on the Cayman Islands or enslaving Nicaraguan children and selling them into prostitution, Mr. Google doesn't know it. I find not a breath of scandal, not a hint of wrongdoing. He's devoted his life to the health and general well-being of poor people in strife-torn little nations."

I shook my head. "We're missing something, then."

He nodded. "I guess the hell we are. We could look some more, but I don't have any more energy for it."

"So now what do we do?"

"I don't know about you," said J.W., "but I'm going to church."

I laughed. "Sure you are."

"No, really. It's Sunday, and I'm going to church."

"You don't go to church," I said. "You're like me. You're a pagan."

He shrugged. "I like the music."

"I like the music, too," I said. "I have several CDs of sacred music. Handel and Haydn, Beethoven and Bach and Mozart. Wonderful stuff. But you don't need to go to church to hear the music."

"You coming with me or not?"

I smiled. "I didn't bring any church clothes. Sorry."

He shrugged.

"Is Zee going with you?" I said. "Want me to stay with the kids?"

"Zee won't go. I won't even ask her."

"You," I said, "are up to something."

He smiled. "Maybe I am. And maybe I'll tell you about it. Nobody dresses up for church anymore, you know."

"If it was my own church," I said, "if there was such a thing as my own church, which there isn't, maybe I wouldn't bother dressing up, either. But if you want me to attend somebody else's church, I'd have to wear a jacket and necktie. To dress casually in somebody else's church would be disrespectful."

J.W. cocked his head at me, then nodded. "That's incredibly old-fashioned of you."

I shrugged. "It's how I was raised."

"I have some extra jackets and ties. They'll fit you."

"Okay, then," I said. "I'll go with you."

J.W. grinned. "Just don't hold me responsible for the music."

Chapter Eleven

J.W.

Bach often bores me, but I like some of his work and that of other composers inspired by Christianity, and I'll attend a church service that offers a mass or an oratorio or other religiously oriented music I've heard and enjoyed. The Island Community Chorus sings such pieces often and well, and occasionally a church choir will give one a shot. Religions have inspired so much great art, architecture, and music that it's almost enough to make you a believer.

That morning, though, I wasn't in church for the hymns.

I also wasn't dressed up for the occasion, although I did wear clean slacks and a clean shirt, both recently purchased at the thrift shop where an unknown-to-me clotheshorse just my size often abandoned good-as-new clothes, which I snatched up if I happened by before someone else got them.

Brady, perhaps because he was used to wearing neckties, looked posh and comfortable in my sports coat.

I gave him an admiring glance as Zee brushed imaginary dust particles from the jacket. Then she stepped back and said, "You look very nice, Brady, so don't be surprised if you get a lot of smiles from wives and frowns from their husbands."

"That's why I don't go to church more often," said Brady. "I don't want to break up families."

"I like a man with a sense of social responsibility," said Zee. She looked at me. "Don't worry. I like you, too."

"Let's go," I said to Brady. "We don't want to miss the opening prayer."

"Or the collection plate."

We went out to Zee's little red Jeep, which she had offered us on the grounds that it was more respectable than my battered Land Cruiser.

It was another sunny day, but low gray clouds off to the east suggested that a weather change might be on the way. As we drove up our driveway, Brady shook his head. "It's been a while since I went to church."

"It'll be good for you," I said.

"Once, when I was in college," he said, "I was walking along a street one Sunday morning when I heard some singing in a church and realized that it was in a language I'd never heard. I went inside and sat in the back so I could stand when everybody else did and sit when they did and not be going up when they were going down and down when they were going up. The church was all gilt and bright colors, and it was obviously a Christian church of some kind, but when the singing stopped and the sermon, or whatever it was, began, it was in that same language that I'd never heard. I stayed to the end of the service, then left and never did learn what kind of a church it was." He paused. "It was as if I'd been to another planet, where things looked familiar but really weren't. Very ethereal."

"How was the music?"

"Very ethereal."

"And the sermon?"

"Ethereal, of course," he said. "It was that sort of day."

"You're more spiritual than I thought."

"Did I ever tell you that I once gave thought to becoming a Trappist monk?"

"No. Did you?"

"No." He laughed. "My religion is fishing."

"Now there's a divine experience," I agreed. "At least when they're biting."

Father Georgio Zapata's church was hardly a cathedral. It was a low wooden building at the end of a short dirt driveway off North Road near the Vineyard Haven–West Tisbury line. The sign at the end of the driveway read: CHURCH OF THE SAINTS AND THE SINNERS. WELCOME ALL. FATHER GEORGIO ZAPATA, PASTOR. I thought the sign looked movable.

"All-encompassing," said Brady, as we passed the sign. "Saints and sinners."

"We both fit in there somewhere," I agreed.

The driveway was bumpy, and the dirt parking area at the end of it was full of potholes and cars. I'm always surprised at the number of people who go to church, though I guess I shouldn't be. The cars were of all ages and conditions, ranging from ancient sedans and pickups to modern SUVs. On the far side of the lot was a big new four-door pickup with *Zapata Land-*

scaping written on the door, along with a logo and a Vineyard telephone number. The pope had a special car, so why shouldn't Father Zapata?

The building was not new. It was a fairly large, shingled, one-story structure that, I suspected, was probably used for some other purpose when not in use as a church. Maybe as a meetinghouse or a warehouse, or as a studio for dance or gymnastics or karate. Teachers of those arts are always trying to find a place to practice them. That would account for the movable sign. It probably only went up when religious services were being offered. On Sunday and maybe one or two other days of the week.

"Just what are we looking for here?" asked Brady.

"Eduardo Alvarez attended this church," I said. "I'm hoping to find somebody who can give me information about who he hung around with or how he managed to get himself killed. If his widow's here, maybe she can point me at somebody who can help me."

I parked the Jeep. Brady and I exchanged arched eyebrows and went into the building.

The church service was being held in a fairly large room that appeared to take up about half of the building. The room was full of rows of folding chairs that faced a low stage with curtains behind and on either side of it. A portable pulpit had been placed on one side of the stage, and on the other was a banner with a white cross on a blue field. In the middle of the stage was a small altar covered with a white cloth and holding a cross carved from dark wood upon which hung a crucified Christ.

At the back of the room was a wall split by a hall-way that led toward the rear of the building. I whispered a guess to Brady that there were bathrooms back there, and that one of the side rooms might be a kitchen. It was the sort of setup often found in buildings used for informal special occasions or as meeting places for clubs, and it reinforced my notion that the place was used by a lot of people for a lot of different purposes.

The folding chairs were filled with people, both adults and children, dressed more formally than I expected. They looked solemn, and many held beads in their hands. There were even a few veils. When we came in, faces turned toward us. Many looked puzzled or curious, but others simply turned back. I thought I saw Gloria Alvarez's face on the far side of the room, but I couldn't be sure. We sat in chairs near the rear of the room, and I found myself studying the backs of many heads. I had a sense of déjà vu, having done just that the previous night.

A murmur of hushed voices flowed into my ears as the worshippers exchanged whispers. Then the murmur quieted, and Father Georgio Zapata emerged from behind a curtain. He knelt and said something in front of the crucifix, crossed himself, then faced the congregation. He again made the sign of the cross and said something in what I thought was Portuguese, and the audience responded in the same tongue. He smiled a charismatic smile and went to the pulpit.

The service started with what I presumed was a Bible reading followed by a song I didn't know. The sermon that followed started mildly and grew in intensity until the ceremony became what seemed to be a combination of revivalist fervor and Catholic ritual. Perhaps if it had been conducted in English I'd have understood it, for although Portuguese was a language I could recognize, I couldn't speak or comprehend it very well.

What I did grasp was Zapata's charm and his passion. As the sermon progressed, his face took on a glow, and his chanting voice filled with persuasive power that first roused his listeners and then brought them, chanting with him, to their feet. I had no idea what they were saying, but their voices and clapping hands made the room shake, and when I looked along the line of people standing and chanting beside me, I could see ecstasy in their faces.

Brady put his lips close to my ear. "Scary." He pointed a finger toward the door, silently indicating the virtue of an early exit.

I nodded but didn't move. I felt as I have felt in a crowd of partisans at a football game—as though I was sitting with a beast with a thousand mouths but no mind at all. Its great univoice was braying, its eyes were brilliant with faith and ardor, and its mighty heart was beating a cadence of zeal that allowed for no doubt or skepticism such as Brady's and mine.

No wonder Brady thought it wise to withdraw.

Then, more suddenly than it had arisen, that fantastic passion peaked and subsided as Zapata's voice flowed over his congregation in soothing, quieting, confident tones that pushed his listeners back into their seats and bent their heads in prayer. Something about the rhythm of the words they intoned with him led me to think I recognized the Lord's Prayer.

The prayer, or whatever it was, ended, and the collection plates moved through the congregation from the front rows to the back. Brady and I were last in line, and we both dropped in bills and watched as the containers of money were carried to the stage and placed on the altar. Then there were more words and the people all moved forward to receive wafers and wine. Then came another hymn followed by a final, soothing prayer given by Zapata, and the service was over.

The participants stood, chatted with their neighbors, collected their children, and began moving toward the door, where Zapata stood, smiling and shaking hands.

I had presumed that Brady would be more than willing to be the first to escape into open air, but to my surprise he nodded toward the back of the building. "You know Gloria Alvarez and Zapata," he said, "but I don't. I think I'll look around while you try to get a line on people who might know something about her husband."

He turned and walked toward the hallway in the back of the building. Aside from the fact that he was several inches taller than most of the others in the congregation, he looked like just an ordinary celebrant whose bladder had been stretched by a long sermon.

As I went toward the door, I saw that Brady had caught Zapata's eye, and when I reached the priest and took his hand, he said, "Mr. Jackson, isn't it? I'm delighted that you and your friend have attended our service. We don't get many Anglos here. May I hope to believe that you speak Portuguese?"

"I'm afraid not," I said, "but I'm glad I came. I can remember when Roman Catholic masses were in Latin, so listening to a service in a language I don't know isn't new to me."

"You seem too young to remember the Latin mass."

"I was a kid," I said, "and my father used to take us to different churches now and then."

"And which did you choose?"

"None."

He smiled his charismatic smile. "Ah, we live in a skeptical age, but I assure you that faith is the way to happiness and a better world. Does your friend share your views?"

"You'll have to ask him when he comes out."

Zapata laughed. "Yes. Perhaps I will. Better, though, not to attempt such a conversion right now, don't you agree?"

I agreed and went on out to the Jeep, where I stood and watched for Gloria Alvarez to emerge from the church.

When she came, though, I almost missed her, because I was staring at a man who had preceded her. He was a big man with a wide face, and he had taken time to talk warmly with Zapata before walking away from me across the parking lot with a smaller, swarthy, companion by his side. I watched him—casually at first, because he seemed to be another of those Anglos whom Zapata had called rare in his congregation, and because he looked vaguely familiar.

But then I really watched him, because when he turned his head to speak to the smaller, bronze-skinned man, I instantly thought I recognized the back of his head as belonging to the man I'd observed listening to Dr. Nathan Lundsberg last night, and in the same moment I recognized him as the same man I'd seen in the photo on Robert Mortison's fireplace mantel when I'd talked with his wife, the soap opera fan. Mortison was one of the names Steve had given me when I visited him in the hospital. Mortison and Harry Doyle. Names that had seemed to scare Steve.

And now Mortison and Lundsberg? Could that be right? How could they be connected? Or had I jumped to a conclusion based only on fleeting glimpses of a face and the back of a head?

I flashed a look at the church's door just in time to see Gloria Alvarez dropping Zapata's hand and walking into the parking lot. I glanced back at Mortison, who was approaching a forest green Mercedes sedan that looked a lot like the one I'd seen in front of his garage, then trotted across the parking lot, dodging potholes, and intercepted Gloria.

"Mrs. Alvarez," I said. She looked startled. "Do you remember me? J.W. Jackson. Zee's husband."

Her eyes were tired, but she tried a smile and said, "Yes, of course." She put a hand on my arm. "Have you found something to show Eduardo was innocent?" Her eyes brightened.

"Not yet," I said. "I'm hoping that you can point out some of his friends from church who might be able to help me. But first, tell me. Do you know that big man over there?" I pointed.

The bright eyes dimmed. "Of course." She nodded. "That is Mr. Mortison."

"Who's that with him?"

Her face seemed to harden. "That? That is Harry Doyle. He works for Mortison. Eduardo didn't like him."

I wondered if I should be wearing a dunce cap. "That's Harry Doyle? I thought Harry Doyle must be Irish. That man looks like a Latino. Are you sure?"

She gave me a look of gentle irony. "Do you think the Irish all stayed in Ireland? O'Connor was Simon Bolívar's Minister of War and O'Higgins was the liberator of Chile. Harry Doyle's people live in Guatemala or Nicaragua, I believe. Am I not right to think that there are even some Irish here in America?"

I gave her a smile. "Yes, I believe that's the case." Across the parking lot, Mortison and Doyle were looking at the church door. I followed their gaze and saw Brady Coyne, testimony of the Irish presence in America, shaking hands and talking with Zapata. Brady then walked toward Zee's Jeep, unaware of the attention he was getting from Mortison and Doyle.

As Brady left the church steps, Zapata looked at Mortison and Doyle and nodded toward Brady's back. Then he looked at me and, seeing that I was watching him, waved and smiled before turning away and shaking the hand of the next person coming out of the hall.

Brady walked on to the Jeep, where he paused and glanced around a bit before spotting me. Then I looked again at Mortison and Doyle and saw that they were no longer studying Brady, but were staring at me. They held my gaze for a long moment, then climbed into the Mercedes and eased out of the lot.

Hmmmm. Something had just happened, but what was it? Had we caught Mortison's attention because we were strangers? Had Zapata signaled them to take note of us, or was that just my imagination?

Gloria Alvarez touched my arm again. "There, coming out now. You see that man? His name is Norman Frazier. He worked with Eduardo in the restaurant. They were friends. Perhaps he can help you."

"Thanks," I said. "I want to talk with him."

I left her and crossed the lot to intercept Frazier. I caught him at his car, an elderly sedan.

"Norman Frazier?"

"Yes?" He was a young guy with a shock of yellow hair. His name, skin tone, and hair all set him apart from most of Zapata's flock, and I wondered if he knew Portuguese. He gave me an uncertain smile.

I told him my name and that I was looking into the death of Eduardo Alvarez, and I watched his face change.

"Terrible thing," he said, opening his car door. "But I'm afraid I can't help you."

I put my hand on the door and held it open. "You were his friend. You worked with him at the Wheelhouse, but the night he was killed you didn't show up for work. Were you with him?"

"No." He slid into the driver's seat.

"Do you know where he went?"

"No."

He tugged at the door, but I held it. "Why so great a no?" I asked.

He'd probably never read *Cyrano* but he knew what I meant. "Let go of the door."

"A man is dead. He was your friend. What happened to him?"

Frazier's face was full of fear. "Stop this. They'll see us."

"Who? Who'll see us?" I looked around, searching for, but not finding, eyes upon us as I held the door open against his yanks and pulls.

"I don't know who they are," he said, "but I know what they'll do if they think I'm talking to you. They did it to him, and they'll do it to me. Let me go!"

"You can talk to me or to the cops," I said. "It's up to you."

"The cops? You think I'm afraid of the cops? Let go! Please!"

"Who are you afraid of?"

"Doyle is one of them. I can feel his eyes on me right now. He's watching me all the time." He gave up tugging on the door and started up the car with a roar.

"Doyle is gone," I shouted over the sound of the engine. "He drove away."

His eyes were wild. "There are others!"

He slammed the car into gear, and the door jerked out of my hand and slammed shut as he spun his wheels and sped, bouncing and sliding over the potholes, out of the lot. I watched him roar away, then walked across to where Brady stood by the Jeep.

"What was that all about?" he asked. "You got everybody's attention, even Zapata's. Most people

206

don't confuse church parking lots with the Indianapolis Speedway."

I looked back at the church, but Zapata was gone, and the last of the worshippers were headed toward their cars, some looking at me as they went.

I told him what had passed between Frazier and me.

Brady thought for a moment, then said, "Do you know where he lives?"

"No, but I can probably find him."

"I'd say it's pretty clear that Mr. Frazier knows something about Eduardo Alvarez," he said. "I think you should squeeze it out of him before Doyle or one of those other people he's afraid of gets to him. Remember what happened to Larry."

How could I forget? "I think you're right," I said, "although I didn't see anybody looking at Frazier. I did see several people who seemed to be interested in you and me, though."

Brady allowed himself a small smile. "Maybe it was because we're an unexpected sight in church, especially one where we stick out like sore thumbs. You know the names of any of the interested parties?"

"Three," I said. "Bob Mortison, Harry Doyle, and Georgio Zapata." I told him what I'd seen pass among them and of their interest in him and me. "And there's another thing," I said. "I'm pretty sure that I saw Mortison up in Chilmark last night, listening to Lundsberg."

His brows arched. "Really? How sure are you?"

"Fairly but not absolutely."

"Enough to act on the assumption that he was?"

I nodded. "Yes."

"Well," he said, "that adds spice to the stew, doesn't it? Mortison was in Chilmark, Doyle works for Mortison, and Frazier is afraid of Doyle. How do you suppose Zapata fits in?"

"They all go to his church."

"So did Alvarez," Brady said, "and he's dead."

"Maybe Frazier knows how and why," I said. "Let's try to find out."

As we drove out of the lot I glanced in the rearview mirror and saw that Father Zapata had come back out of the church and was watching us leave.

"I don't suppose you have a phone book in this car," said Brady, peeking into the backseat. "If you do, I can see if Frazier is listed there and learn where he lives."

"We don't have phone books in our cars," I said, "because we almost never use our cell phone except to call home, and we know that number."

"In another generation or two," said Brady, "babies are going to be born with one hand fastened to an ear, and all the parents will have to do is slip a phone into the hand."

"We'll stop at a filling station and peek at their book."

We drove toward Vineyard Haven while Brady told me what he'd seen when he went to look in the back of the church building. It was just what we'd guessed: two bathrooms, one for men, one for women, a combination kitchen-pantry on one side of the hall, and another room on the other side, notable for the padlock on its door. A storage area, probably, with stuff no one wanted stolen. Did each group that used the building have a key, or was the locked room used by only one organization? If you knew who to ask, you could find out, but who knew who to ask? Zapata, maybe.

On Beach Street we stopped at the first filling station, and while Brady was looking with horror at the price of island gasoline, I was failing to find a single Norman Frazier in the station's phone book.

"My God," said Brady when I climbed back behind the wheel. "How can you people afford to drive cars down here?"

"Prices have gone up even more than usual because of the strike," I said, "but everything on the island costs more than on the mainland because of freight charges. Gasoline always costs fifty cents a gallon more."

"But gasoline comes here by tanker," said Brady, "just like it does to every other part of New England. The delivery cost is no greater here than it is anywhere else."

I ignored this appeal to reason. "Liquor costs several dollars more a bottle because of freight, food costs more because of freight, shoes and socks cost more because of freight. Fortunately for us islanders, we're all multimillionaires, so we can afford the necessities." I pointed to the left as we drove toward Oak Bluffs. "There's the *Trident*. She doesn't look too bad, but there's not much left of her engine room."

"So that's where Alvarez died." Brady looked at the boat as we passed.

"So they say."

"Where are we going?"

"To a restaurant called the Wheelhouse in Edgartown," I said. "Frazier worked there with Alvarez. The woman who runs the place may know where Frazier lives."

Nellie Gray did know. Frazier lived out on West Chop.

We turned around and drove back the way we'd just come, passing the line of cars parked beside the beach between Edgartown and Oak Bluffs, and going on through downtown Oak Bluffs and Vineyard Haven out toward the West Chop Lighthouse. Near the library I pointed out the street at the end of which, long before, Lillian Hellman and Dashiell Hammett had cohabited in a house overlooking the outer harbor. The island now crawled with more celebrities than ever, but Lillian and Dash were still my favorites.

"Maybe the falcon is hidden somewhere here on the Vineyard," said Brady.

"Could be."

"We could use Sam Spade on this case."

"I think Sam works in California," I said. "Maybe we can bring Stoney Calhoun down from Maine. He's as good as Spade."

Brady gave me a blank look. "Who's Stoney Calhoun?"

"I'm not absolutely sure, and neither is he." I slowed down. "In any case, we're here, so it looks like we'll have to handle things ourselves."

Norman Frazier lived in a small house not too far from where Harry Doyle lived. I wondered about that. Did they socialize? Did they even know they were almost neighbors?

My mind was filled with questions and memories. I remembered what Doyle's boyhood pal Steve had said about Doyle asking him to help on a job and the two of them being seen together by Bonzo and Eduardo Alvarez. I remembered, too, Steve's suspicion that Doyle might have been involved with the explosion on the *Trident*. And I remembered Bonzo saying that Steve and Eduardo often argued but never came to blows, because Eduardo didn't believe in fighting.

What were Steve and Eduardo arguing about? Union violence? Blowing up the *Trident*? Maybe Norm Frazier knew. He and Eduardo were friends, and Eduardo might have confided in him. Was that the reason Frazier feared Doyle? Because of what Eduardo had told him?

Frazier's house was on a narrow dirt lane leading off of West Chop Road. It was surrounded by trees and in need of paint. His car was beside the house. I parked in front, and Brady and I went to the door.

I think that if Frazier had had a peephole he probably wouldn't have opened the door, but when I knocked he did open it, just far enough for him to peek out and for me to slide a sandal between the door and the jamb.

He pushed, but Brady and I pushed harder, and we were in his hallway before he could even yell for help, if that was his inclination.

I kicked the door shut and said, "We need to talk, Norm."

He backed away. "No."

We followed him down the hall and into his dingy living room. He backed into an overstuffed chair and sat down hard, seeming to sink into the cushion. I ignored a wave of guilt because I was exploiting his fear.

"I need to know about Doyle and the others," I said in my hardest voice, leaning over him.

He cowered. "Leave me alone. I can't tell you anything."

I poked a thumb toward Brady. "You may not be afraid of me or the police," I said, "but my friend, here, is down from Boston. You don't want to know what he does there, but he can do it here too, if I ask him to. You're playing with the big boys now. Do you understand me?"

He threw a frightened glance at Brady, who, I hoped, was looking tough.

"Jesus," said Frazier, "I don't know what to do. I'm in a mess, but I never done anything."

"You don't have to do anything to be in trouble," I said. "You just have to know something. What is it you know? Tell me quick and save yourself some grief."

"If I say anything," he said, "they'll do something to me! Something bad!"

"We'll do something worse if you don't, and we'll do it right now. Isn't that right, Bruno?"

Brady made a choking sound that he turned into a growl.

"Oh God," moaned Frazier.

"I'm running out of patience," I said.

"All right, all right," cried Frazier, putting up his hands as if to protect himself from attack. "Eddie

Alvarez and me were buddies. Hell, he even got me to go to church with him and tried to teach me Portuguese, you know what I mean? I mean, we were close, and we talked about everything. Some of it was union stuff he wouldn't even tell his wife because, you know, he didn't want her to worry. Well, he told me that he seen Steve Bronski talking with Harry Doyle, and he said Doyle was a bad apple. Eddie was afraid that Steve might get involved in some shenanigan that would hurt the union, and so he tells Steve not to get mixed up with Doyle. So him and Steve get nose to nose, and Steve tells him to mind his own business, says he don't know nothing about Doyle's plans and he ain't gonna get involved anyway, but that he don't want Eddie or that Bonzo guy talking about him and Doyle, because Doyle is working for Mortison, and Mortison ain't helping the union any, and Steve don't want the other union guys to think he's pals with a scab."

"So far you've told me nothing I don't know," I said, narrowing my eyes a little.

Frazier seemed to try to sink out of sight. "Come on. Gimme a break, willya? I'm tryin' to help, ain't I? What happened was, whatever Doyle had in mind when he talked with Steve, it was going down the next Wednesday night, so Eddie tells me he's going to find Doyle that night and follow him and find out what he's doing and keep him from doing it if it's something that'll be bad for the union. I tell him that's probably not a good idea, because Doyle is a bad egg, but Eddie says he don't want any trouble to happen, so he's going to stick to his plan. Well, I didn't want him out there alone, so I said I'd go with him, but I didn't want no trouble either."

He looked up at me with fear in his eyes.

"Continue," I growled. "I want all of it."

"Sure, sure." Frazier nodded vigorously. "So, okay, I drive us up to Doyle's house—he lives a couple blocks from here, you know—and we see his car's still there, so when he leaves we follow him down to the docks, and when he parks, we go down a ways farther and we park, too. Like they do in the movies, you know?"

"Yes," I said. "I know."

"Okay, so anyway," said Frazier, "even though it's dark we can see Doyle carry a suitcase out toward the *Trident,* walking sort of sneaky and like the suitcase was heavy, and Eddie doesn't like whatever it is he sees, so he goes running after him, but I don't want no trouble so I stayed where I was."

Frazier stopped talking and gave me a sick look.

"And?" I said.

"That was last Wednesday night. Eddie didn't come right back. I waited, and after a while I see Doyle headed back to his car. He drives past me and sees me and slows down, but then he keeps going, and just as I'm about to go find Eddie, the *Trident* blows up." Frazier's wide eyes stared up at me. "I ain't got proof, but I think Doyle maybe hit Eddie with something and left him there to take the rap for the explosion, you know?"

"I do know," I said. "Then what?"

"So," he said, "there I was with Doyle knowing what I saw. So he comes over here the next morning and tells me to keep my mouth shut or else, but if I do, everything will be fine and I should just keep doing the things I usually do. But now you've got me blabbing. Jesus! I never should have gone with Eddie that night."

"That explains Doyle," I said. "Who are the others you're afraid of?"

"Honest to Christ," he said, "I don't know who they are, but there's got to be more of them than just Harry Doyle. He wouldn't do nothing like that unless it was somebody else's idea. Why would he? I don't know who they are, but they must know about me, too, and now you do, too. I gotta get away. I can't live a normal life here anymore."

"You sure you don't know who those other people are?"

"No. Yes! I mean I don't know!"

I turned to Brady. "Bruno, maybe you should ask him."

Brady glared at him. It was a truly impressive glare.

"No, wait," cried Frazier. "Doyle works for Mortison, I know that. Mortison knows a lot of people. Maybe it's them. And I've seen Doyle up at church a lot. He don't seem like the churchgoing type, but he goes up there." He looked past me at Brady. "I swear to God that's all I know about Doyle, but I know he didn't blow up that ship without somebody telling him to."

I heard the sound of a car stopping in front of the house, then heard Brady's steps going to a window.

"We've got company," he said. "It's Harry Doyle."

Frazier groaned.

"Have you got a gun in the house?" I asked.

"Gun? No, I ain't got no gun!"

"How about a back door?"

"Yeah, I got one of them."

I put down a hand and pulled him to his feet. "Use it," I said.

He did.

I looked to Brady.

"Bruno," he said. "Is that the best thug name you could come up with?"

"It worked," I said. "Is Doyle alone?"

"I think the guy with him is a genuine thug."

There was a heavy knock on the front door.

"What do you think?" I said. "Should we open that door or go out the back one?"

"Leave this to me," said Brady, and he went to the front door and opened it.

"We want to talk to Norm Frazier," said Doyle, frowning.

His companion stood behind him, looking very large.

"Who wants to see him?" asked Brady, standing square in the doorway.

"None of your business," snapped Doyle. "I want to see Frazier. Who the hell are you?"

"My name is Coyne. I'm an officer of the court. If you have any business with Mr. Frazier, you'll do it through us or not at all. You can start by telling me who you are."

Doyle suggested that Brady perform an impossible task.

"Not everyone enjoys your favorite practices, Mr.

Doyle," said Brady smoothly. "Yes, I already know who you are. We have photos of you in our files." He turned to me. "Isn't that right, Lieutenant?"

"He looks worse in person," I said, my right hand behind my back.

"Mr. Frazier is in our custody," said Brady. "However, we would like to talk with you, too. Maybe you'd like to come with us now and save us the trouble of finding you later."

But Doyle didn't accept the invitation. Instead, he turned on his heel, said, "Come on, Bruno," and walked to his car. The big thug followed him.

Brady watched them drive away, then shut the door.

"Jesus," he said, shaking his head. "Another Bruno. It's hard to believe."

"Maybe Doyle was lying about his name," I said. "Have you ever noticed that there are a lot of liars in the world?"

"It's recently come to my attention," said Brady. "What do you make of this business between Frazier and Doyle?"

"I think Frazier is right," I said. "I think there are other people behind Doyle, and I think we'd better find out who they are."

Chapter Twelve

Brady

We went out to the Jeep. "What do you think?" said J.W.

"I think," I said, "I want to get out of this jacket and necktie and back into my blue jeans. I feel like a damn lawyer."

He looked sideways at me but didn't say the obvious thing. Instead, he started up the car and pulled out of Norm Frazier's driveway. "Far as I'm concerned," he said, "we just solved the mystery of who blew up the *Trident*."

"Doyle," I said. "Maybe on Mortison's orders."

J.W. nodded thoughtfully. "That's if Norm Frazier is to be believed."

"I think you scared him pretty good."

"It was you who scared him, Bruno," said J.W. "I'm not sure fear produces truth the way wine does, though."

"Maybe we should go tell the police what Frazier told us," I said.

"Yeah," he said dubiously. "Maybe." He paused. "There's still too much we don't know. Maybe we

219

should try to follow Doyle and his thug, see where that takes us."

"This red Jeep is kind of noticeable," I said, "and I'm not so sure I want to know what those guys would do if they spotted us tailing them. I think we should try to think things through a little bit before we do something stupid. Besides, this necktie is choking me. Take me home, Jeeves."

"At once, sir," said J.W.

He knew how to get to where we were going, and I didn't, so I just watched the scenery go by. It was a postcard-perfect late-summer Sunday on Martha's Vineyard. A lot of people paid a lot of money for this, but it seemed as if every time I was on the island I ended up getting involved in something unpleasant and didn't have the leisure to pay much attention to the scenery or the weather.

We drove in silence for a little while. Then J.W. said, "They're all connected."

"All these men," I said. "Mortison and Doyle and the priest."

"Yes. And Eduardo Alvarez, and Steve with the broken ankle, and Dr. Lundsberg. Larry Bucyck, too. All of them."

"Doyle killed Alvarez and blew up the boat," I said. "Doyle is buddies with Mortison, and Mortison's was the back of the head you recognized at Dr. Lundsberg's last night."

"And they were all at Father Zapata's church this morning."

"Larry Bucyck got tortured and killed for what he saw at Lundsberg's the other night."

"It looks that way," said J.W. "And we saw even more at Lundsberg's."

"What did we see?" I said.

"We saw men studying a map of the island, for one thing." He was quiet for a moment. Then he said, "Two men have been murdered. Unless I'm way off base, Larry Bucyck and Eduardo Alvarez got murdered because they were in the wrong place at the wrong time. They saw something they shouldn't've seen."

"Whatever they saw," I said, "it had to be pretty important to be worth murdering for."

"And those guys with Uzis tried to murder us last night, don't forget," he said.

"I bet it's occurred to you," I said to J.W., "that you and I haven't exactly been keeping a low profile lately."

He turned and smiled at me. "You mean like getting chased by men with Uzis and showing up in church?"

"It's not that funny."

"Detecting 101," he said. "I learned when I was a cop that sometimes you've just got to keep kicking the bushes and shaking the trees until something falls out."

"And you hope whatever falls out doesn't land on your head," I said.

When we pulled into the yard, we found Joshua and Diana in their bathing suits playing in the tree house. We declined their invitation to join them on the grounds that we still had our church clothes on, and we went inside.

Zee was in the kitchen loading up a picnic basket

with sandwiches and pickles and potato chips and cookies. A cooler was stuffed with ice and cans of lemonade and iced tea and soft drinks. "We're hitting the beach," she said. "You guys want to come?"

J.W. shook his head. "Maybe we'll meet you there later."

She shrugged as if she expected that answer. "Gloria Alvarez and Mary are swinging by to pick us up. I wasn't sure if you'd be back in time with my car, and you know how I feel about driving that clunky old Land Cruiser of yours."

"You can take the Wrangler," he said. "We're back."

I poked J.W.'s shoulder. He turned to me with his eyebrows arched. I gave my head a quick shake.

He frowned at me for a moment, then I saw understanding spark in his eyes.

He nodded and turned to Zee. "Actually," he said to her, "you'd better not take the Jeep. On the way home just now it developed a funny clanking noise under the hood. We probably ought to get it looked at before we drive it anymore."

She cocked her head at him. "Clanking noise, huh?"

"Like a handful of spoons and forks got loose under the hood," he said. "It's good that Gloria's driving."

"Spoons and forks," she said.

He shrugged. "Something's loose. You don't want to get stuck at the beach with a car that won't run. I'll drop it off at Paulie's."

Zee smiled, and it was hard to tell whether she saw through J.W.'s story. "I'll let Gloria drive."

222

The toot of an automobile horn came from out front. "That's Gloria," Zee said. She brushed J.W.'s cheek with a kiss, did the same to mine, then picked up the picnic basket and cooler and headed for the front porch.

"Have fun," J.W. called after her.

"Stay out of trouble, you two," she said.

After she left, J.W. sat on a kitchen stool. "That was fast thinking," he said.

"You thought pretty fast, too," I said. "Spoons and forks. That was good."

He shrugged. "I'm not sure Zee believed me."

"Doesn't matter," I said. "She and the kids aren't in the red Jeep, and that's the point. Bad enough we took it to church this morning, and then to Frazier's house. But don't forget that I left it parked in plain sight in front of Larry Bucyck's house the night before he got executed."

J.W. had a faraway look in his eyes that I didn't interpret as concern for me. I thought I knew what he was thinking. He didn't want his wife and kids in a car that killers would connect to a couple of trouble-makers like us.

"I don't think the thugs with Uzis saw the Land Cruiser last night," he said.

I smiled. "Let's hope not."

"I think we need to do some touring."

"The places on the map."

He nodded. "Let's eat something first."

"And get out of these church clothes," I added.

I changed into my jeans and sneakers while J.W. made us some chicken salad sandwiches. When I got back to the kitchen, I saw that he'd also started a fresh pot of coffee brewing. He knew me well.

We ate at the kitchen table. J.W. had his map of Martha's Vineyard spread out in front of him, and he was frowning at it with narrowed eyes. Now and then he'd push his face closer to it and make a kind of grunting sound, as if he was having a conversation with himself.

I didn't interrupt. If he was drawing some inferences and making some deductions, he'd fill me in when he was ready.

When we finished eating, I filled a big travel mug with coffee, and we went outside. "I'll take the Land Cruiser," he said. "You climb into the Wrangler and follow me."

"What about the spoons and forks?" I said.

"Ha, ha," he said.

"I thought we didn't want to be seen in the Jeep."

"We don't," he said. "Just follow me."

At the end of his road, we turned right onto the Edgartown–Vineyard Haven Road, took another right on County Road heading into Oak Bluffs, and a few minutes later we pulled into a gas station. I stopped the Jeep behind the Land Cruiser while J.W. went inside. I could see him talking with somebody, and a minute later he came out accompanied by a gangly teenage boy who didn't look old enough to drive.

The kid came over to the driver's side of the Jeep. "You can pull around back," he said to me. "Leave it between the Ford pickup and the Mercedes. Lock up and bring me the keys."

I did as I was told. When I delivered the keys to the

boy, he looked at J.W. "Call Paulie tomorrow, tell him what's going on, okay?" he said.

J.W. nodded. "I'll call Paulie."

"We're wicked backed up," he said. "But maybe Paulie—"

"It's okay," J.W. said. "Thanks for finding a spot for it."

J.W. and I got into the Land Cruiser and pulled out onto the road. "That was smart," I said. "Get the car away from the house."

"That kid Billy," he said, "told me their mechanics are backed up about two weeks. All the vehicles that came over on the last ferries before the strike are still here, breaking down, needing new mufflers, new tires, oil changes, and the rental cars and taxis have been on the go all summer. I had to bribe him just to let me leave the Jeep there, and it cost me extra to put it out back where you can't see it from the road."

"A sound peace-of-mind investment," I said.

We headed away from Oak Bluffs on County Road and turned back onto the Edgartown–Vineyard Haven Road heading westerly. A bike trail followed alongside. Pretty soon J.W. slowed down and turned left over the bike trail onto a dirt road. We drove slowly past a couple of shingled houses, and a hundred yards or so later the road ended in a little turnaround. J.W. stopped there and got out of the Land Cruiser.

I got out, too. "What's here?" I said.

He shrugged and waved his hand at the scrubby woods. "One of the places that was circled on Dr. Lundsberg's map is in there somewhere."

"Where are we?"

He spread his arms, encompassing the whole area past the end of the dirt road. "State forest," he said. He was walking slowly around the rim of the turnaround, peering into the woods. After a minute, he said, "Here we go. Come on."

He'd found a narrow pathway leading into the woods. We started following it. It was unmarked and unofficial, just a beaten-down trail that might've been made by deer, not people—except for the occasional discarded Marlboro pack and Miller Lite can along the way.

We'd gone maybe fifty yards when J.W. stopped. "Hm," he said.

"What?"

"The trail goes that way," he said, pointing straight ahead, "but somebody recently went that way." He pointed to the right. "See?"

I looked, and I saw that a bush was broken. The cracked wood looked fresh. Then I saw that some weeds had been stepped on.

"The Great White Hunter," I said.

"The Great Indian Tracker," said J.W. "Please."

I followed J.W., and he tried to follow the track of whoever had veered off the trail, but pretty soon he stopped and blew out a breath. "Lost it," he said.

"Where would they be going?"

He looked around, then pointed. Ahead of us was a gentle rise in the land. "That," he said, "is about as close to a hill as we have here on the Vineyard."

"Let's go up there," I said.

We did. The hill didn't amount to much. It was topped with some scrubby oak and pine and a few big boulders. There was evidence that people had been there. Cigarette butts, a couple of Coke cans, a circle of blackened rocks where somebody had built a little campfire. Kids, probably, finding an isolated place to smoke dope and make out. As low as the elevation was, it was enough to give a long view of the flat Vineyard landscape looking toward the south. You could see all the way to the airport and beyond it to the shimmering ribbon of ocean at the horizon.

J.W. had visored his eyes with his hand, and he was peering around like a sea captain looking for land. "Left the damn binoculars in the car," he muttered.

"What're you looking for?"

"I don't know," he said. "I thought I'd know it when I saw it. Now I'm not so sure. I'm not even sure if this is the place Lundsberg was pointing out on his map."

"Maybe if we check out some of those other spots on the map we can make a connection."

"That's what I'm thinking," he said. "Let's go."

We hiked back to the Land Cruiser. J.W. studied his map for a few minutes, then turned around and drove back out to the Edgartown–Vineyard Haven Road. He went a short distance further, in the direction of Tisbury, and then took a left onto Airport Road.

"This cuts north to south, straight through the state forest near the airport," he muttered, as if he was talking to himself, not me. "I'm looking . . . somewhere along here . . ."

He crept along with the Land Cruiser in first gear, peering out his window at the roadside, and after a minute or two he pulled over and stopped the car.

We got out. J.W. stood there, shaking his head. A

meadow of brown grass and low-growing shrubs rolled away to some woods a hundred yards or so from the road. A stone wall demarcated the meadow from the woods. The meadow was open. The woods were dense.

"I don't know," said J.W. "Any thoughts?"

"Me?" I said. "Nope. So far, about all I would surmise is that Lundsberg was not focusing on buildings or population centers. These two places are the opposite of that."

J.W. nodded. "Remote. Or as remote as you can find on the Vineyard. Places to go to get away from people. You could walk across that meadow and disappear into those woods."

He nodded. "Let's keep looking."

We got back into the car. J.W. spread his map across both of our laps and pointed to one of the circles he'd drawn. The state forest was marked in green, and along its northern edge there was a jog in the outline. J.W. had circled that area. "There's nothing there," he said, jabbing at the circle. "No roads go in. No hiking trails, even. It's just woods and fields. We could poke around in there for a week, and even if there was something to be seen, we might not see it. Let's skip that one and head over here." He pointed to his next circle.

On J.W.'s map, it was located inside the green state forest area off Old County Road in West Tisbury.

As he drove, I followed along on the map. We took a dirt road into the western part of the state forest, and pretty soon J.W. turned onto a pair of ruts that weren't on his map.

The ruts ended abruptly at a line of boulders that

somebody had rolled there to keep vehicles from proceeding any farther. J.W. stopped, and we got out.

On the other side of the boulders a pair of ruts disappeared into the woods.

"Aha," said J.W.

"Quoting Sherlock Holmes?" I said.

"Quoting Kermit the Frog," he said, "who also said, The game is afoot."

"I don't think Kermit said that," I said. "Kermit said, When you come to a fork in the road, take it."

"That was Yogi Berra," said J.W.

"Well," I said, "this appears to be a fork with just a single tine on it, so shall we take it?"

"We shall."

"Lead on, MacDuff."

"Now you're quoting Casey Stengel," said J.W.

The old ruts headed east, back toward the middle of the state forest. The deeper we went into the woods, the narrower was the old roadway, until we found ourselves walking single file along a barely discernible trail.

After ten minutes or so, I said, "You sure this is right?"

"From what I remember on Lundsberg's map," said J.W., "he was pinpointing an area that would be about a mile down this trail. We should be getting to it, whatever it is."

"Are you seeing footprints or anything?"

He chuckled. "I've got my hands full just following the trail."

A minute later he stopped and pointed. "Somebody went up there recently," he said.

The ground sloped upward, and I saw where some weeds had been crushed down as if they'd been stepped on.

J.W. got down on his hands and knees, and after a minute he looked up at me. "There's a heel print here where the ground is soft. It's not that old, either. Look."

I looked, and I saw what he saw. "Looks like a boot," I said. "The edges are pretty distinct. Made within the past couple of days, I bet. You can sort of see the rest of the print. It sinks pretty deep. A heavy person with a good-sized foot made it."

J.W. grinned at me. "Bwana," he said.

We were able to follow the trail of stepped-on weeds, occasional boot prints, and here and there a broken branch, to the top of a little brushy knoll. Through the bushes we could see the ocean off to our right. Straight in front of us, maybe a quarter of a mile away, was the Vineyard airport.

As we stood there on the knoll, a plane suddenly came from behind us, so low that I instinctively ducked. It was a two-engine prop plane, the kind that would carry twelve passengers.

It touched down on a runway and taxied directly away from us.

I turned to J.W. and patted my heart. "Scared me," I said.

He nodded, but his frown told me he wasn't paying much attention to me.

"What is it?" I said to him.

"Look here." He showed me some places where tree branches and bushes had been cut off. They created the opening in the foliage through which we had been looking toward the airport.

"All these other places we've been exploring," I said.

He nodded. "There are a couple we haven't checked out yet, but from where they are on the map, I already know what we'll find."

"Vantage points overlooking the airport," I said. "What do you make of it?"

J.W. shook his head. "Ex-Prez Callahan is flying in tonight, right?"

"That's the rumor."

He spread his hands open, suggesting that the conclusion was obvious.

"You think . . . ?"

"I'd like to know what was in those crates that Larry Bucyck saw them unloading on Lundsberg's dock the other night." He turned and headed back down the trail. "Come on."

I followed him back to the Land Cruiser. We climbed in and J.W. started it up.

"I assume we're going straight to state-police head-quarters without passing Go," I said.

"Why?"

"Why?" I said. "To tell them what we know. To report it to the authorities."

"No," he said. "I mean, why do you assume that?"

"Because it's the prudent and responsible thing to do?"

"And what exactly do we know that we should report?" he said. "That we found some broken twigs in the woods?"

231

"Well, yeah, that," I said, "plus there was Lundsberg's map, and there is what Frazier told us, and there's what happened to Larry Bucyck, and there's Doyle and Mortison, and . . ." I shook my head.

He turned and looked at me. "And?"

"That's not enough?"

He smiled. "You don't know Olive Otero and Dom Agganis the way I do. They're good cops, all right. But they're cautious. By the book. Plus, I've had some, um, run-ins with them over the years. This morning, that fiasco at Lundsberg's place, that was the worst."

I nodded. "That was bad. On the other hand, yesterday we did produce Larry Bucyck's dead body for them."

"Big difference," he said, "a dead body, a few broken branches in the woods."

"I guess when you put it that way," I said, "Olive and Dom are probably fed up with our stories. They probably think you and I have been crying wolf a lot lately. To me it adds up. But without some kind of proof, or somebody who's actually in on it to explain it, it just sounds like . . . supposition."

"That's not what it sounds like," he said. "It's what it is. Supposition. At best. We don't know anything. We've got proof of nothing." J.W. put the Land Cruiser in gear and headed back toward Old County Road. "I got an idea," he said.

"I bet you do," I said. "See if we can find somebody with Uzis to shoot at us."

"That's a good idea, too," he said, "and maybe it'll work out that way. But if we can't make that happen, the least we can do is come up with some concrete evidence we can hand over to Agganis. That'll show him that we weren't hallucinating about what we saw at Dr. Lundsberg's place last night. Then maybe he'll listen to us."

"Good plan," I said, "except where are we going to find concrete evidence?"

"Stick with me," he said.

"Is the game afoot?"

"The game is definitely afoot," he said, "and an arm and a leg."

"Zounds," I said.

He turned right onto Old County Road, heading north toward Vineyard Haven.

"Back to the church?" I said.

He nodded. "I got my lock picks with me."

"As a lawyer and an officer of the court," I said, "I am compelled to tell you that any evidence gained by an illegal search, plus all evidence that results from that evidence, is tainted. Fruit of the poisoned tree and inadmissible in a court of law."

"Thank you, Clarence Darrow," said J.W. "Right now the admissibility of evidence is the least of my concerns."

I shrugged. "Me, too."

Fifteen or twenty minutes later we were on the road that went past Father Zapata's church. When we came to the sandy driveway that angled into the parking lot beside the church building, J.W. slowed down enough for us to see that no vehicles appeared to be parked there. But he kept going, driving slowly past the scrubby woods and an occasional shingled house, and he didn't stop for about a quarter of a mile, where we came upon a low white ranch-style building with swings and seesaws and jungle gyms in the side lot and a sign reading HAPPY TOT DAY CARE out front.

No vehicles were parked in that lot, either. Day-care centers were evidently closed on Sundays.

J.W. turned onto the Happy Tot driveway and drove around behind the building. He nosed the Land Cruiser up to the back of the building beside a Dumpster and turned off the ignition.

He opened the glove compartment and withdrew a black leather case.

I pointed at it. "Your lock-picking implements?"

He nodded and slipped the lock-picking kit into his shirt pocket.

"They teach you to pick locks in the army?"

"Self-taught," he said. He rummaged around in the glove compartment again and came out with a cell phone. He turned it on and looked at it. "Still got some battery. You got your cell with you?"

I patted my pocket. "Yes."

"Got my number on your speed dial?"

"All I've got is Zee's number from last summer when I called you from the ferry landing."

"That's what I meant," he said. "This is her phone."

We got out of the Land Cruiser. J.W. held up the ignition key for me to see, then bent down and shoved it into the dirt under the right front tire. He smoothed over the dirt, then looked up at me with his eyebrows arched.

I nodded.

We began moving through the woods parallel to

the road, heading back to the church. We stayed close enough to the road that we could see passing vehicles, but far enough from it that nobody driving a passing vehicle would see us. When we came to a house, we went around it, keeping trees and bushes between us and the yard. The last thing we needed was to be reported as Peeping Toms or vagrants.

We approached the church from the woods behind it. We moved slowly to the edge, crouched behind some bushes, and verified that no cars had arrived in the lot since we'd driven past. The doors and windows of the building were shut and presumably locked. The place looked deserted.

"I'm going to go in and see what's in that padlocked room," J.W. whispered. "You stand watch out here. I got the phone set on vibrate. You do the same. If anything happens, anybody shows up, friend or foe, hit my cell number, let it buzz twice, then disconnect and get the hell out of here. Slip into the woods and head back to the Land Cruiser. I'll meet you there. If I don't show up in some reasonable amount of time, don't hesitate to just drive away."

"Why are you whispering?" I whispered.

He smiled. "Because we are being furtive and clandestine."

"If you want me to come inside," I said, "vibrate me."

We took another look around, then scooted to the back of the building. J.W. went to the back door. It would open directly on to the front-to-back corridor where the locked room was located.

I crouched behind an azalea bush at the rear corner

of the building. From there I could see the road and the driveway and most of the parking lot. If anybody drove in, I'd spot him in time to warn J.W. and give him a chance to get out.

It seemed to take him forever to get the back door unlocked, but when I looked at my watch, it had been only about five minutes. I didn't know whether that was efficient or bumbling lock-picking, but I was impressed that he'd done it at all.

He looked over at me, gave me a thumbs-up, and slipped inside, where another lock-picking challenge faced him.

I waited there behind the azalea, alternating my attention between my watch and the entry to the church parking lot. I didn't know whether padlocks were more or less challenging than door locks, but another ten or fifteen minutes came and went and J.W. neither reappeared nor sent me a cell-phone signal.

Then a van turned into the driveway.

I didn't hesitate. I hit Zee's speed-dial number on my cell, let it vibrate a couple times, and disconnected.

The van turned its side to me at the front of the building, and I saw that it was Father Zapata's landscaping truck. It reminded me that Larry had seen a van at Dr. Lundsberg's, and men were loading crates into it. I was willing to bet it was the same van.

The van kept going, and in an instant it was out of sight from my spot at the rear corner of the church, presumably stopped directly outside the front door.

I heard the murmur of men's voices. Then two car doors slammed.

More voices.

Somebody came around the corner, heading for the rear of the building. He was coming directly toward me.

I looked at him only long enough to see that he was a big man wearing jeans and a T-shirt and a ball cap with the visor pulled low over his forehead. The cap had the New York Yankees logo on it.

Then I slipped into the woods.

I hid behind the trunk of a big oak tree and watched the big man saunter along the side of the church. He kept moving his head around, as if he expected to see something, or somebody.

I noticed that his left hand was holding a handgun against the side of his leg.

Where the hell was J.W.?

I had the terrible thought that there was no cell-phone reception on this part of the Vineyard, or inside the church building. J.W. was merrily picking away at the padlock on the storeroom door, and a man with a gun was about to catch him in the act.

The man was barely ten feet from turning the corner to the rear of the building when the back door opened and J.W. slipped out. He looked around quickly, then darted into the woods a bare instant before the man with the handgun would have seen him.

J.W. was about thirty feet from me. I stared at him, willing him to look my way. But he kept his eyes on the man behind the church.

When I looked back, I saw that the rear door from which J.W. had just exited had not shut tight. I wondered if the man knew the door had been closed and locked.

This man's job seemed to be to walk around the outside of the church, keeping watch while his compatriots presumably went inside. At one point he seemed to stare directly into my eyes, and it took a powerful act of will not to crouch lower behind my tree. But I knew any slight movement would catch his eyes.

He walked past the back door, paying more attention to the woods than to the building. Then he stopped and turned. He looked at the door, then went up to it. He pulled it, and it came open.

He pulled some kind of walkie-talkie from a holster on his belt and spoke into it. His voice was a rumble, but I could hear urgency in it.

I glanced at J.W. He'd spotted me and was moving his fingers at me.

I jerked my thumb over my shoulder.

He nodded and slipped deeper into the woods.

I did the same, scooting in a crouched-over position through the bushes and between the trees, half expecting shots to ring out behind me.

But none did.

I angled in the direction of the Happy Tot Day Care Center where the Land Cruiser waited for us. I was trotting through the woods, trying to hold back the panic. I found myself panting and sweating hard, and finally I stopped and bent over at the waist to catch my middle-aged breath.

"That was close." J.W.'s sudden voice behind me, practically in my ear.

"Jesus," I said. "You shouldn't sneak up on a man like that. You trying to give me a heart attack?"

"Did he spot us, do you think?"

I shook my head. "I think we're clear. But the back door didn't latch. They'll know somebody was there."

"Yeah, I know." Then he looked at me and said, "Christ. I didn't have time to lock the padlock. They'll know we got into that storeroom, too."

"Well," I said, "at least they don't know it was us. We got away, and they didn't see us. So what was in there?"

"I only got a quick look inside. There was plywood covering the window, so it was pretty dark, but I could see that there were some wooden crates piled up against the wall, just like the ones that you said Larry Bucyck described."

"Crates," I said. "What kind of crates?"

"They had *United States Army* and some kind of serial numbers stenciled on them."

"You think—?"

He nodded. "If I'm not mistaken, those crates contain military weapons."

Chapter Thirteen

J.W.

"We've got to talk to Dom Agganis," said Brady. "Now we've definitely seen enough to make him listen to us. Crates of military weapons? He'll have to take us seriously."

He got no argument from me. We trotted to the old Land Cruiser and got out of there. I thought the Happy Tot Day Care Center was probably glad to see us gone.

As we headed down State Road, Brady said, "Tell me again exactly what you saw in there."

"I'd have seen more if I'd been keeping up with my lock-picking practice," I said. "I should have been inside in a couple of minutes, but it took me too long, and that didn't leave me much time inside. There were those six crates, and I thought I saw a couple of battery packs, and there was other stuff in there like you'd expect to see in a storeroom. A couple of folding tables, some folding chairs, like that. I was just about to try to figure out what was in the crates when the phone went off, and I had to get out of there."

"Were any of the crates open?" said Brady. "Did you see what they held?"

"One had been kind of pried open. Looked like it held a metal tube of some kind. I couldn't tell what it was. Like I said, I'm betting they're weapons of some kind."

"You said the crates were stenciled with the words *United States Army*," said Brady. "Anything else? Any other markings that might tell us what they held?"

I coaxed an image of the room into my mind as I drove. There wasn't much that was new, but I did remember some printing on the crates. "F-I-M-9-2 was stenciled on the sides," I said. "There was more, but that's all I can remember. Does that make any sense to you?"

"No. Nothing."

I switched gears. "Did you recognize the guy with the gun?"

"No. A big guy with a Yankee cap and a pistol."

"Two reasons to be scared of him."

"I'd have been scared," Brady said, "even if he'd been wearing a Red Sox cap."

"Tell me about the car."

"It was a van with the Zapata Landscaping logo on the door."

I felt my eyebrows rise. "Was Zapata there, too?"

It was Brady's turn to look inward and try to conjure up an image from his memory. He frowned and shook his head. "The van had tinted windows, so I don't know how many people were in there or who they were. The only guy I saw was the Yankee fan."

We came to Vineyard Haven and drove on toward Oak Bluffs. The road was full of summer cars, and we crawled over the drawbridge not much faster than we could walk.

"Where do all these people come from?" asked Brady.

"Pilgrims who came seeking the Promised Land, found it, and now can't leave because of the strike. The gods are jesters. What do you think the van was doing there?"

"I bet they were there to clean out that room," said Brady. "Those crates don't hold stuff you normally find in the storage room of a meeting hall. The van was there to haul off the crates."

"If you're right," I said, "by the time we tell Dom what we saw, the evidence will be gone. Just like up at Lundsberg's. If he actually does go to the meeting-house, he'll probably find a bunch of nuns having tea."

But Dom didn't toss us out of his office, and he didn't go find the coven of tea-drinking nuns, because when we walked into the state-police office on Temahigan Avenue, we found a fresh-faced young police officer sitting behind the desk. He looked about twelve years old, and I knew immediately that he was one of the summer cops who come down for the season to help out, and who live in the barracks above the office while they're here. His name, according to a silver plaque on his shirt, was Olaf Nordman.

"May I help you?" he asked. His face was as pink and round as the fabled baby's ass, and he looked as innocent.

"Yes," I said. "I need to talk with Dom Agganis, and I need to do it now."

His baby face became less angelic. "What's the problem? Maybe I can help you."

I instantly knew that he couldn't. I gave him my name and introduced Brady. "We talked with Sergeant Agganis and Officer Otero earlier," I said, "and we're here to give them more of the same story. It's important that we see them right away."

"Sergeant Agganis and Officer Otero are out of the office and won't be back until later," said Olaf. "What's this story about?"

I pointed to the right side of the desk. "There's a tape recorder in there. If you'll get it out, I'll go over everything, old and new. There's a lot of detail, so I think the tape will help."

Olaf made no motion toward the drawer. "Why don't you just tell me your story? If we need a tape of it we can get it later." His voice suggested both patience and repressed irritation.

"We don't have time for this," said Brady, speaking as much to me as to the young officer.

"We'll have to make it," I said. I leaned toward the desk. "All right, from the beginning, here's what's happened." I started to talk, speaking fast and sticking strictly to the facts. After perhaps two minutes of my rapid-fire speech, the young policeman held up his hand.

"All right," he said. "Let me get the tape recorder." He did that, turned on the machine, and spoke into a mike, giving his name and ours and noting the time and place. Then he handed me the mike and said, "Start again."

I did, and with Brady's additions and clarifications, we put the whole tale into the tape, including almost everything we'd seen, done, and heard since we'd last talked with the police. The only things we omitted from our report were our own illegal acts.

When we were through, Olaf turned off the tape recorder and reached for the radio transmitter on the desk.

"We're shorthanded," he said as he pulled the mike toward him, "but I'll see if the Tisbury police can check the meetinghouse."

"Tell them to be careful," said Brady. "There was a guy with a gun up there."

"I'll tell them," said Olaf, and he picked up the phone and did. When he finished making his request, he hung up and turned back to us. "You two had better stick around. Sergeant Agganis will want to talk with you."

"Dom and Olive know us and can find us if they need to," I said. I scribbled our cell-phone numbers on a slip of paper and gave it to the young police officer. "They can contact us at these numbers."

"I suppose I could arrest you," said Olaf.

Brady shook his head. "You have no charges."

"I can probably think of one."

"Don't waste your time," said Brady. "Instead, get hold of Dom and tell him what we just told you. Come on, J.W."

Brady turned and walked out, and I followed him.

"Maybe you should start a religious cult," I said, as we went to the truck. "You're a born leader, fearless in the face of authority, charismatic, and gifted with a golden tongue. Look how easily you got me to follow you."

"Leaders are people who jump in front of crowds that are already moving," said Brady. "I didn't think you planned to hang around waiting for Dom to show up, so I led the way out. I want to get back to your computer."

"Fine. I want to go there anyway to spread out that map again and to collect some hardware. I'm tired of being the only guy in town without a gun. What do you want to do on the computer?"

"I want to get on the Internet," said Brady. "Everything is on the Web if you look long enough and hard enough. We've been running into trouble ever since I came down here, but we don't know what we're dealing with. The bad guys have already killed two people, and the pace seems to be picking up. Things are happening. I feel like I'm in a movie that's being fast-forwarded."

It was barely mid-afternoon, and it seemed as if I'd already put in a couple of days without sleep, but I was also filled with the same sense of accelerating conspiracy of which Brady spoke. I drove home faster than the old Land Cruiser was used to going.

When we parked in the yard and went into the house, I was glad to find that Zee and the children weren't there. My coldest reasoning told me that they were in no danger, but my hottest emotions said that they were. Jung would have considered that conflict normal, but I didn't like it. My feelings are never totally under control, but I'm happier when my mind is running things.

"You know where the computer is," I said to Brady. He nodded and went there.

I went to the gun cabinet, got out the old .38 Smith and Wesson that I'd carried long before, when I'd been on the Boston PD. I loaded it and stuck it in my belt, and then I loaded the little Beretta P80 that Zee had used before she'd graduated to her Colt .45 and become a competitive target shooter.

I put the Beretta on the kitchen table and unrolled my map. I studied it, taking particular note of the circled areas we'd visited earlier. I almost immediately felt my eyes widen.

It is a curiosity to me that I often don't see things that are right in front of my nose. If you move the orange juice six inches from where it normally rests in the fridge, I may think we don't have any. If my car keys aren't in their normal pocket, I ask Zee if she's seen them.

Now I looked at the map and the circled areas marked on it and saw it as if for the first time. I got out my pencil and drew a line joining the areas to one another.

The line became an irregular circle at the center of which was the airport, and the marked areas were each at the end of a runway, set back a short distance in more or less uninhabited spots.

They were all under flight paths for takeoffs and landings.

I looked at the weather gauge on our wall. The

wind was southwest, which is the prevailing wind direction on the island.

I heard a soft whistle from the guest room and then the sound of the printer. A moment later Brady came into the kitchen.

"Take this," I said, handing him the Beretta. "And look at this." I pointed at the map.

"You look at this," he said, accepting the pistol with one hand and giving me some printed pages with the other. "I did a search for F-I-M-9-2. This is what came up." He put the pistol in his pocket.

He looked down at the map, and I looked at the papers he'd given me. There I saw a photo of a pipelike device and an article about FIM-92 Stinger ground-to-air missiles. I scanned the article swiftly and felt adrenaline flow through my veins. The SAM was light, easy to carry, capable of being fired from a man's shoulder, and capable of bringing down an aircraft at altitudes above twelve thousand feet with a three-kilogram penetrating hit-to-kill warhead.

"This has to be what was in those crates," I said, looking up at Brady. "Missiles." My voice sounded odd in my ears, as though it was coming from someone else's mouth.

"And this," he said, putting a finger on the map, "shows where they're going. How many crates did you say you saw?"

I told him and he nodded. "That's one for each of these areas. These guys are planning to shoot down an airplane, and they've found locations to cover every possible flight path."

I looked back at the photo. The more I looked, the more the SAM seemed to resemble the pipe I'd seen in the crate.

"We've got to call the cops again," I said. "These guys must be after Joe Callahan. At least he's the only big shot I know of who's coming here today."

"This is your island, not mine," said Brady, "but even I know it's crawling with VIPs and private jets. Maybe it's not Callahan. Maybe it's somebody else."

"Whoever it is, they want him pretty badly," I said. "But if it's not Callahan, who is it? And who's mad enough to commit multiple murders to get at him?"

"If it is Callahan," said Brady, "what did he do to deserve this much hatred? As presidents go, Joe Callahan had fewer enemies than most. He even pals around with the guy who replaced him, and that guy's in the other party."

You don't have to be guilty of anything to have people hate you. Celebrity in itself can make you a target, and the innocent often only inherit the earth rock by rock.

I went to the phone and called the Edgartown police station. Kit Goulart answered. Kit and her husband, Joe, are both over six feet tall and weigh in at about 290 each. When they walk down the sidewalk, they fill it up. They look like a pair of plow horses headed for the barn. Kit's voice is patient and gentle, the whisper of a woman half her size.

I asked if the Chief was in, and she said that he was. I told her I was on my way down, and she said she'd give him the message.

"Why are we going to the Edgartown police?" asked Brady, reasonably. "Everything we've seen so far happened in some other town."

"Because I know the Chief and he knows me. We need somebody who'll listen to us and not call us crazy."

He raised a forefinger. "You're absolutely right. Let's go."

I did that, and we drove into town where, without too much trouble since it was mid-afternoon and most tourists were still at the beach, we got past the dreaded Stop and Shop–Al's Package Store traffic jam—caused, as are most traffic jams on the Vineyard and elsewhere, by people making left turns. "When I'm king," I said to Brady, "I'm going to ban left turns."

"I know, I know," he said. "And you're going to ban small dogs, high heels, and pay toilets, too. I don't think I've heard you say that more than a thousand times."

"It's a sound platform for revolution," I said. "You have to admit that."

"I own a smallish dog," he said, "and Evie looks amazing in heels."

"I'm not a fanatic," I said as we passed Cannonball Park. "There are exceptions to every rule."

We turned right on Pease's Point Way and parked in front of the police station beside a cruiser. Because of Homeland Security, the Patriot Act, and other antiterrorist laws and practices implemented after the 9/11 attacks in New York and Washington, the front door of the police station is now locked and you have to push a buzzer to get in. This is because you never know when some international terrorist organization might decide to attack the Edgartown police station.

Now that I thought about it, the fact was that Brady and I were there to tell the Chief that we believed a terrorist group of sorts was planning a missile attack on the Martha's Vineyard Airport. Another of life's ironies.

I punched the buzzer, and Kit Goulart looked out at us, smiled, wiggled her fingers, and pushed the button that opened the door.

"The Chief is in his office," she said, waving a massive hand in that direction.

We found the Chief sucking on his favorite briar. It was not lighted, because he only smoked out-of-doors, but like all pipe smokers, he found the oral stimulation of chewing the stem to be almost as important as the taste of the tobacco smoke. I knew all about that, having once been a pipe smoker myself and still having a nose that, when I caught a whiff of smoke from a passing pipe, tried hard to lead me after the smoker, inhaling deeply.

"What can I do for you?" he asked.

"We're the Cassandra brothers," I said. "We can't find anybody to believe us."

"I'm tempted to say that's understandable, but I won't," said the Chief, and waved us to two chairs. "Speak. I don't have much time, so don't waste it."

Talking fast, I told him about agreeing to try to clear Eduardo Alvarez's name and about what I'd learned from Steve Bronski. I didn't tell him about how Steve happened to break his ankle.

Brady told him about coming down to see Larry Bucyck and what Bucyck had told him, and about us finding Bucyck's body the next day. We both told him about what we'd seen and done at Lundsberg's house on Menemsha Pond and what we'd found there the next morning when we'd returned with Olive Otero. We told him what had happened at Zapata's church and about our encounter with Harry Doyle after we'd talked with Norm Frazier. We showed him our map and told him what we'd seen when we tried to find some of the marked sites. I told him what I'd seen in the storage room of the meetinghouse. I didn't mention picking the locks. We told him of our conversations with the state police, and finally we told him what Brady had learned on the computer, and of our conviction that conspirators intended to use surface-to-air Stinger missiles to shoot down an incoming plane, and that our best guess was that Joe Callahan was the target. We wrapped up our presentation by reiterating the links we'd noticed among Zapata, Mortison, Lundsberg, and Doyle.

When we were done, the Chief studied us with an unfathomable expression. He'd been in the cop business for most of his life and was past being surprised by anything human beings were capable of doing.

Then he nodded. "It doesn't take much to make a killer out of a guy who's normally nice as pie. Maybe the ties between those guys go back to Nicaragua. Mortison lives down here in Katama, so I know a little about him. He's always been a hard case, but he got harder when his brother got himself killed when one of those militia outfits attacked a mission hospital down there in the jungle. Now you tell me that this Dr. Lundsberg ran clinics in Nicaragua and that Zapata was working down there before he came on up here. What I don't get is what all that's got to do with Joe Callahan."

"Maybe I do," said Brady. "Early in Callahan's first term, he didn't immediately cut off aid to some of the right-wing political movements that his predecessor supported. By the time he did, there'd been a lot of killing by militias, and it was financed by us. Only Callahan's best pals have forgiven him. It was a bad mistake."

The Chief glanced at his watch. "If you're lying about all this, somebody will want you both in jail. If you're just wrong, they'll probably still want you there. But I believe you saw what you say you saw."

I felt relief flow through me and remembered having the same feeling when I was a kid accused of breaking a window I didn't break and having my father believe me. But I had no time to luxuriate in being believed, because the Chief was already reaching for his phone and saying, "We have a time problem. Joe Callahan is flying in on a private jet, and he's supposed to land in about an hour. I'm going to assume that those six crates are gone from the meetinghouse by now. We have to get our people out to these sites immediately."

His face remained unemotional, but I knew he was wondering if he had enough time and personnel to get the job done. The island cops were already stretched thin by the strike and by Larry Bucyck's murder, to say nothing of maintaining law and order among 100,000 August people who were rowdier than usual because they didn't like being trapped, even though they were trapped in Eden.

I stood and touched the map in front of him. "The

wind is from the southwest," I said. "I don't know if wind direction means much to pilots these days, but I imagine his plane will be landing from the northeast, coming into the wind over Oak Bluffs and the high school on its approach."

Brady, who'd gotten up and followed me to the desk, nodded and pointed. "So, if you can't cover all of the sites, maybe you should concentrate on those on the northeast. These two sites are the closest ones." He glanced at me, then back at the Chief. "We've been to one of those places. We can take you there. It'll save you some time."

"No," said the Chief. "You two have done your duty already. Leave this up to the people who are getting paid to do the work." He raised a hand to silence us, then picked up the phone and spoke into it. His voice was very professional. His words were straightforward and tolerated no argument. He finished one call, punched a button on his phone and made another, then another and another. When he finished the last call, he got to his feet, folded our map, jammed it in his pocket, then started toward the door, waving us out in front of him.

As we passed Kit, she said, "Do you have enough men?"

"We'll have to make do with what we've got," said the Chief.

She frowned, but nodded. "Well, be careful out there."

"I will," he said.

As we walked outside beside the Chief, Brady said, "How many people know Callahan's ETA?"

254

"I don't know," said the Chief, opening the cruiser's door. Then he paused and looked at Brady. "You're right. If this scheme is what it seems to be, somebody must have given that information to the bad guys."

"Who told you?" I said.

"I got a call from Washington. The Secret Service still protects ex-presidents. Callahan will have some agents with him on the plane. There aren't many secrets in Washington. When the dust settles we'll have to find the tipster. I'll worry about that later."

"Have you got enough men to cover all those sites?"

"I have enough for the ones under the approach, at least," he said. "I'll try to collect more." He pointed his finger. "You two stay out of it. I have enough to worry about without worrying about you, too."

He got into the cruiser and drove away.

Above us, the innocent blue sky held clouds whiter than newborn lambs, and the sun shone down onto a world that should have been devoid of murder.

I looked at Brady and quoted the old saw: "'Nature may be violent, but only man is vile.'"

He nodded, then squinted up at the sky. "Am I imagining things," he said, "or are those clouds blowing in a different direction than they were when we got here?"

I looked up at the woolly lambkin clouds and felt a chill.

The wind had changed. Now it was blowing from the northeast.

The Chief would be covering the wrong sites.

Chapter Fourteen

Brady

We stood there outside the police station looking at the sky. The clouds off to the northeast were roiling and boiling, and they seemed to be piling up and turning darker by the minute.

"You heard any weather forecasts lately?" I said to J.W.

He shook his head, still frowning at the sky.

"It's almost the end of August," I said. "The beginning of the nor'easter season along the New England coast."

He nodded. "They sometimes come in fast this time of year." He put his forefinger in his mouth, then held it up. "It's a northeast wind, all right." He pointed at the big oak tree that grew in front of the police station. "See how the leaves are showing their undersides? That means a storm is coming."

I looked at the tree. The top branches were swaying in the freshening breeze, and the undersides of the leaves looked silver. "So Callahan's plane won't be approaching from the northeast," I said. "It'll come from the opposite direction."

J.W. blew out a breath. "The Chief will have the wrong sites covered. We've got to tell him."

"Don't you think he'll figure it out?"

"He might. But we can't take that chance. Come on."

He turned and headed back to the station, and I followed him. He poked the button, and when Kit Goulart hit the buzzer, we went inside.

"What now?" Kit said.

"You've got to get ahold of the Chief," J.W. said.

She frowned at him. "He's doing something pretty important. As you know."

"This is about that. Get him on the radio. We don't have any time to waste."

"What exactly is it about?"

"The wind has changed. Now it's coming out of the northeast."

"You want me to give the Chief a weather report?"

"It's important," said J.W. "He'll understand."

She nodded, then picked up the microphone from the console beside her, poked a button, and said, "Chief, come in, please." She paused, scowled at the phone, then said, "Chief? Are you there? I have information for you." Another pause. "Chief, come in, damn it." She looked up at the ceiling for a minute, then looked at us. "He's not answering."

"We don't have any time," said J.W. "Keep trying. Tell him about the wind. Tell him it's coming from the northeast. Do you understand?"

"Of course I understand," said Kit.

"Or call the state police," said J.W. "Call somebody.

Tell them they've got to go to the southwest circles on the map. The Chief will know what that means." He touched my shoulder. "Come on." He turned and strode out of the station.

I followed him. Back outside, the sky directly overhead was still blue and dotted with puffy white clouds. But the breeze had picked up a little more, and a dark cloud bank was building on the northeast horizon. The temperature seemed to have dropped ten degrees in the past few minutes, and the air felt damp and heavy. The storm was coming fast.

J.W. was heading for his Land Cruiser. I followed him, and we climbed in.

"You got a plan?" I said.

"Not much of one. Somebody's got to check out those sites on the southwest end of the island. If Kit can't get ahold of the Chief in time, that leaves us." He started up the car.

"We gave the map with your circles on it to the Chief," I said.

"I've got another map in my glove box."

I opened the Land Cruiser's glove box. There were many maps in it.

I found one of Martha's Vineyard and opened it on my lap. This one, unfortunately, did not have any circles on it. "You remember the places from what you saw at Lundsberg's?" I said to J.W.

He tapped his head. "I got the map of Martha's Vineyard here." He leaned over, frowned at the map, then poked at it with his forefinger. "Here," he said, "on the road to Scrubby Neck Farm. And here, on

Deep Bottom Road. The Chief should have the others covered. But not these. These are on the opposite side of the island."

"We better get going, then."

He turned onto the road.

I was remembering how the plane had come zooming in over our heads when we were out scouting the circles on the map. I wondered where the wind had been blowing from when that happened. Maybe we were wrong about this wind direction business. I was pretty sure airplanes took off into the wind. But maybe they landed with it behind them.

Well, it didn't really matter. With one of those FIM-92 Stinger missiles you could shoot down an airplane from anywhere on the island. J.W. had seen six crates in the storeroom at Father Zapata's church, and Dr. Lundsberg had circled six areas on his map. Six sites, six missile shooters, each capable of bringing down an airplane twelve thousand feet away. That was more than two miles.

"Holy shit," I muttered.

"What?" said J.W.

"I don't think the wind direction makes any difference to these guys," I said. "I bet there's a missile launcher at each of the six sites. I bet they intend to shoot all six missiles at Callahan's plane."

J.W. looked at me. "So if five of them are stopped, or misfire or something, there will still be a sixth, and that'll be enough."

"More than enough." I looked at my watch. About fifteen minutes had passed since the Chief told us that Callahan's plane was expected in about an hour.

"We've got three-quarters of an hour. Can we get there in time?"

"Gonna be close in this old crate," he mumbled.

"What's the plan?"

With one eye on the road, he leaned over and poked a finger at the map. "I've got an idea of the layout here," he said, indicating the road to Scrubby Neck Farm, "so you can drop me off there. Then you'll head over to this spot." He tapped the other place on Deep Bottom Road. "I figure we can get to this first spot in about fifteen minutes, leaving you another fifteen or twenty to find the other place."

"You better step on it," I said.

He stepped on it. There was plenty of Sunday-afternoon island traffic on the road, folks on their way to or from the beach with no deadlines or obligations or any reason to bother traveling at the speed limit, but J.W. nosed up close to the slow vehicles in front of us until they got the hint and pulled over so he could pass them. Still, time seemed to be moving faster than we were.

"Got your weapon?" said J.W.

I patted my leg where Zee's Beretta was a heavy, awkward lump in my pocket. "I do," I said, "though I'm not sure how it will stand up against a Stinger missile."

"You've shot people before," he said.

"A couple," I said. "I didn't enjoy it, but they were fully prepared to shoot me."

"You did what you had to do," he said. "I hope you're prepared to do it again. The trick is, don't hesitate. Don't think about it. Shoot first, think later. Just

261

aim for the middle of him and keep pulling the trigger until you run out of bullets."

"I can do that," I said. "How about you?"

"These people intend to assassinate the former president of the United States. What do you think?"

"That," I said, "answers my question. Can't you drive a little faster?"

We were on the Edgartown–West Tisbury Road, heading west. As we put a little distance between ourselves and Edgartown, the traffic seemed to thin out, and pretty soon we had an empty road ahead of us. I noticed that J.W. had nosed the needle of his speedometer past sixty. The old Land Cruiser was shimmying with its effort.

"We get stopped by a cop," I said, "we'll surely be late."

"We get stopped by a cop," he said, "we can tell him what's going on and get some help."

"If he believes us."

"Which he probably wouldn't," said J.W. "On the other hand, this is one date we can't be late for. Too late even by one minute and it's all over."

A few minutes later J.W. slowed down, then took a left turn onto a dirt road. It cut through woods and meadows. No houses or other buildings.

I squinted at the map and saw that he was aiming for Scrubby Neck Farm. "You know what you're doing?" I said.

"I think I've got an idea where their launching area is."

J.W. took a left and then another left, and then we found ourselves at the end of the road.

262

He stopped and climbed out of the Land Cruiser. "Can you find your way back from here to the road?"

I nodded.

"Okay. Take a left turn on Deep Bottom Road. You should find a trail going off to the left into the woods. Go." He patted his hip, where he'd tucked his Smith and Wesson .38 into his belt, gave me a thumbs-up, and headed for the woods in back of one of the house lots.

I scrambled over the console into the driver's seat, and suddenly I was alone in J.W.'s Land Cruiser with a puny handgun in my pocket and the life of a former president of the United States in my hands.

I looked at my watch.

I had about twenty-five minutes. Not enough time to ponder the significance of what I was doing.

I found my way back onto the Edgartown–West Tisbury Road, turned left, and began looking for Deep Bottom Road.

I thought about J.W. By now he was sneaking through the woods toward some general area he'd seen on the big map at Dr. Lundsberg's house the previous night. If we were right, there would be a man with an FIM-92 missile launcher there.

I blinked away the image of J.W. and his .38 shooting it out against a man with a weapon powerful enough to blow up an airplane. I had to focus on what I was doing.

I found Deep Bottom Road and turned onto it. It was a narrow dirt road that cut through some scrubby woods. I slowed down to a crawl and looked hard. Off to the left, the land rose to a little lumpy hill. A good vantage for shooting down airplanes.

After a few minutes, I spotted some old ruts leading into the woods. This had to be the place.

My first thought, in the interest of time, was to take the Land Cruiser as far over those ruts as its four-wheel drive would allow.

Then I thought about the noisy old Land Cruiser whining along in four-wheel drive with its bad muffler and all its rattles and clanks. I wondered if I could drive it very far without alerting the man I expected would be waiting on top of the hill. I couldn't take that chance.

So I pulled it over to the side of the road and got out. Now the clouds blanketed the sky and the wind was whipping the tops of the trees. The air was dense with moisture. Soon it would rain.

I began to hurry down the rutted road, and I'd gone about halfway when I heard the murmur of a man's voice. I stopped in my tracks and listened. I couldn't make out his words, but his voice was low and conspiratorial.

I slipped off the ruts into the woods and began to ease my way from bush to bush parallel with the rutted roadway until I saw him. He was a young black-haired man wearing work boots and camouflage pants and a black T-shirt. His back was to me so I couldn't see his face. He was sitting on a big boulder with a cell phone pressed against his ear and a cigarette dangling from the corner of his mouth.

An Uzi leaned against the boulder he was sitting on. It was an ugly thing, all function, no form, just a mechanism of black metal that could spit out bullets so fast they made one continual blasting noise. It

264

didn't have a stock. You didn't bother holding it to your shoulder and aiming. You just held on with both hands, kept your finger on the trigger, and let the bullets spray, the way I had done the previous night when J.W. and I were fleeing from Dr. Lundsberg's place. I remembered the feeling of lethal power in my hands when I held that Uzi that was spitting bullets at the speed of sound. I didn't want those bullets spitting at me.

I was about thirty yards from the guy. If he didn't turn around, and if I could avoid stepping on a twig or flushing a partridge, maybe I could sneak up behind him.

No other plan occurred to me, so that's what I decided to do.

I kept one eye on the man and one eye on each place I set down my foot. The freshening wind and the damp air helped muffle the sound of my movements.

I found myself drenched with sweat, even though the air was cool. My middle-aged heart was hammering in my chest, and I had the random, panicky thought that if a stroke or a heart attack killed me, ex-President Callahan would also be a dead man.

Luckily, the area around the boulder where the guy with the Uzi sat featured tall pine trees, and the soft ground was cushioned with years of fallen brown needles.

I was no more than ten feet from his back when he snapped his cell phone shut, stood up, and stuffed it into his pants pocket. He took a final drag off his cigarette, dropped it onto the ground, and half turned toward me as he stamped it out under his foot.

I crouched behind a tree trunk and held my breath as he yawned and stretched. Then he turned away from me, tilted back his head, and gazed up at the dark sky.

I slipped Zee's Beretta out of my pocket, flicked off the safety, got my feet under me, took three quick steps, and levered my left forearm around the man's throat before he knew I was there.

I yanked back as hard as I could. I held nothing back. I wanted to crush him.

He gurgled in his throat and grabbed and scratched at my arm with both of his hands.

I jammed the muzzle of the Beretta into the soft place under his right armpit. My finger tightened on the trigger.

"*Do it,*" I told myself.

But I couldn't.

He was clawing at my arm where it was levered around his throat. I felt him growing weaker.

I lifted the Beretta and smashed the butt down on top of his head.

A moan started in his chest and rose up into his constricted throat. It stopped there, and the man's entire body shuddered and twitched.

Then he went limp in my arms.

I eased him to the ground. He lay on his left side, motionless. I looked at his face. I thought I might have seen him in Father Zapata's church, but maybe not. He was a stranger to me.

I wondered if I'd killed him after all.

I bent down and pressed my fingers against the side of the man's throat. I found a fluttering pulse. I kept my fingers there, and after a minute his pulse seemed to strengthen.

He'd wake up with one helluva headache.

I hoped he wouldn't wake up for a while, because I wasn't done. I still had a job to do, and I couldn't afford to take the time to tie him up.

I stuffed the Beretta into my pocket. At that moment, the unconscious man's phone rang.

I fished in his pocket, where I'd seen him put it, pulled it out, opened it, and grumbled, "Yeah?"

"Everything all right?" said a deep voice. He spoke with no accent.

"Uh-huh," I grunted.

"Fredo?" he said. "That you?"

"Yeah."

"Well, okay," said the voice. "I thought I heard something."

I mumbled, "Umm," and shut the phone, figuring if I tried to say more I'd be pressing my luck.

I knelt down and stuffed the phone into the pine needles under the boulder. Maybe it would provide some kind of evidence later.

When I stood up and looked at my watch, a raindrop hit the back of my hand.

Callahan's plane was due in about five minutes.

I picked up the man's Uzi. A path wound up the slope. I started to follow it. I expected to find a man with an FIM-92 missile launcher on the hilltop.

The rain moved in quickly. It came aslant on a sharp northeasterly wind. The trees swayed and creaked, and almost instantly the ground under my feet was soft and moist.

I made no effort to move silently. I held the Uzi in both hands with my finger on the trigger and followed the path quickly up the hill.

The man was standing on the far side of a clearing. He was looking intently through an opening in the foliage toward the airport. The Stinger was mounted on his right shoulder. It was a simple-looking device— a tube about four feet long extending back over his shoulder, a square piece braced against the front of his shoulder with a handle and a battery pack and what I assumed was a trigger mechanism. He had it aimed upward at about a forty-five-degree angle, and he was squinting through a sight of some kind. He held the handle in his left hand. His right hand fingered the trigger.

I stood in the path, partially hidden by the close-growing bushes. He stood on the other side of the clearing about twenty feet away. His back was to me, and he seemed to be concentrating on what he was seeing through the sights of his terrible weapon, but even under the cover of the wind and rain, there was no way I could get close enough behind him to grab him by the throat and whack him on the head before he saw me.

Then I heard the drone of a jet engine. It seemed as if it was directly overhead. I looked up, but the plane was higher than the low-hanging storm clouds.

I wondered if Callahan's plane would decide not to try landing in this weather. But I doubted it. Instrument landings were routine.

The sound of the plane's engine faded into the

clouds. I guessed it was circling, preparing to make its final approach.

The man with the Stinger was pointing his weapon up at the sky, and I remembered that he didn't need to aim it, that its infrared homing mechanism would take care of that. As I understood it, all he had to do was launch the missile in the general direction of the plane. Its high-tech capabilities would do all the fine-tuning.

It looked to me as if the man was about to shoot.

"Hey!" I yelled.

He whirled around to face me, and in that moment I saw that it was Harry Doyle.

Chapter Fifteen

J.W.

When you live on an island you're always conscious of the weather, especially of the wind and of tropical storms moving up the coast or brewing between Africa and the Caribbean. Although we all keep track of the latest forecasts, they are rarely of much help to us residents of Martha's Vineyard, because island weather often is quite different from mainland conditions. Also, in spite of the fact that the island's land mass is only around 120 or so square miles, it's not uncommon for it to have completely different kinds of weather only a few miles apart. My house in Edgartown can be in a blazing hot summer sun, but if I drive to South Beach to cool myself in the surf I can find a thick fog with a chilly wind blowing. Or I can leave home in a steady rain and find dry roads in Vineyard Haven or bright sun in Chilmark.

And, as in all of New England, there is truth in the old saying, "If you don't like the weather, wait a minute." So when the wind veered and the storm clouds came roiling in from the east, I was not surprised, but I wished Thor had kept his hammer quiet for a bit longer.

As Brady drove away, I was filled with a desire to be many places at once, to be invincible and invisible. But I was here and very mortal and touched by an urgent fear. I knew I had no time to waste if I was to find the missile site I knew was near.

But where was it? I was within the circle I'd drawn on our map, but the landscape was new to me. Oh, to be Sherlock Holmes, capable of deducing truth from the scantiest clue, or Lew Wetzel, unerring in his tracking skills.

But I was neither, and my time was running out. The high branches of the trees were beginning to sway, and the temperatures began to drop as the gray clouds passed under the sun.

I was on a sandy road leading toward South Beach. I started trotting down the road, looking for fresh tire tracks. Somewhere off to my right, not too far from the road, was the site I sought. I'd seen the size of the crates holding the missiles, so I was sure that they and their operators had been brought in by car and that the car would still be in the area to provide them with a swift escape from the search that would certainly follow the crash of the plane.

Other people used this road to get to their houses, so the car must be parked out of their sight. Maybe behind an abandoned building or in a grove of trees.

I watched for any sign of tire tracks leading off the road but saw none. I trotted on, because I could think of nothing else to do. I had odd imaginings. One of them was a genuine wish for a helicopter. If I had a helicopter I could find those guys in two minutes. Another was a vision of a plane exploding in the air and sending fiery pieces of metal spinning to the ground. A third was of me running headlong into a man with an Uzi, who immediately turned it toward me. I felt an additional rush of fear and stumbled when I thought of that, but I kept going.

It seemed that I'd been trotting forever when I finally saw where some tire tracks had turned off the road to the right. I glanced that way and saw no sign of the car, but the soft sand and the bent grass led my eyes toward a thick cluster of tall oak brush. I imagined eyes looking at me from the oaks, like those of lions lying in the tall grass of the veldt, invisible to their prey, so I trotted on down the road as though I was out for an afternoon jog. When the road bent out of sight, I left it and cut to the right, running, bent over, eyes sweeping the trees ahead of me.

Then, believing that a guard must certainly be somewhere near the car, I slowed and moved ahead more carefully. My advantage was that I knew he was there but he didn't know I was there. I made a wide circle out around the cluster of oak brush, glad that the wind was rising and filling the forest with sounds to cover those I was making.

Suddenly I saw a van with the Zapata Landscaping logo. It was hidden from the road by the oak brush and had been turned and was parked facing back toward the road. I froze and let only my eyes move. I saw nothing more at first, but then I saw movement. A man was coming toward the car from some site farther into the woods. The sureness of his stride suggested that he was walking on a trail. Or maybe his confidence was based on the Uzi slung on his shoulder.

I instantly recognized him as the man I'd seen at the meetinghouse when I'd slipped away into the cover of trees after Brady's warning phone call.

In the movies, machine-gun-toting villains are always blazing away at pistol-packing heroes and missing them a thousand times before getting popped off themselves by a single round from the hero's trusty handgun. But I didn't think that was a likely scenario if I challenged the guard's Uzi with my old .38, and for a moment I was in a whirlpool of thought, desperately wondering what to do.

Then I heard, or imagined I heard, the distant sound of a plane somewhere off to the southwest, and knew I had no time to waste. Turning, I scurried back to the road, then ran from there toward the cluster of oak brush shouting, "Zapata! Zapata! Abort! Abort!" The sound of the plane grew louder, and I heard, too, the faint sound of what could have been firecrackers, but I believed was gunfire coming from the direction Brady had headed.

Rounding the brush, I came face to face with the guard. The muzzle of his Uzi looked like the entrance to the Holland Tunnel, but I ignored it and shouted, "It's been called off! I just heard from Lundsberg! Callahan's not on this plane! Use your phone! Stop Zapata before it's too late! If he shoots down this plane, the cops will get us before we have another chance! Hurry!"

The big man stared, not knowing what to believe.

"Call him! Quick! If he shoots that missile, we'll never get another chance at Callahan!" He still hesitated, and I screamed, "Jesus Christ, man! Do you want us all shot or in jail for nothing? Here, gimme that phone!" I reached for it.

But he suddenly believed and brushed my hand away. He tipped the Uzi up, dragged out his phone, and shouted into it. "Zapata! Don't fire! Repeat, don't fire! Callahan is not, repeat not, on this plane! Lundsberg says to abort! Do you hear me? I said abort! Do not fire. Callahan is not on this plane! Abort! Abort!"

He turned and stared up the path as if to will his voice to reach Zapata even faster, and when he did I snaked out the .38 and laid it as hard as I could on the side of his head. He went down like a felled ox. I found a pistol in his pocket and put it in mine, and then I grabbed the Uzi and ran up the path.

At its end, in a small clearing on the far side of which branches had been cut away to more clearly reveal the airport runway, stood Zapata, holding a weapon that I took to be the missile launcher. It was pointed toward the ground. The air was full of sound as a jet plane roared over our heads, descended, and touched down. Zapata was watching it, half turned away from me. It had begun to rain, and the noise of the plane and the rain and the rising wind hid the sound of my footsteps as I approached him. Or perhaps he presumed that I was the guard. In any case, he didn't turn until I was close to him. When he did, I leveled the Uzi at him and said, "Put down that launcher. Don't make me kill you."

His face went pale. He hesitated so long that I almost fired. Then a bitter smile appeared on his face. "If I squeeze this trigger, I imagine both of us will be blown to bits," he said. "What do you think?"

I thought he was right. "We will be," I said, "but Callahan won't."

"I think we're at a standoff," he said.

When you absolutely know that you're going to die and there's nothing you can do about it, fear disappears and you become quite detached. "No," I said. "You're all through right here. You can take me with you, but this is the end of it. Put down the weapon and we can both live."

"Are you so brave?" he said. "Does life mean so little to you?"

I shrugged, wondering what Zee and the children would do without me. I wished that I could be there to see. "I'm not brave," I said. "I want to live. I hope you do too."

"I'm trying to decide whether I can lift this thing and shoot you with it before you can shoot me."

"I don't think you can."

He seemed to consider his options carefully. Then he said, "Neither do I," and he bent and lowered the launcher to the ground.

"Step away," I said. "Do you have any other weapons?"

"No." He stepped away from the launcher.

"I believe you, but I'm going to search you anyway. Don't do anything to make me nervous."

I searched him and found not even a pocketknife. I used his bootlaces to tie his hands and then, remembering the firecracker sounds, used his cell phone to call Brady's phone, breathing between my teeth.

I felt weak when I got no answer, and fear for

Brady brought a chill of bitterness toward Zapata and his crew. What had happened over there?

I rang off, called 911, and told them where I was and what had happened. Then I walked with Zapata back down the path to the van, where I used the guard's bootlaces to truss him as well. He was still alive, but he was bleeding from one ear. I felt very cold and indifferent toward both of them.

I sat Zapata against a tree and studied him. His dark eyes were full of thoughts.

"What was this all about?" I asked. "What did Joe Callahan do to make you so angry that you'd kill a plane full of people just to get at him?"

"In war they call civilian casualties collateral damage," he said. "They are the price that must be paid for justice."

"What justice? Callahan was one of the most humane presidents we've ever had."

Zapata's face tightened. "Humane? He supported the death squads in Nicaragua."

"Not for long," I said. "He got rid of them during his first months in office."

"Too late," he said. "Did you ever hear of the Santa Anna Mission Hospital? I was working there with Nate Lundsberg and Lou Mortison."

"Nate?" I said. "Dr. Lundsberg, you mean?"

Zapata nodded. "He's an amazing man. A saint."

"Who's Lou Mortison?"

"Bob Mortison's younger brother. Nate was the doctor and Lou and I and Nate's wife, Julia, were his assistants. We were the only medical team in the area, but the CIA had it in their heads that we were supporting the guerrillas. They couldn't send the army, because that would be bad politics, but they could send the death squads, and that's what they did. They killed all our patients, and they killed Lou, and they killed Julia, though not before they raped her, and they burned the place to the ground. Nate and I managed to escape." He looked up at me with passionate eyes. "We've been waiting thirteen years for justice."

"You've killed at least two men who didn't deserve it," I said. "Where's the justice for them?"

The flame faded from his eyes. He looked at the ground. "You mean Alvarez and Bucyck. I didn't know about them until after it happened. That was Harry Doyle's work. We never should have brought him into the group, but he's loyal to Bob Mortison. We needed someone as tough as Harry is, and he would do anything for money. It was his idea to use the missiles, too."

"Where did you get them?"

"Harry got them. Apparently there were so many made and shipped around the world that nobody knows how many are still out there. I don't know where he got them, but he says there are more if we need them." He lifted his eyes. "I'm not sorry about the missiles, but I'm sorry about those two men and the other innocent people who would have died on the plane. I hope you can believe that."

I could believe it.

"I guess I understand Larry Bucyck," I said. "He was onto your plan. But why Eduardo Alvarez? Why blow up the *Trident*?"

"It was looking like the strike might get settled without Callahan," he said. "We needed to unsettle it to get Callahan down here. It was Mortison's brainstorm. Blow up the boat, make it look like the strikers did it, and they'd all walk away from the table. Alvarez just happened to be in the wrong place at the wrong time."

"I guess to hell he was," I said.

The guard groaned and moved a little bit.

I listened for the sound of cars bringing the police, but heard none.

I thought about men like Zapata and Lundsberg. Good men normally, heroic, even, but capable of wickedness almost beyond comprehension. And more than capable of seeing their evil as necessary and therefore moral. I remembered reading about Hitler's last days in the Berlin bunker when he still believed that he'd been right in everything he'd done and that one day the world would come to recognize that.

God save us from idealists. They're more dangerous than fiends.

But was I much different? I was ready to shoot Zapata in cold blood because he was willing to kill a plane full of people I didn't think should be killed. We all must have some thinly covered instinct to destroy anyone or anything that seriously threatens our vision of life as it should be. Show me a sufficient danger and I'll show you my fangs. My avatar, if I have one, has bloody claws.

Then I thought about Brady. What had happened with him? Who had loosed that sputter of shots?

I heard the *whump-whump* sound of helicopter

blades, and soon a Coast Guard copter came swinging toward us over the trees. It circled above us.

Then I heard the sounds of automobile engines, and I stepped around the cluster of oak brush to a spot where I could see the road and watch Zapata at the same time. A state-police cruiser came into sight, and I waved it down. Dom Agganis stepped out and came toward me as other cruisers pulled up behind his and other men stepped out, some of them in civilian garb—chinos and summer shirts hanging loose over their belts. Clearly feds in their Vineyard casual duds.

"Are you all right?" Agganis asked.

"I'm fine."

"Any casualties?"

"A guy with a sore head. You might want a medic to look at him."

"What happened here?"

I told him, and he nodded.

"All right," he said. "We'll take it from here. You can start by handing over that Uzi." He nodded back toward the cruisers. "There are guys from Washington here, and they'll want a report."

I'd forgotten I had the Uzi. I gave it to him, along with the pistol that had belonged to the guard. "There's an armed missile in a launcher up yonder," I said, pointing up the path. "You might want somebody who knows what he's doing to disarm it."

"Good thought. Where's Coyne?"

I pointed west. "Deep Bottom Road. He went to check out another possible missile site. I heard what sounded like shots, and he doesn't answer his cell phone. I've got to get over there."

"Leave that to us." He put a big hand on my shoulder, squeezed it, and turned back to the cruiser, where Olive Otero stood with four feds. "Come on."

When we got to them, he told everyone what I'd told him and said, "You take over here, Olive. Cuff Zapata and call an ambulance for the other guy. I'll be back."

"I'm going with you," I said.

"No you're not," said one of the feds. "You're coming with us." He showed me a grim face and a Secret Service shield.

"Fuck you," I said, reaching for the door handle of Dom's cruiser.

"No," said Agganis, stepping between me and the door. "Someone just tried to kill Joe Callahan, and these guys work for him. They need to know exactly what's been happening around here. You go with them." His voice was gentle but firm. "We'll go find out what happened to Coyne."

"I don't know who's over there," I said, "but one of them may have the machine gun I heard."

He waved two policemen over and told them to follow him. Then he turned the cruiser and drove away with other cops and federal agents following him.

Now it was raining a small misty rain. It had been raining for a while, but I'd barely noticed.

"Come with us, Mr. Jackson," said a man in a summer shirt.

I hesitated, then got into a cruiser. One man drove, one sat beside him, and one sat on either side of me in the backseat. No one said much as we drove to state-police headquarters in Oak Bluffs.

Someone offered me a cigarette, but I shook my head.

I spent two hours at the station going over the events of the past few days, then going over them again, and then going over them yet again, sometimes remembering things I'd forgotten to mention before and sometimes forgetting to mention things I'd said earlier. When they finally got through with me, they seemed angry, but satisfied.

"All right," said the chief among them. "Mike, here, will take you home now. We'll probably want to talk with you again. One thing. Don't talk with the press about this business. Let us get a handle on it first. It's a matter of national security."

"Okay," I said. "Now, please, take me up to see what happened to Brady."

"No. We'll take you home."

"I'll need my truck. It's up where Brady is. My wife's car is in the garage."

"Good. That'll make it easier for you to stay home. You can get your car tomorrow."

"Come on," said Mike. "Your wife is probably worrying about you."

She probably was, and I didn't want her to. I worry her enough under normal circumstances.

"All right," I said.

Mike drove me home in silence and left the house the same way.

The rain shower had passed over, and I was sitting on the balcony with a drink when Gloria Alvarez's car came into the yard and deposited Zee and the kids and a ton of beach stuff in the yard before driving away again. They'd had a long day on the sand.

"I'll be up as soon as I shower," called Zee, waving at me.

After a while she came up, glass in hand. She was bright and clean and shiny, but her eyes were full of care. She gave me a kiss, then sat down and raised her glass. "Consider yourself clinked and tell me about your day, if you think I should know about it. Where's Brady?"

I wanted to tell her everything, and I did. When I was through, Zee shook her head and slid close to me. She put her arm around me. "You could have been killed. You scare me. Now I'm worried about Brady."

"So am I. The plane landed, so Callahan is all right, but I can't remember whether I heard the shots before or after that."

"Dom should tell us what happened. He shouldn't make us wait."

I could imagine several reasons why he might not want to tell us anything. None of them was good.

Zee felt the tension in my body and tightened her arm around my waist. "I find it almost impossible to believe that anyone would want to harm Joe Callahan. He's such a good man."

Being good never saved anyone, as the saints and martyrs can attest. "It's over now," I said. "Callahan's safe."

"But is Brady safe?" Zee had tears in her eyes. "If he isn't hurt, they won't charge him with anything, will they?"

I thought that, the law being what it is, Brady, and I, too, for that matter, could be charged with some crime or other, but I wasn't worried about that. I was worried about that flurry of shots that I'd heard.

"I imagine Brady's fine," I lied. I felt I was on the lip of the Void, ready to fall.

We sat close together in the fading evening light and looked out over the gray waters of Nantucket Sound where the sailboats were easing toward harbor under the low dark sky. In spite of the sultry summer heat, the earth seemed without form, and darkness was upon the face of the deep.

What had become of Brady?

Chapter Sixteen

Brady

I was looking straight into the gaping muzzle of
Harry Doyle's missile launcher.

Instinctively I ducked sideways and dropped into a
crouch. In the same motion, I braced the Uzi against
my hip and pointed it at him. "Drop that thing,
Harry. Do it now."

He looked directly at me, and his lip curled into a
hateful smile. "Fuck you."

Then he turned and pointed the business end of the
Stinger at the sky.

Overhead, the drone of the plane materialized,
grew louder, then faded, making another circle before
it landed.

"Put it down," I repeated.

Harry Doyle ignored me. He hunched his shoulder, squinted his eye, peered through the sight on his
weapon, and tracked it across the sky above us like a
skeet shooter swinging on a high-flying clay pigeon.

If he launched the missile in the general direction of
Callahan's plane, the missile's heat-seeking guidance
system would do the rest, and it would be all over.

I held the Uzi tight in both hands, held my breath,

and pulled back on the trigger. The sudden burst of noise exploded in my ears.

The missile launcher fell from Doyle's shoulder onto the ground. His face and chest blossomed red. He windmilled his arms, staggered a few steps backward, then crashed into the underbrush. He twitched a couple times, then lay as still as death on the rain-soaked ground.

I let the Uzi fall from my hands. My entire body began to shiver and tremble. I tilted my head to look at the sky. The rain was cold on my face, and my mind was empty of thought or feeling.

A few minutes later, out of the wet silence, came the sudden deafening roar of a big engine, and then a jet airplane broke through the low clouds just a few hundred feet directly over my head. Its landing gear was down and its lights flashed bright colors in the rainy afternoon twilight. I watched it sink toward the slick runway of the Martha's Vineyard Airport. My fists and jaw were clenched tight as I waited for the blast and explosion of airplane and Stinger missile colliding in the air.

President Callahan's jet dropped toward the runway, touched down, bounced slightly, then slowed in a roar of backdraft and a screech of rubber-on-wet-tarmac. At the end of the runway it turned and taxied over to the terminal.

He had made it.

My entire body was a clenched fist. I didn't know how long I'd been holding my breath. I let it out in a big cathartic whoosh.

And then all the strength seeped out of me. My

head felt like it wanted to lift off my neck and drift up into the sky. I let myself drop to the ground, and I sat there hugging my legs with my forehead on my knees.

I took a dozen slow, deep breaths and waited for the adrenaline overdose of the past few minutes to drain away. I was dizzy and nauseated and utterly exhausted. The rain, and the realization of what I'd just done, washed over me.

After a few minutes I forced myself to lift my head and look around.

Harry Doyle hadn't moved. He was sprawled on his back. His chest bloomed with red splotches. The Stinger missile launcher lay on the ground beside him.

I crawled over to him and pressed my fingers against his neck, searching for the pulse I knew I wouldn't find. Two of the Uzi bullets had hit him in the face—one just under the left side of his nose, the other above his right eye.

I wondered what destiny in Doyle's life had decreed that he should end it here in the rain on a scrubby-oak knoll on the southwestern side of Martha's Vineyard, a failed presidential assassin, killed in the nick of time by a wills-and-estates lawyer from Boston with an Uzi.

Callahan had made it. His plane wasn't shot down. That was the important thing.

I fished my cell phone from my pocket, pecked out the number for J.W.'s cell, hit Send, held it to my ear.

It bleated once, weakly. Then nothing.

I looked at it. The battery was dead.

Well, J.W. knew where I was. Assuming that he

was all right, sooner or later he'd tell the police, and they'd come.

I had the Land Cruiser. But I wasn't going anywhere. I couldn't leave the crime scene. The place where an assassin and his sentry had set up his ambush. The place where I'd given one a concussion, at least, and killed the other.

I made my way back down the path to where the sentry had been. He was still lying where I'd left him. I knelt beside him. I could see that he was breathing.

I poked his shoulder. "Are you awake?" I said.

His eyelids fluttered, but he said nothing.

I don't know how long I knelt there in the rain. My sense of time had deserted me, and I might have drifted off into some kind of postadrenaline stupor, when I heard in the distance the unmistakable *thump-thump* of helicopter blades.

A minute later the slamming of a car door jerked me upright.

The police was my first thought.

Harry Doyle's compatriots was my second thought. More men with Uzis and missiles. More assassins.

I still had Zee's Beretta in my pocket. I pulled it out and slipped behind some bushes.

Then I heard the static of a police radio and saw the strobing blue light flashing through the wet woods.

I put the Beretta back into my pocket, stepped out onto the opening, put both hands on top of my head, and shouted, "I'm Brady Coyne. I'm a friend. Don't shoot me."

A uniformed cop came up the path. He held a

police assault shotgun at his hip. He stopped when he saw me, raised his shotgun to his shoulder, and aimed it at the middle of my chest. "On the ground," he said. "On your belly. Right now. Put your hands behind you."

I did what he said.

Then there were two of them. The first one stood over me aiming the shotgun at my head. The other one patted my pockets, found the Beretta, took it out.

Then he grabbed my arm and hauled me onto my feet.

"Who are you?" said the cop with the shotgun. I'd never seen him before. He looked like he should still be in high school.

"My name is Brady Coyne," I said. I pointed up the path. "There's a dead man up there. I killed him. He was going to shoot down the president's airplane."

The two cops looked at each other. Then one of them went jogging up the path.

He came back a minute later. "There's a dead guy up there, all right," he said to his partner. "And there's an Uzi and some kind of missile launcher, too."

The other cop walked over to the edge of the clearing and spoke into his cell phone. Then they led me down the path and put me in the backseat of the cruiser that was parked a little way down the dirt roadway.

About ten minutes later another vehicle, this one an unmarked SUV of some kind, nosed its way up the road and pulled to a stop beside the cruiser. Dom Agganis got out of the front seat. Two men in chino pants and golf shirts stepped out of the back. They both had close-cropped hair and smooth faces and cold eyes. One was blond. The other looked Hispanic. They had broad chests and narrow waists and big biceps. FBI or Secret Service, I guessed.

They talked to the two uniformed cops for a minute. Agganis stood off to the side, apparently deferring to them. Then one of the cops opened the cruiser door, grabbed my arm, helped me out, and stood me there facing Agganis and the two guys in plain clothes.

Both of them flashed a badge at me and mumbled their names. All I caught was the title "Agent" before each name.

"You're Coyne?" said the light-haired one.

"Yes. Brady Coyne."

"You're Jackson's pal."

"Yes."

"Did you kill that man?" He pointed his chin up in the direction of Harry Doyle.

"Yes."

"Did he fire upon you?"

"No, not exactly. He—"

"Hang on a minute," he said. He cleared his throat, told me I was being held on suspicion of murder, then recited the Miranda warning. "Do you understand?"

"I studied it in law school," I said. "But, listen—"

"Do you understand?" he repeated.

"I understand. Yes. You're not arresting me, are you?"

"We're holding you for questioning. Obviously you are in jeopardy."

"Obviously I did a good and necessary thing."

"A man has been murdered," he said.

"It wasn't murder."

"So do you want a lawyer?"

"I am a lawyer."

He rolled his eyes.

"I don't need a lawyer," I said.

"Okay," he said. "I ask you again. Did you shoot and kill that man?"

"I did, yes. You'd hardly call it murder, though."

He almost smiled. "Tell me about it."

"I don't know where to begin."

"Begin at the beginning."

I shrugged. "I'm not sure where the beginning is. When Larry Bucyck called me, I guess."

"Larry Bucyck, who was murdered yesterday?"

"Yes."

"Good," he said. "Begin there."

So I did. I began with Larry's phone call and concluded with our discovery of the crates that held the shoulder-mounted Stinger surface-to-air missile launchers.

"We'd heard Joe Callahan was coming to the island to mediate the strike," I said. "We guessed those Stingers were intended to shoot down his plane. We told the Edgartown chief of police about it, showed him the circles on our map, and he went off to cover the northeastern approaches to the airport, but then the wind shifted. So J.W. and I figured we better try to cover the southwestern approaches. I left him off and came here. Whacked the guy with the Uzi on the head, snuck up on the other guy up there with the

Stinger, Harry Doyle's his name, and when we heard the plane overhead, he pointed that thing up into the sky. So I shot him with the Uzi."

When I finished my recitation, the two agents looked at me for a long minute without blinking. Then the Hispanic one turned to Agganis. "This make any sense to you?"

Agganis shrugged. "I knew about part of it. The rest of it fits, yes."

"Okay," said the blond agent, "except this man here killed that guy." He turned to one of the uniformed officers. "I want you to take him to the station and hold him until we get there. We're going to have to talk to him some more."

"I told you everything," I said.

"You're a lawyer," he said. "You know how it works."

I shrugged, and they loaded me into the cruiser.

When we'd backed down to the road, the cop in the passenger seat turned around, pointed at J.W.'s old Land Cruiser that was still parked on the shoulder where I'd left it, and said, "That yours?"

"It's J.W. Jackson's. I was driving it."

"Gimme the keys."

I fished the keys from my pocket and handed them to him through the wire mesh that separated us. He slipped out of the cruiser, got into the Land Cruiser, and we all headed back to Edgartown.

They stuck me in an interrogation room, gave me a mug of coffee, and left me there to watch the hands on the wall clock creep around the dial. It reminded

me of waiting for the end of the school day in one par-
ticularly boring last-period junior high school history
class.

Finally the two agents showed up. They asked me
to tell my story all over again, this time into a tape
recorder. They interrupted me frequently for clarifi-
cation and detail and chronology. They wanted to
know everything.

I assumed some state and local cops, and some
Secret Service agents, too, maybe, were watching and
listening through the one-way glass.

After a while, their questions convinced me that
they weren't going to prosecute me. They didn't
seem very interested in what I'd done out there in the
woods that afternoon. It was the assassination plot
that they wanted to know about.

It was almost nine in the evening when they finally
let me go. I told them I planned to head back to
Boston the next day, that I'd be staying with the Jacksons that night, and gave them a card with my home
and office numbers on it.

They gave me the keys to the Land Cruiser and
told me it was parked in the side lot. Then they both
shook my hand.

"Thank you," said the blond agent. "Your country
owes you."

"You did good work," said the Hispanic agent.
"You and Jackson."

"I'll be sure to tell him," I said.

"Yes," he said, "but, um, don't talk to the media
about any of this, okay?"

I looked at him. "Why?"

It was his turn to look at me. "It's . . . sensitive."

"You mean embarrassing?"

He gave his hand a little flip, as if to say it was obvious. "National security."

I smiled. "I do believe in a free press."

He opened his mouth to say something.

"And please don't threaten me," I said.

He gave me a cold-eyed smile. "Oh, we never threaten, Mr. Coyne. We don't need to." He pattted my shoulder. "Again, many thanks for your help today. You were heroic. Drive carefully, okay?"

When I pulled into the Jacksons' driveway, I saw J.W. sitting on his front steps under his porch light.

He got up and came to the car. When I stepped out, he said, "You're all right."

"I am. Yes. I'm fine."

"I tried to call you," he said. "Several times. I was worried."

"I'm sorry," I said. "My phone died. I tried to call you, too."

"So what happened?"

"Why don't you get me a beer? Then we can exchange stories."

"Excellent plan," he said. We walked toward the house. "They didn't throw you in the clink?" he said.

"Nope. They considered it, then decided that I'm a hero. So are you."

"Yeah," he said. "I got that line, too. By way of convincing us not to talk to the media."

"I'll tell anybody who asks that you're a hero," I said.

294

Zee was in the kitchen. When I walked in, she came over and hugged me and kissed both of my cheeks. "You're all right," she said.

I smiled and nodded. "I sure am."

She returned my smile. "I'm glad," she said.

J.W. fetched beers from the refrigerator. We took them up to the balcony, where we sat and looked out at the starless Vineyard night. He told me about his encounter with Father Zapata. He'd managed to take control of the situation without killing anybody, which I thought was especially heroic of him. I told him about my confrontation with Harry Doyle, and how I hadn't been able to avoid killing him.

J.W. sympathized. He figured it would bother me for a long time, and I sensed that he was right.

Somewhere in the midst of our recitations, he went down and got more beer for us, and when our story-telling wound down and those bottles were empty, he said he was sure I must be hungry and there was plenty of food left over from their supper.

I told him that I hadn't noticed, but now that he mentioned it, I was famished. "I better call Evie first," I said. "Can I use your phone?"

"Grab another beer from the fridge if you want," he said. "Use the phone on the desk in your bed-room."

"Can you ferry me back to America tomorrow?"

"If you can stand another wet ride on the catboat, absolutely. Maybe we'll get up early, go fishing before we leave. You up for it? Tide'll be perfect at first light."

"Irresistible," I said.

I found another Samuel Adams lager in the refrigerator, took it into the guest room, and sat at J.W.'s desk. I drained half of the bottle before I pecked out my home number on the phone.

When Evie answered, I said, "It's your wayward roommate, reporting in."

"Oh, jeez, hi," she said softly.

"Hi, yourself," I said.

"Are you all right?"

"Why wouldn't I be?"

"I worry, that's all. Last time I talked to you, you told me your friend Larry had been killed. So it should come as no surprise that I imagine things."

"I'm fine, babe. I'll tell you all about it when I see you."

"All about what? What do you mean?"

"Larry. What happened. That's all."

I heard her blow out a breath. "The Vineyard is all over the news, you know," she said. "President Callahan flew in to settle the strike, they're saying, like God coming down in a machine to tie up the loose ends in a Greek tragedy, restore order out of chaos, and both sides have agreed to sit down with him. The place must be crawling with Secret Service."

"Yes," I said. "I suppose it is."

"Coincidence," she said. "Larry getting killed right before the ex-president arrives."

"I guess so."

She paused. I figured she expected me to say more, but I didn't. I didn't want to talk about it. Not yet. Not to Evie, at least not on the telephone.

"Well," she said after a minute, "I hope you and J.W. managed to do some fishing, anyway."

"Not yet," I said. "We've been kind of tied up with the whole Larry thing. We might sneak out at first light tomorrow."

"They figure out who did it? Larry Bucyck, I mean."

"I think they've got a good idea," I said. "They don't tell me anything."

"So when are you coming home?"

"Tomorrow. After fishing. J.W.'s gonna sail me to Woods Hole, assuming Callahan hasn't gotten the ferries up and running by then."

"Be careful, Brady. I do worry."

"I'm always careful," I said, trying to keep all irony out of my voice.

Chapter Seventeen

J.W.

I have a friend who's traveled more than I have and who, when the world is too much with him and time is out of joint, catches a plane to Albuquerque, rents a car, and drives toward Colorado until he finds some lonesome dirt road leading away from the highway into the desert. He drives along that dry, barren track deep into the gigantic, indifferent wilderness, then parks and walks away, across the empty, burning land, for an hour or more before turning back to his car. When he gets there, thirsty and tired, all of his self-pity and all of his notions that things should be different than they are have been burned out of him, and he's ready to return to the real world and be content in spite of its cruelties. He calls it Desert Therapy.

The sea plays that role for me and probably explains why I live on an island. Like the desert and the mountains out west, the ocean is huge and powerful and dangerous and beautiful and totally indifferent to the desires of man. When I walk its beaches or sail over its mysterious waters, my illusions about how things should be are washed away, and I'm purified. It promises me nothing, and though it is always awesome and can be violent, it is never evil and is often unimaginably beautiful.

Fishing is also purification. You cast your line and you either catch fish or you don't, and you have to accept your fate or be a fool. If you're the sort of person who has to catch fish to be happy, you should do something else.

Both Brady and I liked to catch fish, but we didn't have to catch them to be content. Early the next morning, on South Beach, we offered our lures to the bluefish we knew were out there and watched the eastern sky brighten as the earth turned until, like a great orange ball, the sun rose into the sky. We caught no fish, but it made no difference, because our fishing had, for a while, made us one with the universe. We had not said much, because we didn't need to.

We were home in time to join Zee and the kids for breakfast.

"I notice that my car is still missing," said Zee, as I piled more pancakes onto her plate. She poured maple syrup over them and licked her lickable lips. Zee, to the amused annoyance of her women friends, can eat like a horse and never show it.

"I'll get the car," I said, "and then I'm going to sail Brady back to America. You can all come along if you don't have anything better to do."

"Yay!" said the children in unison, mouths full of pancakes. They liked to sail and would, I suspected, eventually become better at it than I was.

"Well, I'm certainly not going to stay home alone," said Zee. "While you guys go get the Jeep, I'll fix us all some lunch."

So two hours later we were all in the *Shirley J.* easing out past the town dock in front of a small southwest breeze that overnight had replaced the northeast wind that had so affected us the previous day. The dock was lined with people fishing and watching the alternating On Time ferries pass back and forth across the channel between the village and Chappaquiddick carrying cars and trucks, three at a time, to the far Chappy beaches. Some people waved, and we waved back.

Behind us, the harbor was full of summer boats, some already running up sails. Above us, the new sky arched high and blue. We passed between the ferryboats, then jibed to the right and went out past the lighthouse. There, as we approached the large yachts anchored in the outer harbor, we jibed again and on a broad reach headed out into the sound. It was a perfect day for sailing a small boat such as ours.

I gave the tiller to Brady and watched Zee adjust the sheet until the big mainsail was pulling perfectly. The Oak Bluffs bluffs slowly grew closer, and the thin line on the northeastern horizon that was Cape Cod became clearer as the morning mists burned away.

"Sing us a sailing song, Uncle Brady," said Diana.

The rest of the crew thought that was a splendid idea, so Brady gave us a rendition of "High Barbaree" and then an encore of "The Golden Vanity," and he got a round of cheers and applause.

"Now it's someone else's turn," he said, after blowing kisses to his fans.

So I sang "Lowlands," and the kids sang "Barnacle Bill the Sailor," and Zee sang "Henry Martin," and we all sang "Across the Wide Missouri," and we ended up singing ourselves all the way to East Chop.

The wind came up a bit, and there were occasional whitecaps around us, but the tide was running west and helped carry us smoothly into Woods Hole, where we made fast and said our good-byes to Brady.

"Are you okay?" I asked him after he'd gotten kisses from Zee and the children and a farewell hug from me.

"I'm fine," he said, "but it'll be good to get home to Evie."

"Put it behind you," I said. "You did what you had to do."

"I know that in my head," he said, "but my feelings aren't so sure."

"That's because you're a good man, and not a cold-blooded killer."

He gave my shoulder a gentle slap and walked away.

We Jacksons climbed back into the *Shirley J.* and cast off. The wind was now in front of us, and the tide, though it was easing, was there as well. I put the wind on the starboard bow and the tide on the port bow and thus managed slow progress, close hauled, back toward the island. Zee went below and came up with her lunch basket. Sandwiches and soft drinks for all hands. When we finally got off West Chop, the tide was flat and we made better progress. The children took turns on the tiller, with me helping them out when it got too much for them, because a catboat can demand a pretty strong hand at the helm.

We sailed past the entrance to Oak Bluffs harbor and down along the state beach between O.B. and

Edgartown. The beach was filled with people and bright umbrellas. All around us sailboats and power-boats were making white wakes in the blue water.

We were back at the stake by mid-afternoon and home again in time for snacks and drinks—martinis for Zee and me, lemonade for Joshua and Diana—and smoked bluefish pâté on crackers for all. The big people sat on the balcony, and the little people sat in the tree house.

"Pa?"

I looked across to where Diana was perched in the big beech tree. "What?"

"Can we sit with you and Mom in the balcony?"

"No. The balcony is only for big people."

"Can we someday?" she said.

"When you're a big person," I said. "Not before."

"Pa?" said Joshua.

"What?"

"Can we have a dog?"

"No. No dogs. We have cats."

The kids both giggled loud giggles. I'd been set up. They'd known the answer before they'd asked the question.

Zee sat close to me. "How are you feeling?"

I put an arm around her. "Good. I feel good."

Three days later, the strike was over. Joe Callahan had proved to be the magician everyone had hoped he'd be, and the big boats were running again, making extra trips to carry everyone who wanted to go back to the mainland.

Not much had appeared in the papers regarding the

attempt on Callahan's life, but there were already rumors, because too many people knew something about it, and eventually there'd be trials.

"Will you and Brady have to testify?" Zee asked.

"Maybe. Prosecution witnesses."

"Will Brady face charges?"

"I'm sure they'll be dropped if they're ever brought at all. After all, he not only saved Joe Callahan's life, he saved everyone on that plane. They should give him a medal."

"They should give you one, too."

"I already have enough medals," I said, reminded of the old ones from Vietnam, in the bottom drawer of our bedroom dresser. "Besides, you know what they say about awards."

"Yes, I do," she said. "You've told that joke more than once."

"You're sure you don't want to hear it again?"

"I'm very sure."

The children were off at a neighbor's house for the afternoon.

"Say," I said to Zee. "How'd you like to go fishing? We have a couple hours before we have to pick up the kids."

"An excellent thought," said Zee, getting up immediately. "The tide is wrong, and it's the wrong time of day, but what the hell? Let's do it!"

As I was taking the rods and tackle box out to the Land Cruiser, the phone rang. When I got back into the house, Zee was holding the receiver in her hand. She looked at me. "Are you busy tomorrow night?"

"No."

She spoke into the phone. "We'll be glad to come. Thanks. See you then."

"Who was that?"

"That was Joe Callahan's right-hand man inviting us to dinner with the Callahans tomorrow night. Apparently the prez thinks he owes you something."

"What's he serving?"

"He didn't say."

"We can take him some bluefish pâté. I doubt if he has any of that on hand."

"If he thinks he's grateful now," said Zee, "he'll *really* be grateful for that."

"As well he should be."

Then we strapped the rods on the roof of the Land Cruiser and headed for the beach.

Chapter Eighteen

Brady

On the drive up from Woods Hole I plugged my cell phone into the jack in my car and tried calling Evie at her office, but her secretary said she was in a meeting and didn't know how long she'd be. I asked her to tell Evie that I was back in America, heading home, and would see her when I got there.

A half hour or so later, just as I was crossing the Sagamore Bridge, my cell phone jangled.

"Are you all right?" Evie said when I answered.

"Why wouldn't I be all right?"

"There are stories coming out of Martha's Vineyard," she said.

"What kind of stories?"

"About President Callahan flying in during a storm. About a terrorist roundup."

"Terrorists, huh?"

"Alleged terrorists," she said. "That's how they say it. An alleged terrorist plot. There are no details. It seems to be in the realm of rumor. No official person says anything except 'no comment.'" She hesitated. "I don't suppose you know anything about such things."

"Why would I know?"

She chuckled. "Because I know you and I know J.W., and you told me about Larry Bucyck getting murdered, and I just bet you do, that's all."

"What time do you expect to be home?"

"You're changing the subject."

"Not really," I said. "I'm just thinking that the proper way to tell you about my adventures would be on our patio with gin and tonics, not over the phone while I'm trying to negotiate the traffic on the Sagamore Bridge."

"Six," she said. "I'll be home around six. I'll make a point of it."

"Meet me on the patio," I said.

"Yes," she said. "It will be very good to see you."

I was sitting in one of our Adirondack chairs out on the patio with Henry, our dog, lying beside me, and a pitcher of gin and tonics full of ice cubes and lime slices on the table. Henry and I were watching the goldfinches peck thistle seed from the feeder.

I couldn't shake the memory of gripping the cold metal of that lethal Uzi in my hands and holding down the trigger and watching the red blotches blossom on Harry Doyle's face and chest.

When Evie came out the back door onto the patio, she said, "Hi, honey."

I turned and looked at her. She looked terrific. "Hi, babe," I said.

She started to come to me. Then she stopped. "Brady," she said. "What's the matter?"

"Nothing's the matter," I said.

She came over, sat on my lap, put an arm around my neck, and kissed my cheek. "You look so sad," she said softly. She nuzzled my face and squirmed in my lap. "Oh, my dear man," she whispered.

"It's okay," I said. I pressed my face into her hair. "I'm not sad now."

"Do you want to talk about it?"

"Maybe later."

She picked up my hand and pressed it against her breast. I could feel her heart beating.

She put her mouth against my ear. "We could . . ."

I turned my face so that my nose touched hers. "Here?" I said.

"I've really, really missed you," she whispered. "I was so worried." Her arm tightened around my neck, and her hand pressed hard against mine where I held her breast, and then she tilted her head and touched my lips with hers. Her eyes were wide with the question, and then her mouth opened against mine, and she said, "Oh," deep in her throat, and then she shifted and lifted her skirt and moved to straddle me, and pretty soon there was nothing but Evie, and I felt whole again.

I beat Julie to the office the next morning. I got the coffee going and shuffled through the mail and the messages she'd left on my desk, and I was happy to conclude that my presence would have been redundant if I'd been in my office on Friday and Monday instead of down on the Vineyard.

When Julie came in and saw me sitting at her receptionist's desk sipping coffee and reading e-mails off her computer, she said, "Oh, hello. How lovely that you could come to work today."

"The coffee's ready," I said. "May I pour a mug for you?"

"Sure," she said.

I got up, filled Julie's mug and topped mine off, and headed into my office.

Julie followed me. We sat at the coffee table, Julie on the leather sofa, me in the leather chair.

"What's up?" she said.

"What makes you think something's up?"

"You don't get in early, make the coffee, and pour mine for me unless something's up."

"I need to tell you some things," I said, "and I need to leave some things out, and I want you not to ask me about the things I'm leaving out. Okay?"

She shrugged. "You're the lawyer," she said. "I am merely your employee. I do what you say."

"Ha," I said. "You are hardly mere, and mostly it's I who do what you say."

"What's up?" she said.

"Larry Bucyck was killed while I was down on the Vineyard."

"Killed," she said.

"Murdered, actually," I said.

"Our client."

"Yes."

"Oh, dear." She looked at me over the rim of her coffee mug. "I want to ask what happened, and why, and what it means, and if it had anything to do with all the news coming from the Vineyard about President Callahan and the ferry strike and terrorists."

I didn't say anything.

"But I won't," she said after a minute. "I won't ask. Okay?"

"Okay," I said. "Here's what I want you to do. Larry owned some property in Menemsha that I assume is worth quite a bit. I want you to check on the deed and title to that property, and I also want you to see if Larry had a legal will. I can't even remember if we ever did one for him, or how his divorce affected the status of his estate."

Julie nodded. "I can do that. No problem."

"Also," I said, "there's a person named Sedona Blaisdell who lives there in Menemsha. See if you can find her number and get her on the phone for me."

"Sedona, huh?" She cocked her head and arched her eyebrows. "Pretty name. Somebody you, um, met down there?"

I smiled. "Yes."

"Evie know about her?"

"Evie knows about everything," I said.

"Oh, I'm sure."

She left the office, and a few minutes later the console on my desk buzzed. I picked up the phone, and Julie said, "I have Mrs. Blaisdell on line one." She emphasized the "Mrs."

"Thanks," I said. I poked the button for line one and said, "Sedona?"

"Yes?" she said.

"It's Brady Coyne, from—"

"I remember you," she said. "Of course. How are you?"

"I'm fine. I was just wondering how you were making out with Larry Bucyck's animals."

"No problem," she said. "Rocket is living here with us, and my husband actually seems to like him. I'm feeding the pigs and the chickens, which I don't mind at all, but eventually we're going to have to figure out what to do about them."

"I should have an answer for you within a day or two," I said. "That's why I'm calling. Is that all right?"

"No rush as far as I'm concerned."

"I appreciate it," I said.

"It's the least I can do for Larry," she said.

After I disconnected with Sedona Blaisdell, I called the state-police station on the Vineyard. I asked for Dom Agganis or Olive Otero.

Olive came on the line. "Mr. Coyne," she said. "You again."

"I'm back in Boston," I said. "Out of your hair."

"Good. What can you do for me?"

"I'm wondering about Larry Bucyck's body."

"The medical examiner has it right now. I expect he'll be done with it pretty soon. We've solved that particular crime."

"Who did it?"

She hesitated, then said, "I don't see any harm in telling you. It was that man Harry Doyle. The man you killed. Several, um, witnesses independently told us about it. Mr. Bucyck saw things he shouldn't have seen, and these witnesses saw him see them, so they sent Doyle to be sure that Mr. Bucyck couldn't interfere with their plan. If they'd been smart, they would've sent somebody to take care of you and J.W. Jackson, too."

"So the ME is ready to release Larry's body?"

"As soon as he knows to whom he can release it."

"I'll get back to you on that," I said. "Please don't let him do anything without checking with me."

"You ask a lot, Mr. Coyne." She hesitated. "But I suppose all of us down here are indebted to you. You and J.W. Yes, I'll talk to the medical examiner."

"I appreciate it," I said.

On Thursday came the news that President Callahan had successfully mediated a settlement to the ferry strike. When I talked to J.W. a couple days later, he said that finally things seemed to be returning to normal. Summer people were deserting the island like rats from a sinking ship, the bluefish were blitzing off South Beach and Cape Pogue and Lobsterville, and J.W. was laying in a winter's supply of his famous bluefish pâté. He and Zee were looking forward to the autumn, he said, and maybe Evie and I would come down for a few days and compete in the Derby.

He told me that he and Zee had been invited to dine with ex-President Callahan. "I bet I could wangle an invitation for you," he said.

"You kids go ahead, have fun," I said. "Give the prez my regards."

J.W. asked me if any law enforcement or Homeland Security types had harassed me. I told him no. He said they probably would.

And they did, on the following Monday, just a week after I returned to America. A female agent named Hanover, a no-nonsense blonde woman of about forty, and her partner, a bald guy named Keene with gray eyes and a gray suit, appeared in my office and said they wanted me to go with them.

I asked if I should bring a lawyer with me.

They assured me that I wasn't being accused of anything. They were simply gathering information.

I said okay.

They escorted me to the FBI building in Government Center in their black Ford Taurus, led me into a room with no windows, sat me at a rectangular table, and proceeded to depose me. There was a stenographer there, and several other people to whom I wasn't introduced.

Agent Hanover asked all the questions. She didn't seem very interested in the details about the man I'd shot to death, which was a relief. Her questions kept swinging back to Dr. Lundsberg, and pretty soon I caught onto the fact that he had eluded capture. They guessed that he'd slipped away from the island Sunday afternoon before President Callahan's plane arrived and all hell broke loose, perhaps on the big boat that J.W. and I had seen at his dock on Saturday night, and they thought he might have made it to sanctuary in someplace like Guatemala or Nicaragua, where extradition would be difficult, if not impossible.

Lundsberg, I inferred, was the mastermind of the assassination plan. The various agencies were quite sure they'd rounded up all the other conspirators— Mortison, Zapata, and a dozen or more others.

But Lundsberg was the prize, and he'd gotten away.

I couldn't infer much else from the questions Agent

Hanover asked me. They were all questions of fact. She didn't ask for my opinion or analysis or judgment, which was okay by me.

And when we were finished, she didn't thank me, either for my forthrightness at answering her questions or for my small part in preventing Callahan's airplane from being shot down with a Stinger missile.

I guessed I wasn't going to be given a commendation. That was all right. They weren't going to prosecute me, either.

It took me about three hours to drive from my townhouse on Mount Vernon Street on Beacon Hill in Boston to Marcia Bucyck's log home on a hilltop in East Corinth, Vermont. I'd called the previous day, told her what had happened to Larry, and asked directions to her place.

We sipped iced tea on her front porch, which looked down on the rooftops and the single white church spire of the village. She had a long blonde braid with streaks of gray in it, and she wore blue jeans and a pink T-shirt and sandals. A pretty middle-aged woman with a soft smile and intelligent blue eyes.

She told me that her two children, hers and Larry's, a boy named Blake and a girl named Summer, had both gone back to college. She'd been married to a man named Sullivan for a while after her divorce from Larry, but it didn't last very long.

I told her how Larry had carved out a little Walden for himself in a patch of woods on Martha's Vineyard, how he raised chickens and pigs, how he made a tasty quahog chowder and a deadly apple-pear-and-rose-hip wine, how he built stone sculptures that I guessed would stand there for eons, the Stonehenge of future generations, and as Marcia listened, she gazed off toward the village and tears brimmed in her eyes.

I told her that the ME was holding his body, and I gave her a number to call. And I told her that Larry's will bequeathed everything to her, or if she'd pre-deceased him, to his two children equally, and that I'd handle the legal end of it if she wanted.

She smiled and said she'd appreciate it.

I told her that two real estate appraisers had esti-mated the market value of his seven acres in Menemsha at around two and a half million dollars and that Larry's five pigs and eleven hens and one mostly basset hound were being cared for by Sedona Blaisdell, and I gave her Sedona's phone number in Menemsha.

Marcia thought she'd sell the property. She could use the money to pay for Blake's and Summer's col-lege expenses, and their graduate school, too, if that's what they wanted to do. She'd give the animals to Sedona Blaisdell if she wanted them.

Then while we sipped iced tea, we talked about Larry, our memories of him. Marcia said she sup-posed she'd never really stopped loving him.

Now, with the kids off to school, she was alone. She had a vegetable garden and some good neighbors and plenty of books, and she guessed she was begin-ning to figure out what Larry was seeking down there in Menemsha.

"It's really what we all want," she said. "Robert

Frost called a poem 'a momentary stay against confusion.' That's about the most we can hope for out of life, isn't it? A good poem?"

I nodded. "If we're lucky, if it is a good poem, and a good life, it begins 'in delight and ends in wisdom.'"

"Also Frost," said Marcia.

I nodded, finished my iced tea, glanced at my watch, and stood up. "I better get going," I said. "Long drive."

She followed me to my car, and when I held out my hand to her, she ignored it and hugged me.

Then I got in my car and pointed it south, to my home in Boston, to Evie, and to my own stay against confusion, however momentary it might turn out to be.

RECIPES

Brady Coyne's Slow-Cooked Brunswick Chili

Brunswick stew originated in the Appalachian south around two hundred years ago. Its main ingredient was squirrel, but it became a catch-all for whatever kinds of meat happened to be available—chicken, pork, beef, raccoon, deer, opossum, bear, turkey, partridge— and local vegetables such as okra, corn, and various kinds of beans. Bubbling over campfire coals in a big cast-iron kettle, Brunswick stew was a favorite of hunters and trappers as well as big families on small budgets.

Brady originated his variation, Brunswick Chili, one autumn several years ago when his freezer accumulated gifts from several hunting friends—ground elk, venison scraps, moose steaks, and rabbit. It's also good with store-bought stew beef (chuck) and pork rib meat (include the fat) in combination (or not) with ground beef and pork. The spirit of Brunswick stew encourages infinite variations depending on what's handy, so sometimes Brady adds corn or substitutes limas or chickpeas for kidney beans, and if he happens to have a couple of

319

leftover andouille sausages in the fridge, he cuts them into pieces and throws 'em in as well.

He prepares it in the morning, lets it simmer in his slow cooker all day, and serves it with biscuits or French bread, a green salad, and mugs of a local micro-brewed lager.

J.W. concedes that it is delish.

6 pounds available meat in any combination, cut into small (½-inch or smaller) cubes

1 cup all-purpose flour, plus flour for dredging

2 tablespoons (approximately) chili powder, for dredging and to taste

1 tablespoon (approximately) paprika, for dredging and to taste

1 tablespoon (approximately) cumin, for dredging and to taste

Olive oil

2 large yellow onions, quartered and sliced, plus 1 large yellow onion, slivered, as garnish

8 cloves garlic, diced

1 green pepper, diced

2 (16-ounce) cans black beans, drained

1 (16-ounce) can red kidney beans, drained

2 large cans diced tomatoes or 8 plum tomatoes, quartered

1 cup red wine or beer

2 tablespoons Worcestershire sauce

Shredded Cheddar cheese, as garnish

1. Dredge the meat cubes with flour, chili powder, paprika, and cumin, brown on all sides in olive oil

    in a hot skillet, then dump into your slow cooker along with all the cooking juices.

2. Combine the quartered and sliced onion, garlic, and green pepper, and sauté in the olive oil in the skillet until the onion is transparent. Add to the meat in the slow cooker.

3. Empty the drained cans of beans and the diced tomatoes into the slow cooker.

4. Add the beer or wine and the Worcestershire.

5. Add the chili powder, paprika, and cumin to taste.

6. Stir and mingle all the ingredients, cover, and let the slow cooker, on its lowest setting, do its thing for 8 to 10 hours while you go fishing.

7. Serve in bowls and sprinkle the shredded cheese and slivered onion on top.

Serves 8.

MEDALLIONS OF BEEF IN COGNAC CREAM

A simple, elegant recipe. The steaks ooze flavor and melt in your mouth. You can substitute sirloin tips for the tenderloins and use half-and-half instead of the cream, but don't leave out the cognac!

    4 (4 ounces each) beef tenderloin steaks
    Salt and cracked pepper
    2 tablespoons olive oil
    2 tablespoons unsalted butter
    2 shallots or 1 small onion, chopped
    ¼ cup cognac

½ cup whipping cream
Fresh parsley, as garnish

1. Sprinkle the steaks with salt and pepper. Combine the oil and butter in a large skillet and heat over medium heat until the butter melts. Add the steaks and cook 5 minutes on each side. Remove the steaks to a serving platter and keep warm.
2. Drain all but 2 tablespoons of drippings from the skillet. Sauté the shallots in the drippings until tender. Add the cognac and cook over medium heat, deglazing the skillet by scraping the particles that cling to the bottom. Gradually stir in the whipping cream and cook until heated. Pour the sauce over the steaks and garnish with the parsley.

Serves 4.

ABOUT THE AUTHORS

The late PHILIP R. CRAIG was the author of nineteen novels in the Martha's Vineyard Mystery series. A professor emeritus of English at Wheelock College in Boston, he loved the Vineyard and lived there year-round with his wife, Shirley.

WILLIAM G. TAPPLY is the author of more than thirty books, twenty-one of which are Brady Coyne mysteries. He has also written several books about fishing and the great outdoors, and he is a contributing editor for *Field and Stream* and a columnist for *American Angler.* A professor of English at Clark University in Worcester, he lives with his wife, novelist Vicki Stiefel, in Hancock, New Hampshire.

9 781451 624939